WARRIOR SOUL

DAVID BARBUR

COUGAR ROCK PRESS

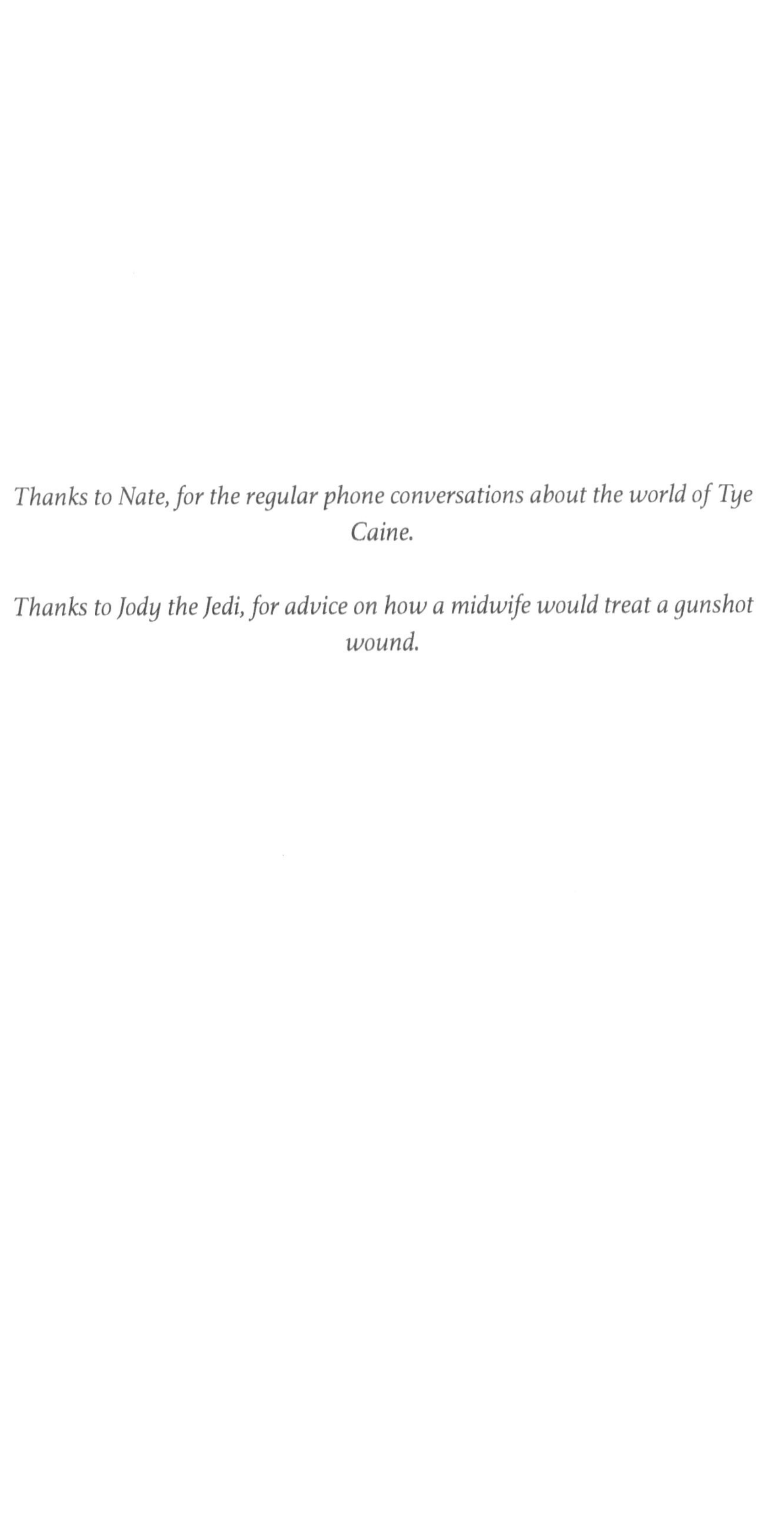

Thanks to Nate, for the regular phone conversations about the world of Tye Caine.

Thanks to Jody the Jedi, for advice on how a midwife would treat a gunshot wound.

1

Tye Caine shifted his shotgun into his left hand and knelt to look at the footprint.

The early-morning breeze blew up the hill, and the ever-present hiss of the river in the valley's bottom competed with the songs of black-capped chickadees. The sun was just peeking over the horizon, promising to warm the spring air that was still chilly from the night before.

Tye didn't recognize the track in the patch of bare ground, muddy from last night's rain. The track was fresh. He could see every detail of the worn lugged boot sole. He put his foot next to it. Whoever made the track was a much bigger, heavier person than him. The impression in the mud was deep.

He stood and turned a slow circle, scanning the thick forest around him. His right hand crept back onto the stock of the shotgun without him even thinking about it.

Normally, he didn't walk around his property with a shotgun, but he'd woken that morning with a sense of foreboding, and as he passed his pickup in the driveway, he'd stopped to retrieve the battered old Mossberg from the locker in the back of his truck, feeling foolish as he'd done it.

The track was at the northern border of the property where he lived. On the other side of the property line were thousands of acres of private timberland. There was no reason for anyone to be up here. It wasn't hunting season, and they were half a mile from any of the gravel roads that snaked their way through the timberland.

Other than the birds, the surrounding forest was still. He couldn't shake the feeling of unease he'd had since he awakened. It wasn't a feeling of being watched so much as a feeling of building pressure, like a storm was coming.

Tye cast about for more sign. Other than the single clear track, there was scant evidence of the person's passing. Sticks littered the forest floor, but none were broken. There were no impressions or damage in the soft patch of moss that would have been the logical next place for the person's foot to fall.

Tye was a tracker, and over the years he'd trailed hundreds of people while working search-and-rescue cases. He'd developed a sense for people who were woods-wise, people who were aware of the sign they were leaving behind. Other than the single clear track that screamed like a billboard in the middle of the forest, the person had left very little sign of their passing through. It was hard to believe that was an accident, and it was even harder to believe they hadn't left the track in the mud expressly for Tye to see.

Tye walked a wide circle around the northern edge of his property, walking slowly and quietly. There was plenty of sign where deer passed through every night, and the wide trail through the low-growing vegetation of the valley's resident black bear just awakened from her slumber, but he had to strain to follow the trail of the human. He pieced together the trail from a bent piece of vegetation here, a faint partial impression on the forest floor there.

There were motion-activated wildlife cameras strapped to several trees here on the edge of the property. Tye enjoyed keeping track of what wildlife visited his land. It was like a window to another world. The trail he was following led right to the camera.

With a last look around, Tye slung the shotgun over his shoulder and pulled the memory card out of the camera. Using a card reader attached to his cell phone, he scrolled through the pictures.

He was greeted with shots of several blacktail deer, and a good-sized black bear snuffling around in the undergrowth looking for morsels to sate her spring hunger. Normally he would have examined each picture closely, trying to identify each animal and enjoying the nuances of their behavior when they were unobserved by humans.

Now, he swiped through the pictures, glancing at each one long enough to make sure there was no human figure, until he reached the end.

There, only inches in front of the camera, was a human hand with two fingers extended in a "V" sign.

The time stamp was only an hour and a half ago.

There were no other pictures on the card. Clearly, the person had been aware of the camera and had avoided being captured by the lens, other than when they'd stuck their hand in front of it.

Tye transferred the pictures to his phone, then put the memory card back in the camera. He was debating following the trail north into the woods on the other side of his property line when he heard an engine coming up his driveway. It was several hundred yards away, but the sound carried in the still air. He thought he recognized the sound of the engine as belonging to his girlfriend Kaity's Jeep.

Frowning, he checked his phone for a message from her. Nothing.

He turned and followed the trail down the hill. There was probably nothing wrong, but he couldn't shake the feeling of dread that had been following him around all morning like an unwanted black dog.

He listened as the Jeep climbed the steep driveway, then heard the crunch of tires on the gravel of the new extension to the driveway that had just been installed. The engine cut out, and he heard a door slam.

Aside from his worries, it was a fine spring morning. Tye was looking forward to some sunshine after a long, gray winter. The bare branches of the alder and big-leaf maple trees were swelling with buds poised to unfurl. He knew in a matter of days the landscape would be transformed into a riot of green, and after months of dreary sameness, every morning he would step out his door to a new landscape.

He turned toward the trail that would take him down the hill and home. Normally he walked through the woods at a slow, stealthy pace. Now he wasn't running, but he didn't care as much about the noise he was making, either.

He wondered if he was overreacting. A car pulling up his driveway shouldn't have been cause for alarm, but over the last several months, he'd been shot at, stabbed, and nearly drowned as he worked to find people missing in the dense wood of the Pacific Northwest.

The trail ended at the T-shaped intersection of his driveway. The driveway led through the trees to the county road at the bottom of the valley. To his left was the house that belonged to his friends Gary and May. His property was to the right.

As he walked down the freshly laid gravel of his new driveway, he recognized the tracks of Kaity's Jeep, then he walked around a corner and saw it parked behind his pickup truck.

She was nowhere to be seen, but from inside his yurt, he heard soft music playing, one of her favorite albums. He relaxed. Apparently, nothing was wrong.

The camper shell on the back of his pickup was unlocked, so he made quick work of stowing the shotgun inside. He didn't want Kaity to see him with it. He felt foolish parading around the property with it.

Just past the new gravel was a freshly cleared flat spot. Electrical conduit and plumbing pipes stuck out of the ground, and stakes and twine marked the outline of where their new tiny home would be delivered a few days from now.

Past that, a narrow footpath led through a patch of alder trees, and his yurt came into view. The little green octagonal shelter blended into the woods. It had been home for a few years.

Kaity was squatting in front of the wood stove, blowing a small flame to life, when he walked in. Here in the dense trees, it would take a while for the sun to warm the yurt.

She shut the doors to the stove and stood. She was almost as tall as him, with a shock of short black hair sticking out from under her fleece cap.

"There you are," she said and hugged him.

"Hey," he said. "What's up?"

"The tiny-house company wanted me to re-check some final measurements. I know you could have done it, but I thought I'd run out here real quick before work and surprise you."

Kaity worked as a librarian in the city of Vancouver, Washington, nearly an hour's drive away. She split her time between staying with Tye here in the yurt and her house in town.

"That's a lot of driving to take some measurements," he said.

"That's not the only reason I came." She kissed him.

Tye pulled her to him, all the other concerns of the day forgotten. He took her right hand in his.

"You don't have to wear the cast anymore?" A few weeks earlier, she'd fractured her hand punching a man in the face. Considering he'd helped kidnap both of them, the guy deserved it.

"The doctor says I'm good to go, as long as I don't punch anybody again." She looked at the time on her phone. "I have forty-five minutes before I have to leave for work. I have some great ideas about how we could spend the time."

Before he could reply, a car door slammed outside. He flinched and turned toward the door.

"Whoa," she said. "You're jumpy. What's wrong?"

Out of reflex, he almost said, "I'm fine," but bit the words off before they came out of his mouth.

"Don't be a typical dude and tell me you're fine," she said. "You've been a little edgy the past few days. What's going on?"

He sighed and felt his shoulders slump.

"I'm sorry. Somebody has been walking around up at the northern edge of the property. I found a track, almost like they meant for me to find it. And they messed with my trail camera."

"There's no hunting season right now. Kids screwing around?" she asked.

"It doesn't feel that way," he said. "I've been feeling off in general, like something is about to happen."

"Do you have the card from the camera?"

He pulled the card out of his pocket and handed it to her. Kaity's backpack was sitting on the bed. She unzipped it and took out her laptop and stuck the card in the slot.

"Let's see," she said as she scrolled through the pictures. "Deer. Deer. Owl. That's cool. Another deer. And somebody flashing a peace sign at the camera. I guess that's better than if they'd just used one finger."

"Maybe I'm making too big a deal about this," he said.

She turned and put a hand on his cheek. "You realize your intuition has kept us from getting killed a couple of times, right? I think we should pay attention to this."

"Thank you." He felt a lump in his throat that surprised him. All his life he'd had visions and feelings about the future but had kept them hidden from most people.

"It might be good to take your mind off it for a while, though." She pulled him to her again. "Forty minutes until I have to leave for work. Tick-tock."

As he bent over to kiss her, he heard footsteps on the gravel.

"Really?" Kaity said.

"It's probably Gary or May. Hopefully, it will be something quick," Tye said.

He didn't bother to wait for a knock, just opened the door and stepped outside.

It was his friend Gary, who lived in the house at the other end of the driveway. He was a tall, sinewy, bearded man, with a long ponytail of dark hair falling down his back. He wore stained work clothes and heavy leather boots.

"Hey, Tye," he said. "Hey, Kaity," he added when she peeked out the door. He looked back and forth between the two of them. "Sorry to interrupt, but you know the neighbors down the hill? Deborah and Vivian?"

"Yeah. Deborah is the one that just had surgery, right? May is helping her out."

"Yes. Them. Deborah thinks she may have shot somebody last night. They were trying to break into the house, and they ran off into the woods."

Tye sighed. "I'll get my stuff."

2

———————

Deborah and Vivian lived down the hill on the other side of the county road, next to the river. Tye parked his truck beside Gary's barely running International Scout.

"I was going to give Vivian a ride to work," Gary said as he shut off the Scout. "Their Subaru is in the shop. Something with the transmission."

The river noise was a constant murmur down here. Behind Deborah and Vivian's two-story log home, the river ran in a deep canyon carved by eons of water flowing down out of the mountains to the east.

"This is beautiful," Kaity said as she climbed out of the passenger side of the truck. She turned in a circle, taking in the giant Douglas fir trees that ringed the house. "This place hasn't been logged in the last 50 years like ours has. I guess ours will look like this someday."

Tye stopped for a moment, other concerns forgotten. He and Kaity were buying a tiny home to place next to his yurt, but it was the first time he'd ever heard her use the words "ours." He was struck at that moment by how much he just liked looking at her. She was wearing a fleece cap, a puffy jacket, and stained hiking pants, and he found her attractive because of all that, not despite it.

She caught him looking at her and smiled.

The door of the house swung open and a slender woman in her sixties wearing a pants suit stepped out.

"Thank you for coming," she said. "I didn't know what to do. Deborah doesn't want to call the sheriff." She bit her lip and rubbed her hands together. A little brown dog peered from around her ankles and gave a low growl.

"Hush, Chester." She bent over and the little dog jumped in her arms. "Why don't you all come in? It will be easier to show you than to try to explain."

Vivian and Deborah had moved in only a few weeks earlier. Moving boxes and cans of paint were stacked in the hallway. Vivian led them into a living room with floor-to-ceiling windows that looked out over the river below. A stocky woman with short gray hair was on the couch. Her foot was in a plastic boot and propped up on pillows.

There was a glass-paned door leading out to a wood deck outside. A splintered bullet hole marred the frame just above the doorknob, and the glass door was spiderwebbed.

"Well, I don't see a body," Gary said.

"Not sure I hit him," Deborah said.

"What exactly happened?" Tye asked.

"I haven't been able to sleep since the surgery two days ago." Deborah gestured at her foot. "I've been sleeping out here on the couch so I don't keep Vivian awake. Last night, Chester was super restless, whining and barking at the door."

As if to confirm her story, Chester gave a low growl.

"So I went and got my pistol," Deborah continued. "And I just sat here on the couch. I thought maybe it was a bear, and if I saw it, I'd fire a couple of rounds out the window to scare it off."

That wasn't exactly how Tye would have handled the situation, but at least the steep hill across the river would stop any errant bullets.

"Then somebody started jiggling the handle to the back door. There was no moon, so I only saw an outline, but it was a person, not a bear."

"What did you shoot at them with?" Gary asked. "That's a big hole."

From the couch cushions, Deborah produced a stainless-steel revolver. It had a massive frame but a short, stubby barrel. Tye drew back a little when she whipped it out, but she had it pointed in a safe direction, and her finger was off the trigger.

"It's a .480 Ruger Super Redhawk Alaskan," Deborah said.

"What the hell do you shoot with that?" Gary asked.

"Pretty much anything I want," Deborah answered. "Up in Alaska, I carried it when I worked on the pipeline, in case of bears."

She opened the cylinder and handed the gun to Gary, who ejected six fat cartridges into his palm. Each one was the size of his thumb.

"Looks like you replaced the round you fired."

"No sense walking around with a gun that isn't full-up."

"I reckon." Gary set the gun down on the side table.

Tye walked over to the back door and squatted to look through the bullet hole. Kaity stood beside him and looked out the window.

"I'd expect to see a bunch of blood if she hit anybody," she said.

"Or just a body on the porch, considering the size of that hand cannon." Tye looked over his shoulder at Deborah. "We could walk around and see if there's anything to see."

"I'd appreciate that," Deborah said. "I would have gone outside at first light, but you know..." She gestured at her foot.

"Yep. I get it." Tye opened the back door gingerly, lest all the glass fall out. He stepped back out into the sound of the river, followed by Gary and Kaity. Despite his care, a few shards of glass fell out of the door.

"We ought to tape that up for them," Gary said.

"Yeah, we can do that," Tye said. He surveyed the damage. Where the bullet had exited the door frame, it had blown out big splinters, then traveled through one of the porch supports, nearly cracking the two-by-four in half. From there it had presumably sailed across the river, where hopefully it had buried itself in a tree trunk or the dirt of the hillside.

"If we have occasion to visit them in the night, let's make sure we announce ourselves," Tye said quietly.

Gary and Kaity both nodded.

"There's a drop of blood," Kaity said. She pointed at the deck.

Tye squatted to look. The splotch of blood on the deck board was about the size of a quarter. The center wasn't dry yet.

"Not enough for a bullet wound. Must have gotten hit with a splinter from the door," Gary said.

"Or some glass," Tye said.

"Here's another." Kaity was tracking the droplets down the steep stairway that led to the river below. Tye and Gary followed along. Kaity had been working on her tracking skills, and Tye was content to let her take the lead. They were mindful of the rotten boards on the stairs that hadn't seen any maintenance in a long time.

"It's a shame this house sat empty for so long," Gary said. "It will be a nice place once Deborah and Vivian get it spruced up."

"They have their work cut out for them," Tye said.

"I think he crossed the river," Kaity said from the bottom of the stairs.

Tye joined her at the river's edge. There in the narrow strip of sandy beach between the bottom of the stairs and the water, he saw an indistinct set of prints heading toward the house, and another set heading back.

"Yep. That's a bold move right there," Tye said. "Big guy. Maybe some kind of moccasin on his feet. He definitely crossed the river."

"That seems super dangerous," Kaity said.

"He wouldn't have been able to do it a week ago," Tye said.

The river was only twenty yards across at this point. Right now, it was shallow, a little over knee-high in a few spots. A week ago, during the height of the spring snow melt, it would have been up to Tye's shoulders, and the current would have been raging.

"I think I see a spot on the other side where he climbed out," Kaity said.

"That's an odd damn way to burglarize a house," Gary said. "You wouldn't be able to carry much away across the river. Even though the water is low, I'd hate to try that crossing in the dark."

"It makes me wonder if he had something more nefarious planned," Tye said. "That water is still pretty cold. I don't particularly want to wade across, but I reckon I could drive to the other side there, work my way down the bank, and try to pick up the trail from there."

Kaity pulled her phone from her pocket. "I should have left for work five minutes ago."

"I can go by myself," Tye said.

"You mean, you want to go alone through the woods, trailing a potentially violent criminal?" Kaity asked. "Because that's worked out so well the other times you've done it."

Gary sighed. "I'm supposed to dig some trench for the new house's sewer line, but it could wait a few hours. I could back you up."

"So, we're getting involved in this?" Kaity asked.

"They're neighbors," Gary said.

"Yep," Tye said. "They're neighbors."

3

———————

"Did Kaity drive out here before work just so she could see you?" Gary asked as they drove across the Dole Valley Road bridge over the river.

"She did," Tye said.

"You better not screw this one up," Gary said. "She's a pretty good catch."

"I agree," Tye said. He slowed the truck to let a doe and two fawns walk across the road in front of him. The houses out here were spread far apart on five- and ten-acre parcels, separated by dense stands of Douglas fir trees where no one had logged in decades and even denser stands of red alder where folks had sold their timber.

They passed a dilapidated house on the left side of the road. Tye slowed automatically to look the place over, as it belonged to some friends. It needed a coat of paint, but it didn't look like anyone had caused any mischief in the owner's absence.

"How are Miss Natalie and her mom, anyway?" Gary asked.

The previous summer, Tye, Kaity, Gary, and May, Gary's wife, had rescued a young girl named Natalie from a kidnapper.

"They're still staying with George and Brian," Tye said. "I guess Natalie still has nightmares if they try to stay in their house."

"I can't blame her, seeing as how she was snatched right out of the backyard," Gary said.

"I think it's easier for Marsha not to drink if she's not the only adult in the house, too," Tye said. Marsha, Natalie's mother, had been battling a drinking problem when they met her. "I think she and Brian are hitting it off pretty well, and old George is happy to have some company out on that property of his."

"Sounds like a happy ending for everybody," Gary said.

"I met Kaity because of it."

"When you two are old and gray, you can tell people how you met because you found her in the middle of a forest trying to rescue a little girl. It's a much better story than 'We met in a bar.'"

Tye laughed. He slowed the truck down to turn east into the Yacolt Burn State Forest. The roads here were gravel but well-maintained, so he was able to keep some speed.

The forest was actively managed for timber production. The large stretches that had been recently clear-cut looked like moonscapes, with muddy ground and big piles of branches and other debris. Interspersed with the cuts were big stands of mature timber. Tye had learned not to get too emotionally attached to them because it was only a matter of time before they fell before the saw.

He drove through the intricate network of gravel roads without stopping to consult a map. Over the winter, he'd spent a lot of time on these roads, sometimes with Gary, sometimes with Kaity, often alone. Part of it was a desire to know the surrounding landscape. Part of it was a practical need to scout the area for the fall hunting seasons. Tye tried not to eat any meat aside from deer and elk he killed himself.

The other reason was he'd needed time to think. The last six months had been a roller coaster. He'd been involved in helping solve Natalie's kidnapping, which had led to Tye and Kaity establishing a search-and-rescue consulting business. After that, they'd been involved in solving two murders in rapid succession: one on an island in Puget Sound and another in a wilderness area up in the mountains.

On top of all that, his relationship with Kaity, which had started as a slow burn, was now proceeding at a breakneck pace. Sometimes he found it hard to believe they were building a home together.

Finally, he stopped a hundred yards away from an old metal gate across the road. Tye parked the truck in between two trees so it wasn't blocking the road and shut off the engine.

He and Gary both stepped out of the truck and quietly eased the doors shut rather than slamming them. Then they stood quietly for several minutes, moving as little as possible, saying nothing.

Before he started a track, Tye liked to establish a baseline of animal behavior for the land he was walking on. The animals here were used to occasional vehicle traffic, but still, the simple act of driving the truck down the road had created a disturbance. The longer they stood there, the more birdsong Tye heard in the immediate area. A Douglas squirrel stuck its head out of a bush, studied them intently for a few seconds, then decided they weren't worth raising an alarm and skittered up a tree trunk.

A gentle breeze brushed his cheek. The sun was warming the air in the river valley below, so as they descended, their scent would be blowing uphill. They would be less likely to spook animals like deer and elk.

Satisfied that things had settled down, Tye opened the camper shell as quietly as he could so he and Gary could fetch their gear.

"I was thinking of taking the gauge," Gary said quietly.

Tye nodded and unlocked the storage compartment under the bunk. Gary withdrew the old Mossberg shotgun, fed five rounds of buckshot into the magazine, and put a pouch containing some extra ammunition in the thigh pocket of his cargo pants.

Tye settled a sixteen-liter Hill People Gear backpack on his shoulders and eased the back of the camper closed. If something went wrong, he had a decent chance of surviving a wilderness emergency with the Buck knife on his belt and the lighter in his pocket, but the little backpack carried enough gear to give him several extra layers of security.

Tye took a knee and examined a mud puddle on the dirt road. Recently, two other vehicles had passed the spot where Tye had parked the truck. One had been a motorcycle, with knobby off-road tires. The other had most likely been a truck, judging from the width of the tread.

"If I'm reading this mud puddle correctly, it looks like a truck and motorcycle drove in, but only the truck came back," Gary said.

"That's the way I see it," Tye agreed. "There's a chance the motorcycle tracks were fouled by the truck on the way out, but I don't think so."

Tye walked up to the gate and soon found the spot where the truck had been parked, and not far away, the impression of the motorcycle's kickstand in the dirt.

"Three people total," Tye said, pointing at the tracks. "Two were in the truck. One on the motorcycle. All three walked around the gate."

"But only two came back," Gary said from where he was kneeling by the gate. There was a narrow opening between the gate post and an alder tree, just wide enough for a person to squeeze through.

Tye craned his neck and walked bent over from where the motorcycle had been parked, to the truck tire tracks. "I'm pretty sure the two that came back loaded the motorcycle into the back of the pickup."

"But the motorcycle rider didn't come back up the hill," Gary said.

"Nope. Those riding boots he was wearing leave a pretty distinctive track."

"Well, this is damn curious," Gary said.

"It is," Tye agreed.

"I need to go get that ditch dug, but now my curiosity is piqued."

"Mine too. Let's see where the trail takes us."

They walked around the gate and set off down an abandoned road that was overgrown with weeds and small saplings. This stretch of forest belonged to a local conservation land trust. The hundred-acre parcel had been slated for development for a housing development, until the deal fell through and the land trust bought it. Tye was grateful every morning when he woke up and saw a stand of alder trees across the river instead of a bunch of houses.

The land was open to the public but was rarely visited because it was tucked away on the far side of the state forest through a maze of roads. As they walked down the old road, Tye saw plenty of deer and elk tracks, but no trash, broken glass, or empty shell casings that were all too frequent signs of human passage around here.

The only human sign was the trail of the three people that had walked in and two that had walked out. Discerning the age of a track was more of an art than a science. Most of the tracks were mere impressions in the weeds, but occasionally, Tye would find a partial impression of a boot print in a muddy spot. The vegetation was just starting to spring back up, and the marks in the mud were crisp, with plenty of detail. That suggested to Tye the tracks were hours old, and not days.

Tye and Gary fell into a rhythm born of long practice. Tye looked a few feet ahead, watching for the next set of tracks. Gary followed a few feet behind, shotgun cradled in his arms, looking out in the distance for threats. During their search-and-rescue days, they had mostly looked for people who wanted to be found, but not all cases were what they seemed at first glance. Some people went into the woods because they wanted to cover up a crime and didn't take too kindly to being followed.

The trail was consistent the whole time. Three men walked in. Two walked out. It led in the exact direction Tye had intended to go. The old road switchbacked down the slope until it came to a flat area overlooking the river. Soon, they were directly across the river from Deborah and Vivian's house.

There was a fourth set of tracks leading up from the beach. Tye pointed at them and squatted to take a closer look. Gary stayed standing, looking around them in all directions.

The new tracks were big. When Tye put his size-ten boot down in comparison, it was dwarfed in size. Just like the tracks at Deborah and Vivian's house, the tracks lacked any crisp features. Now Tye was even more sure whoever had made them was wearing moccasins or something similar.

Tye stood shoulder to shoulder with Gary but facing in the opposite direction. This way they could talk in low tones and see all around them.

"Those are the same as back at the house," Tye said. "I don't see any more blood, so he must have not been hurt very bad."

"Interesting. Keep going?"

"We've come this far."

Gary nodded, and they resumed tracking. As they moved east, they left the thick stands of alder trees behind and moved into a grove of stately old cedar trees that had escaped the chainsaw. Under the alders, the understory had been a thick riot of low-growing plants, but here, the ground was too shaded for most plants to grow, and it was much more open.

There was a well-defined game trail here, so broad and clear it could have easily been mistaken for a human-made hiking trail. Judging from the dozens of old and new tracks, Tye figured a herd of a dozen elk used this trail at least weekly.

Something shiny caught Tye's eye. He bent to find a shell casing, still shiny and clean. It was odd-looking. Most handgun cartridges were short, often less than an inch, and were cylindrical. Most rifle cartridges were over an inch and a half and had a bottle-necked shape, wider at the base than the neck.

This one was only a little longer than a pistol cartridge but had the bottleneck shape of a rifle case. Tye found a twig, stuck it in the neck of the casing, and lifted it to his nose. The smell of burnt gunpowder was strong. The head stamp on the base of the cartridge read ".300 BLK."

"Recognize this one?" Tye asked.

Gary looked away from scanning the surrounding woods. "I think that's one of those new cartridges the guys who like to play commando are shooting. Wonder what they were shooting at."

Tye put the case back where he found it. He jerked his chin down the trail. "We keep heading this way, we'll likely find out."

The hair on the back of Tye's neck was standing up, for a reason he couldn't quite put his finger on. As they'd moved east down this trail, the birds had gotten more quiet. Now no birds were singing immediately around them. He could hear a lone robin in the distance behind them, but that was it.

He tapped his ear and looked at Gary, who nodded. He'd noticed it too. They moved a little slower, taking more care to scan up ahead with each step.

The shadows were deep here. The sun hadn't quite climbed high enough in the sky to illuminate the river canyon. Tye couldn't make out the dark shape on the ground beside the trail up ahead, but in his gut, he knew what it was.

In a few more steps, they were close enough to tell that it was the body of a man wearing motorcycle boots. He was still and lifeless. The morning breeze ruffled his hair, but there was no other movement.

Gary sighed. "I guess I'm not gonna get to dig that ditch today after all."

4

"He sure looks dead," Gary said. They were still twenty feet away from the body. The man looked young, not quite thirty, and had short blond hair. He wore a gray nylon motorcycle jacket and pants. The jacket was unzipped, and Tye was pretty sure he could see a big bloodstain on the lighter-colored t-shirt he wore underneath the jacket.

"I reckon we should make sure," Tye said. "I'd hate to find out the guy had a little life left in him and then expired after we left to get help."

"Fair point. On we go then."

Tye took a moment to pull on a pair of nitrile gloves from the first-aid kit in his backpack, then they walked up to the body. Tye was no stranger to dead people, but he dreaded it every time he had to deal with something like this, and his stomach roiled.

As they drew closer, Tye saw a black Beretta handgun on the ground next to the man. The hammer was back, and Tye made a note to give it a wide berth. The man still hadn't moved.

"Hey, buddy, you okay?" Tye asked, knowing it would be futile. He felt the man's neck for a pulse. Nothing.

"He's still a little warm," Tye said. The smell of blood was strong.

Tye pulled the jacket away from the guy's chest and abdomen. As he'd thought, it was covered with blood. There was a round wound on the side of his ribcage.

"Looks like a bullet hole to me," Gary said. "Is there an exit?"

Tye lifted the other side of the jacket. "Don't see one. We'd have to roll him over to be sure, but I doubt it."

"Transverse shot across the chest. Probably mashed up both lungs, maybe even hit the heart," Gary said.

"Quick," Tye said.

"Quick," Gary agreed. He pulled his cell phone from his pocket. "And unlikely to be self-inflicted. I don't have a signal down here in the river canyon. I guess we'll have to walk on back up to the top of the ridge."

They were just as careful walking out as they were walking in. Tye figured the shooter or shooters were long gone, but they stayed cautious just in case.

"We're going to have to tell them about Deborah cranking off a round at her intruder last night," Gary said. "Although I doubt the dead guy back there is the result of her shooting."

"I agree on both counts," Tye said. "If she'd hit him with that big .480, it would have gone clean through him, and maybe a couple of other people if they were in the way. There's no way this guy ran very far with that wound. He was shot right here."

"Yep. I'm trying to piece all this together in my head," Gary said.

"It looks like the dead guy rode his motorcycle and parked at the gate before walking into the woods. Two people in a truck followed him. At some point, the motorcyclist wound up with an extra hole in him, and the two people from the truck hiked back up the hill, packed his motorcycle into their pickup truck, and drove away."

Tye held a piece of blackberry bush aside for Gary to slip through. The day was warming up, and both men were sweating as they climbed the hill.

"Seems like an awfully convoluted way to steal a motorcycle," Gary said.

"I agree," Tye said. "And around the same time, somebody

wearing moccasins waded across the river and tried to get in Vivian and Deborah's house, before being met with a round of that little miniature howitzer Deborah is toting around. At which point they hightailed it back to the other side and walked deeper into the forest."

"I find it hard to believe all these events aren't connected," Gary said.

"That would be one big damn coincidence," Tye said. "Check your phone. We're almost out of the canyon."

Gary pulled his phone out. "Yessir. I've got two bars. That should do it." He dialed 9-1-1 and spoke with a dispatcher, who asked the same questions two or three times. Gary didn't even try to give directions to the spot where they were standing. Instead, he made arrangements to meet a sheriff's deputy at an easy-to-find intersection of two major forest roads.

"I sure didn't wake up this morning expecting all this," Gary said as he shoved his phone back into his pocket. "Let's get a move on. There's a deputy close by for a change."

The deputy was waiting for them when they arrived at the intersection. Her nametag read "Fitzpatrick," and she seemed young enough to get carded if she tried to buy beer, but she was efficient and professional, taking their identification and a brief statement as they stood by the side of the road.

"Detective Evans will be here shortly," the deputy said. "She wants us to wait for her before you lead us to the body."

"Evans. Is she the detective that investigated when that fellow kidnapped Natalie and May?" Gary asked.

"She is," Tye said.

"And the murder of that fellow up in the Indian Heaven Wilderness last fall?"

"Yep. Same one."

"You two ought to be on a first-name basis."

"I think her first name is 'Detective.'"

The sheriff's deputy busied herself with paperwork in her car, always keeping half an eye on Tye and Gary as she worked. Gary called May and explained what was going on.

It occurred to Tye that he should text Kaity. Tye was just over thirty years old, but in many ways, he felt like a member of a much older generation. He had rarely used a cell phone until recently. Kaity had been perturbed with him more than once because he'd forgotten to check his phone for hours when she was trying to get in touch with him.

We found a dead guy on the other side of the river, he laboriously typed on the too-small keyboard.

She replied almost instantly. *Seriously? Who is it? Did Deborah shoot him?*

He was shot. Not by Deborah. He had to go back three times and erase typing mistakes.

What makes you think it wasn't Deborah?

Tye stared at the screen, trying to figure out how he could explain the ballistics differences between Deborah's giant handgun and the .300 Blackout via text. He was saved by the appearance of an unmarked sheriff's department SUV.

Detective here. Have to go, he managed to peck out without any mistakes before hitting "send."

Detective Evans was in her forties, with close-cropped hair and a perpetual frown. She wore a pantsuit, with a Glock handgun and a badge clipped to her belt.

Tye walked over, feeling like a sheepish little kid for some reason.

"You," Evans said. "Maybe I should get you a punch card. If you find ten dead bodies, you get a free cup of coffee or something."

"I feel like it's more like they find me sometimes," Tye said before he had a chance to think about what was coming out of his mouth.

Evans put her hands on her hips and sighed. "Doyle says I should trust you."

Doyle Creely was a retired sheriff's department detective and Tye's friend. He'd mentored Evans at the beginning of her career.

"I'd like to think Doyle is a good judge of character," Tye said.

"Hence my willingness not to see something nefarious in the fact that you keep stumbling over dead bodies in the woods." She moved to the back of her SUV, opened the hatch, and sat on the tailgate. "This, of course, happened right as I was leaving court. Tell me everything while I put some boots on."

She fished a pair of heavy lugged boots out of the back of her vehicle and put them on while Tye explained the morning's events.

"So, your neighbor cranked off a round at somebody trying to break into her house, and then you found a freshly dead body in the woods across the river. Maybe I can have this wrapped up in time for a late lunch." She pulled a backpack and camera bag out of her SUV and slammed the hatch.

"I don't think the round that killed that guy came from my neighbor's gun."

"What? You're a ballistics expert now? I appreciate that you found a shell casing by the body, but this place is littered with shell casings. I passed two piles of shot-up appliances on my way in."

"I'm not a ballistics expert, but I've seen enough animals shot with big-bore revolvers to know a skinny dude like that would've had a giant exit wound from a slug that big and heavy."

Evans rolled her neck around with an audible crunching sound. "Okay. I'll keep an open mind. Let's go on a nature hike."

Tye led the way to the trailhead. As they walked, Tye explained the tracks and sign he was seeing. Evans at least seemed to take him seriously, while the younger deputy looked at him like he was crazy.

"You can really tell all that from marks in the weeds?" Fitzpatrick asked.

"Mr. Caine here is a famous tracker," Evans said. "He was even on a TV show. I don't have any idea how to use any of this in court, though."

"Oh," Fitzpatrick said. "That's why you look familiar. You're the guy from Supermodel Survival."

Tye closed his eyes and took a deep breath. Ever since he'd been on the reality TV show, he'd regretted it. The money hadn't been worth it. He'd had to fight to get paid, and he'd become resigned to the fact that he'd forever be "that guy on the show with the supermodel."

Tye had to take off his sweatshirt as they re-traced their steps back to the body. The sun had warmed the air down here at the bottom of the valley. Now that the morning rush was over, the birds had settled down and the forest was quiet. Dead body or not, Tye liked this stretch of woods. It was far enough from a road that there was no trash, and nobody used it for target practice.

"The body is just up here on the other side of those trees," he said, hoping everyone would drop the subject of the TV show.

Evans slowed down and started taking pictures of the scene as they walked. She even took pictures of some of the impressions in the weeds that Tye pointed out, placing a photographic ruler next to each one.

"Here are some clear prints in the mud," Tye said. He squatted next to them and pointed. "See the motorcycle boots, moccasin, and other shoe prints? All four people walked through this muddy patch."

"This I think I can use," Evans said. She took pictures of everything.

"I think the two guys from the truck shot the guy in the motorcycle jacket. Then the guy in the moccasins walked up later, saw the body, then turned around and walked off. There was a little bit of a breeze after midnight last night. It blew the alder cones into the boot-prints. But the moccasin prints were made after the alder cones fell."

Evans nodded. "I guess that makes sense."

"Here's the shell casing," Tye said and pointed it out. Evans pulled an evidence marker from her backpack, placed it next to the casing, and took a picture.

"The crime scene guys will pick that up and bag it," Evans said. It sounded like she was saying it to herself as much as everyone else.

"And there's the body," Tye said and pointed.

Evans told them to stay back. She walked up slowly, taking pictures as she went. She bent over the dead man, pulled his jacket aside, and let it drop. She moved around to better see the dead man's face, and to Tye, it seemed like she recoiled, as if she'd seen something she hadn't expected. Tye didn't know what to think of that. There hadn't been any injuries on the man's face, and he was sure Evans had seen plenty of dead bodies before.

She stood for a minute, taking deep breaths as if collecting herself, then walked back to Tye and Gary. "Okay. Maybe there's some merit to your ballistics theory."

"Did you know that guy?" Gary asked.

Evans gave him an odd look, like he'd caught her doing something she wasn't supposed to. "The medical examiner will make the official identification. We still need to talk to your neighbor. The medical examiner and crime scene team will be here in another half an hour. Until then, we're going to get your statement written down." She pulled a roll of crime scene tape from her backpack and handed it to Fitzpatrick, who started stringing it from tree to tree.

"We already explained it once to Fitzpatrick and a second time to you," Gary said.

"We're the cops," Evans said. "We've got to hear it at least three times."

"Well, let's get started. I've got a ditch to dig," Gary said.

5

———

"I can't believe they took my gun," Deborah said.

It was well after noon, and Tye and Gary were boarding up the shattered back door of Deborah and Vivian's house. Deborah seemed to appreciate the help, but also clearly didn't like anyone but her working on her home. She was giving lots of obvious advice that Tye and Gary were trying to take with good grace.

"I imagine they'll give it back at some point after they run some tests," Gary said around a mouthful of nails. He was hammering a piece of plywood over the back door opening where the glass had been.

Tye finished sweeping up bits of broken glass. "That ought to do it. I reckon we should hit the road soon."

Vivian walked in from the kitchen, holding Chester in his little dog carrier. Tye wasn't sure what breed of dog Chester was, but he suspected he was the result of a wild evening between a chihuahua and a large rat. Right now, he looked thoroughly nonplussed to be confined.

"All we have to do is put Chester in the truck, and we'll be ready to go," Vivian said. "I so much appreciate this."

"I still don't see why we can't stay in our own home," Deborah said.

Before Vivian could answer, Tye leaned the broom against the wall and said, "Well, let's go then. It's getting late." He and Gary had listened to the same argument play out several times now. Tye wanted to help his neighbors, but he was in no mood to listen to the same conflict again.

Thankfully, Deborah let it go and crutched after them as they headed out the door. Tye's pickup was a crew cab, so there was plenty of room to settle Vivian and Chester in the back seat, while Deborah rode up front.

The sun was going down as he drove up the river valley. This had been one of those days that seemed to take forever but then was over before he knew it. They'd waited around in the state forest for hours, repeating their stories to another detective and the medical examiner. Tye firmly suspected it was a stalling tactic to keep them fixed in one spot while Evans interviewed Vivian and Deborah.

They'd returned from the forest to find Deborah fuming over the seizure of her gun and Vivian flatly refusing to spend another night in the house until the police figured out who the dead man was. There wasn't enough room in either Gary and May's trailer or Tye's yurt for two more people and a dog. They'd pitched in helping not only clean up the damage to the back door but also finding a place for the couple to stay.

They'd done it without even stopping to consider whether they should. Tye and Gary had been friends for a long time, and whenever they knew somebody needed help, they tended to do it just by reflex.

"We appreciate the help," Vivian said from the back seat. From the seat beside him, Deborah nodded.

"Least we can do," Tye said. "It's bad timing, all this happening right after you move into a new area."

They were quiet for the rest of the drive. Tye took a turn north and drove through the little town of Yacolt, noting with interest that the lone restaurant was open again. It looked like the new owner was selling tacos, which was a welcome change from the greasy menu from the previous owners. Then he turned west and wound his way through a series of back roads into the hills. He turned on a gravel driveway and drove through an open gate.

They passed a barn, came around a bend, and there in front of them was an old farmhouse, well-kept and full of light. On the other side of the driveway was a sizable travel trailer, also lit up. Tye parked as close to it as he could.

A tall man in his sixties wearing work clothes stepped out of the trailer and waved.

"Hello, George," Tye said as he got out of the truck.

"You're just in time. I got all the linens changed out, the water tanks are full, and the heater is turned on." George Hollis was well over six feet, with shoulders that could fill a doorway and scarred blacksmith's hands. He was also one of the most generous men Tye had ever met.

Deborah managed to get out of the truck and on her crutches without assistance. Tye opened his mouth to make introductions, when the screen door to the house slammed open and a passel of children and a dog ran out and surrounded him.

Tye stumbled as a little girl ran up, hair flying behind her, and wrapped her arms around his waist.

"Tye! It's been so long since I've seen you!"

"Hello, Natalie. I think it was just last week, but it's good to see you, too."

Natalie's twin brothers were both talking at once. One brother was trying to show him a coyote skull, while the other was holding up a bow and arrow he'd carved from a fallen piece of hazel wood. Tye knew their names were Caden and Alfie, but he still struggled to tell them apart. All the while, the family dog, a pit bull mix named Killer, barked joyfully and ran around in circles, wagging her little stub of a tail.

A woman appeared in the doorway, silhouetted by the light spilling from the door.

"Kids, come on back and stop bothering Mr. Tye. There's pie."

"Pie!" both brothers exclaimed at once and sprinted for the door, leaving some blessed silence in their wake.

Natalie took Tye's hand shyly. "I'm glad you're here. Where's Kaity?"

"She had to work. She told me to tell you hello and to say she misses you."

"That's nice."

Killer belied her name and flopped on her back for a belly scratch. Tye obliged for a few seconds, then walked toward the house with Natalie.

"Do you still have bad dreams? About the Dark Man?" Natalie asked.

Natalie had just turned eight, but Tye couldn't bring himself to condescend to her. She was wise beyond her years in a way that was a little unsettling.

"I do," he admitted. "Even though he's dead, I still see him in my dreams."

"My therapist seems to think it's all in my head, but I don't. I think he's real. I think he's still out there."

A breeze blew across the back of Tye's neck, and he shivered. "I suspect you might be right, although it might not be wise to tell your therapist that."

She nodded. "I play along. The Dark Man scares me, but when I'm around good people, people that love me, there's no room for him in my head."

Tye felt a lump in his throat. Natalie had just perfectly articulated something he'd been trying to put into words for weeks. The dreams haunted him only when he was alone, in dark moments when he felt like no one else understood.

The inside of the house smelled like pie and coffee. Marsha, Natalie's mother, looked healthier every time Tye saw her. When he'd first met her, she'd been struggling with drinking, and the kids had been left to fend for themselves. Now she was studying to be a medical assistant and looked clear-eyed.

"I don't know how many times I've told you not to put the coyote skull on the table," she was saying as Tye walked into the kitchen. "Oh, hello, Tye. There's pie and coffee."

"I'd love some." He took a seat at the table. The boys were unusually quiet, their mouths full of pie. "Is Brian working?"

Marsha sat a piece of apple pie and a mug of coffee in front of him. "He picked up an extra shift at the vet clinic. They like him down there."

"He's good with animals," Tye said. As they talked, he realized at one point in his life, sitting and making small talk would have been uncomfortable. But now that he'd left his old life of moving from outdoor job to job, sleeping in the back of his truck, and had now settled into a place, this all felt perfectly natural.

"We have some news," Marsha said. She held out her hand to show him a ring with a small diamond.

"Congratulations," Tye said. "When's the big day?"

"Later in the summer so we have time to go on a honeymoon before school starts. George is going to watch the kids for us."

"That's nice of him." Tye had almost said "brave" but changed it at the last second. The twins were now competing to see who could eat their pie without using their forks or their hands. They were just lowering their faces to their plates and eating.

"You two stop that!" Marsha grabbed an ear in each hand and hauled them over to the sink to wash them off. Natalie rolled her eyes and took a bite.

The door swung open, and George walked in, hanging his coat on a peg by the door and kicking off his boots.

"I've got them settled for the night," he said. "I think Vivian's scared, and Deborah's pretty angry."

"That's about the size of it," Tye agreed.

Marsha put a piece of pie and a cup of coffee down in front of George and shooed the kids out of the kitchen.

"Time for bed," she said.

"I want to hang out with Tye," Natalie protested.

"Tell you what," Tye said. "You go get ready for bed, and I won't leave until you've had a chance to say good night."

That seemed to mollify her, and she followed her mother and mostly scrubbed brothers upstairs.

"Things seem to be going well here," Tye said to George.

"It's been a blessing. This house was going to be mighty empty with just me in it. They set their wedding date on the anniversary of Henry's death. They didn't realize it, and I didn't say anything. He'd want something good to happen that day."

Tye didn't know what to say. Henry Longstreet had been George's partner for decades, long before it was even safe for two men to live together in a rural area such as this. Henry had been killed last summer by Natalie's kidnapper.

"But enough of that," George said. "How are you, Tye?"

"Fine," he said by reflex and took a sip of coffee.

George looked at him over the rim of his cup. "You've touched some evil things in the last year, my friend. Henry fought those same things for decades. Fundamentally, he was a good man, just like you. But it troubled him, more than he would say at times."

Tye moved his pie around on his plate for a while before he answered. "I have dreams still. About a dark figure."

George nodded. "As did Henry. As does Natalie. I imagine it would be difficult to go to a psychologist and talk about your experiences fighting a man who might have been more than a man and sought to suck the very life energy out of people."

Tye laughed. "Yeah, and let's not forget that I sometimes seem to see people who are dead."

George had never asked him if he saw Henry, and the question hung between them, unspoken, for a while. The truth was, Tye had dreamed of Henry Longstreet while he'd been unraveling the mystery of Natalie's kidnapping, and since then, Henry had been absent, as if satisfied that his work was done.

"Well, I just want you to know that the front gate is always open to you, and there's always coffee to be made if you want to sit around this table and air some things out. After living with Henry for so long, I doubt there's anything you could tell me that I would find shocking."

"I appreciate it."

"There's also the matter of Henry's books and research. There are some strange things in there. Books that cost a fortune. Sometimes I'm tempted to burn it all, but I wonder if someday we might need it. I wonder if there are answers for you in there."

"I don't think I'm ready for that yet," Tye said. "But thank you." He'd almost said he wasn't strong enough but again changed his words at the last second.

The sound of pounding feet on the hardwood floor preceded Natalie's entrance to the kitchen. She was wearing sparkly unicorn pajamas, and her breath smelled of mint toothpaste.

"I almost forgot! I drew you a picture."

She handed him a piece of construction paper with a crayon drawing.

"That's me in the center. That's you and Kaity holding my hands. And there's that bad man down there."

Tye unfolded the paper and spread it on the table. It was a remarkably good likeness of both Tye and Kaity. She'd captured Tye's beard and general scruffiness quite well, and Kaity's shock of black hair stuck out from her watch cap, just like in real life. They were both much taller than Natalie.

The dark man in the corner looked just like the black silhouette in Tye's dreams, only with X-marks for eyes, and his tongue was hanging out of his mouth. Somehow, Natalie had rendered the ominous figure harmless and almost comical with her drawing.

"That's awesome," Tye said. "Kaity will love it. I'll hang it up in our yurt." He noted he'd said "our" with a little thrill of pleasure.

"Oh... Are you two living together?" Natalie said with a piercing look that seemed way beyond her years.

"Sometimes," Tye said. "Not all the time."

"Maybe you two could get married on the same day as Brian and Mom. It could be a double wedding!"

Tye laughed. "Well, we're not making any plans yet." He yawned. "It's getting late, and I have work to do in the morning. I have to get home."

She hugged him. Tye winced a little when she jostled the long scar on his ribs, a leftover from the knife wound he'd suffered during Natalie's rescue. It had healed poorly, with the scar adhering to the tissue underneath, and sometimes when something brushed against it, it was like an electric shock.

As he hugged Natalie, he realized it had all been worth it.

"Good night, sleep tight," he said as she drew back.

"Don't let the bed bugs bite," she finished for him and giggled before turning to run up the stairs.

Tye shook George's hand.

"Don't be a stranger," George said.

"I won't."

6

———————

Tye had known the coffee was a mistake but had drunk it anyway. He was wired on the way home and knew he wouldn't sleep for hours.

So instead of going straight home, he pulled over at a spot along the river. Over the winter, he'd installed a lock box in the center console of his truck. Now he opened it and withdrew a little five-shot Smith and Wesson revolver, also a recent purchase that had cost him a small fortune.

Tye had never been one to carry a gun around town. He often toted a pistol while he was out in the woods, but he was perturbed at grown men who felt a need to parade around the local shopping center with a Glock on their hip. Recent experiences had left him with a desire to be armed more often, though.

The little revolver went in a nylon holster that all but disappeared in the front right pocket of his hiking pants. He pulled a flashlight from the charging cradle mounted under the dash of his truck and stuck it in his pocket, then dimmed the truck's dash lights as far as they would go. Then he drove the rest of the way home.

He drove past Deborah and Vivian's house and into his driveway, but instead of driving up the hill, he pulled in just far enough not to block the county road and parked the truck. He pressed the button that disabled the truck's dome light, so it wouldn't come on automatically when he opened the door, then stepped out into the night.

The night air was cool enough he was grateful to be wearing a jacket. Off in the distance, a barred owl hooted a couple of times, then the only noise was the sound of the river. By habit, Tye tended to wear clothes in muted gray, brown, and green. Tonight was no exception, and as he slipped away from the truck, any observer would have been hard-pressed to see him in the dim light of the quarter moon.

Tye walked down the country road, then turned onto Deborah and Vivian's property, walking beside the driveway so he could avoid the gravel. The thin-soled minimalist boots he wore made little sound in the wet grass. He stayed in the shadows, pausing to look and listen as he walked around the house with his hand in his pocket on the grip of the little revolver.

On the back deck, he didn't have to be that quiet because the noise of the river covered the sound of his footfalls. From the front of the house, he'd noticed that there was a lamp left on in the living room, but from here it was barely visible. The south-facing windows were heavily tinted to keep the cabin from heating up from the summer sun. Even with the lamp on inside, it would be impossible to tell if someone was sitting in the living room.

The sound of a heavy engine carried on the night air. Tye paused, waiting for it to pass. Traffic on their road late at night was uncommon this time of year. Come summer weekends, teenagers would often drive into the national forest at the end of the road to party at all hours of the night, but in the spring, things were usually quiet.

He heard the crunch of gravel under tires as the vehicle stopped in Deborah and Vivian's driveway. Then the engine shut off. Tye walked around the house, to the side away from the carport and the driveway, and peeked around the corner.

In the moonlight, he could see a pickup truck blocking the driveway. It was impossible to tell the make or model, or even the color, but Tye got the impression it was jacked up, with a suspension lift and off-road tires. Two people were walking down the driveway. One was squat and broad, the other taller and slender. It was too dark to see facial features or even clothing, but Tye was certain they weren't sheriff's deputies called by a neighbor who had seen him lurking around the house. He wasn't sure whether to feel relieved by that or not.

He crept back to the center of the west wall of the house, careful not to brush against the bushes and make noise. If their goal was to break in, they would have little reason to come to this side of the house. The front door was on the north side, there was a door from the carport on the east side, and the boarded-up back door was on the south. There was no way into the house on this side other than smashing a window and crawling in. Tye figured if the two broke into the house, he'd wait for them to get inside, then run to their truck. It would be awfully hard for them to get away after he slashed their tires and called the sheriff.

He stood there with his back against the wall, flashlight in one hand and his revolver in the other. He heard the faint scuff of a foot on gravel, then the clomp of a boot on the wooden deck. At least one of them was on the deck right around the corner from where Tye was standing.

"What the hell did he want, wading across the river like that?" The man's voice was deep and gravelly and boomed through the night air, even though he was trying to whisper. "I thought maybe he was going to break in and squat in the house, but it's almost like he was meeting Cody here so he could go find something."

"I don't know. Maybe just to visit. He's crazy, so who knows what goes through his head?" This voice was also male, but softer and less distinct. "If we'd caught up with him just ten minutes earlier, we could have punched his ticket before he crossed the river."

"Yeah, those night-vision goggles of yours made it easy to follow him. He never knew we were there," the gravelly voiced man said. "You ever been here before?"

"Just that one time."

There was the sound of the back doorknob rattling. "Locked. I guess there's no reason to go in. Look at that hole. I almost dropped a load in my pants when that bullet came through the door."

"Yeah. I didn't even know anyone had moved in. It's been empty for so long. Sure scared those two old women, though. They lit out and haven't been back since." Tye wanted to get a look at them, but there was no way he could poke his head around the corner of the house without being spotted. They were only a few feet away. He held still and tried not to breathe too loud.

"Why did you want to come here anyway?" gravel-voiced man asked.

"I guess it was kind of dumb. I just wanted to see what he wanted. It's crazy, him coming back here after all this time." Tye had to strain to hear the other man over the sound of the river. Tye was certain he would recognize the first man's gravelly voice. But there was nothing distinctive about the other man.

"Let's get out of here. It's still early enough that a neighbor could be up."

"I guess we could go ride the roads on the other side, maybe catch him out in the open. Maybe he'll try to cross the river again." There was the sound of feet on the deck again, moving away from Tye.

The other man said something Tye couldn't make out, and the gravel-voiced guy gave a low rough laugh. Tye stole up to the northwest corner of the house in time to see the two of them walking back to their truck. It was too dark to make out any new details, but he did see that the shorter guy was the one that got in the driver's seat, so it was probably his truck. They were wise to the trick of turning off the dome light as well, because the doors opened and shut without the light coming on. Tye had hoped to get a glimpse of their faces.

The engine started, and the truck backed out of the driveway to turn toward the west, the direction it had come from. Tye was glad, because if they'd gone the other way, they would have seen his truck parked just off the road. Whether they would have found it suspicious or not, he didn't know.

He gave it a few minutes, then returned to his rig. He slid behind the wheel, debating what to do. He could follow them, but there was no way to drive along the forest roads on the other side of the river without using headlights. He'd have to risk being visible for miles or risk running into a ditch. There was no way to follow the two without being seen. If they had already killed one man, there was a pretty good chance they'd be willing to kill him too.

Instead, he drove to the top of his driveway and stopped where it split. He shut off the engine and climbed on the top of the camper shell. From here he had an excellent view across the river. Instead of always checking the time on his phone, Tye wore a watch with hands that glowed in the dark. He noted the time and settled in to wait.

He'd remembered to put his phone in his pocket before climbing up, so when Kaity called him for their evening chat, he didn't have to climb down off his perch.

"So, what's going on, nature boy?" It was good to hear her voice.

Briefly, he outlined the events of the day, watching the ridgeline to the south as he talked.

"Wow. So, you were standing just around the corner of the house from them? That could have been bad. You didn't get a look at them or a license plate?"

He'd already told her he hadn't seen them or gotten a plate, but sometimes it seemed like she just needed to confirm the things he'd already said. "Nope. Too dark. I wonder how hard it would be to find out who lived in the house before Deborah and Vivian bought it."

"Is that your way of asking me to get my librarian on and do some research?"

He laughed. "I guess it is. Yeah." In the distance across the river, he saw a pair of headlights sweep through the trees. He looked at his watch. Right on time.

"Technically, you don't have to have librarian superpowers to do a property records search, but I feel like this is one of those things that I could do in twenty minutes that might take you longer."

"You're being charitable when you say it might take me longer." Tye sometimes felt like he belonged in another time. Barely over thirty, he was much more confident and competent working with his hands or roaming the woods than using a computer.

"I'll do it tomorrow. We're short-staffed, so I had to close the library tonight, then I'll turn right back around and open it tomorrow. Don't these people know I have a boyfriend? I miss you."

"I miss you too. I appreciate your help with this." Across the river, the lights appeared and disappeared as the vehicle drove behind trees and around corners.

"At first light, I'm going to help Gary dig a ditch, then I thought I would saunter over across the river and see what I can figure out about the man that was standing on Deborah's back porch when she shot at him."

"So, you're sure that wasn't the dead guy?"

"I'm certain. The fellow that prowled their house was wearing moccasins, and the dead man was wearing motorcycle boots. I'm also certain Deborah didn't kill that fellow. Those heavy hard-cast bullets would have punched a hole clean through him and left an exit wound the size of your fist."

"Yuck. So, I guess we're going to stick our nose into this?"

"I intend to. This is a little too close to home. It's not just that Deborah and Vivian are our neighbors. This is right down the road from my home. The home I'm hoping to share with you pretty soon." As he said it, it was like some fierce fire had been lit inside of him. He realized the unspoken thing that had been bothering him all day long: this wasn't just about Deborah and Vivian. Everything Tye owned could fit in the back of his pickup truck, and he could walk away from most of it without a second thought. But he'd die before he let anything happen to Kaity, Gary, or May.

"Will you take Gary with you?"

"I was planning on it. I remember a time when you weren't so sure about Gary."

"That was after I found out he'd killed somebody but before I got to know him. He's kind of like a really big dog. He can hurt somebody if he needs to, but he won't unless he has a reason to." Gary had once killed a man who had been threatening his sister. Few people knew it, and those that did often had trouble believing it after they met him.

"I'll let him know you compared him to a dog."

"Please don't. I think if I was less tired, I could come up with a better analogy." She yawned. "I have to go to bed. Please be careful tomorrow."

"I will. I promise. I love you."

"I love you too. Good night."

He shut off the phone. The truck across the river was still driving around. He felt like there was little point in sitting there and watching them do it any longer, so he drove over to the parking place in front of his yurt. Normally he would have just walked right in, but tonight, he did a circle around the outside, shining his flashlight occasionally to check for tracks or other sign. He didn't see anything.

Inside, he checked around and found nothing disturbed. Technically, he could lock the door when he left, but first, he'd have to find the key. Tonight, he just latched it, something he rarely did. He'd always considered the yurt as a place to take shelter from the elements. The heavy canvas walls were stout enough to keep the rain outside and the heat from the wood stove inside, but he'd never worried that they offered scant protection from someone who intended to do him or Kaity harm.

He often read a book before bed, but tonight, he was just too tired. Still, it was a long time before he fell asleep. Instead of locking the little revolver in his pocket back in the truck, he'd put it on the table beside the bed. The sights had little tritium vials that glowed in the dark, and he spent quite a bit of time staring at those three little dots in the darkness before sleep finally came.

7

———————

Tye had gone to bed dreading the dream he knew would come. Sometimes the fear of dreaming kept him awake, tossing and turning, staring at the ceiling, anxious about what would happen. Lately, he'd resolved to just go to sleep and let the dream happen so he could get it over with.

So, it was a relief when he found himself standing in the entryway of Deborah and Vivian's house. Only, the house was as it had been before they moved in, rundown and in need of paint and a good cleaning. The place had sat empty for years. Tye had often driven by and wondered what the story was, but he'd never bothered to find out.

The house smelled like chili, and when he walked in, he saw a pot simmering on the stove. He stood in the middle of the kitchen and turned in a circle. The walls were covered with old, flowered paper that looked dated from the 1960s, and the appliances were goldenrod.

The living room was dim. The walls were covered with cowboy art. Tye didn't have much of a sense for art, but he could tell some of it was bad. An old Martin guitar leaned in one corner and a battered Winchester 94 rifle hung over the mantle. There was a functional minimalism to the place that Tye liked.

Tye saw movement out of the corner of his eye, but when he whirled around, there was nothing there. He thought he heard the slightest sound of a footfall, so he walked over to the bottom of the stairwell. All he saw was a steep flight of steps, the finish worn off the wood in the middle of each tread from decades of use. No one was there.

When the dreams first started, Tye had been terrified. Now he almost saw them as a puzzle he had to figure out. One day, he'd been roped into babysitting Natalie while her mother took the two boys to a doctor's appointment. He'd watched as she navigated a complicated first-person point-of-view computer game where she walked around and unlocked various mysteries by shifting levers and pressing buttons. It had struck him how much the game was like one of his dreams.

The upstairs was all one room, an old attic that had been turned into a bedroom. In juxtaposition to the downstairs, this one seemed to be the abode of a teenage girl. There were posters of music acts Tye vaguely recognized from years before. A shelf was overstuffed with fantasy novels and Dungeons and Dragons game books, some of which Tye had owned himself in his youth.

The walls were painted a pastel yellow, which probably helped brighten the place up, since the only source of natural light was the two small windows at either end. The room was roughly finished; not all the drywall was well done. In places, Tye could see the seams where the panels hadn't been well taped. There was no closet, just a battered old armoire with clothes spilling out of its open door.

Tye stood in the room and turned in a circle. He felt like there was something he was supposed to find here, but he didn't know what.

"I could use a little help," he said. Even though he knew it was a dream, he felt foolish talking in an empty room. Natalie's game had come with a button she could press to get a helpful hint, and Tye felt himself wishing for one of those now.

He didn't see or hear anything, but suddenly, his nose was filled with a floral scent that he almost recognized. Honeysuckle? Jasmine? Something like that. From outside he heard the barred owl hoot three times, and a chill passed over him. It felt like the temperature in the room had dropped twenty degrees in a matter of seconds.

There was a shuffling sound from the stairs, and he turned toward them, wondering what was about to present itself, when the smell of flowers was replaced with the smell of dirt. Tye felt like he was being suffocated, like earth was being forced down his throat. His vision went gray around the edges, and the room swam in front of him.

He sat upright in his bed in the yurt, covered in sweat but shivering. The inside of the yurt was freezing. He hadn't lit a fire because the nights had been staying warmer, but he felt like he was on the verge of hypothermia.

As his feet hit the floor, he heard an owl from outside, hooting three times. The air inside the yurt felt stuffy and close, and he still felt like his nostrils were stuffed with dirt. He pulled on a pair of pants and a hoodie and stepped outside.

It was warmer outside than it had been in the yurt. The night was quiet, the silence only broken by the whisper of the river in the valley below, then the owl hooted three more times. Tye saw a dark silent shape fly over the yurt, then it vanished into the trees.

For a moment, Tye felt like he was in two places at once, both back in the attic bedroom of Deborah and Vivian's as it used to be, and here, outside his yurt. Then the smell of dirt was replaced with the smell of the young Douglas fir trees that grew around him. Their sap was starting to flow and filled the air with a pine scent, with an almost citrusy undertone that he loved. He stood there breathing in the night air and grounding himself in the place where he was standing.

"I don't know what I'm doing. I need help." The thought arose and was out of his mouth before he could think about it.

Tye stood there for a long time, listening to the woods, but there was only silence.

8

———————

"I think Detective Evans recognized the dead guy," Gary said as he threw a shovelful of dirt onto a tarp.

Tye grunted as he dug his shovel into the ground. It was wet enough to be soft, but there were still plenty of rocks. "I certainly got the impression something surprised her. Not sure what. She's a police detective, so surely dead guys aren't a mystery to her."

They both dug in silence for a few minutes. They'd been at it since it was light enough to see. Fueled by a breakfast of elk sausage, eggs from the chickens that were rooting through the ground around them, and homemade biscuits, they'd managed to dig the trench in just a couple of hours. Now they were a couple of feet from the stake that marked the endpoint.

"I guess on the one hand we could just let the police handle this," Tye ventured.

"But on the other hand, if some fellow comes creeping around here when May is home by herself, there isn't going to be a sheriff deputy sitting in the driveway to take care of business."

"That's kind of what I was thinking too," Tye said. "I've been pretty creeped out lately, between the footprints at the top of the property and now this thing over at Deborah and Vivian's house."

Gary dropped the last shovelful of dirt on the tarp. "It was going to cost me almost five hundred bucks to rent a trencher for this job. I reckon that means our labor is worth a couple of hundred dollars an hour. I think we should treat ourselves to a six-pack of nice beer, instead of the usual cheap stuff."

Tye leaned against his shovel. "Sounds like a plan."

It took only a few minutes for them to change clothes and switch modes from homestead hard labor to wildland tracking. Tye greatly preferred the latter. Recently, Kaity had brought a book titled *A Hunter in a Farmer's World* into the yurt, dumped it unceremoniously in his lap, and said, "Here. Read this."

He was still digesting what he'd been reading, but he was glad he no longer felt like a failure for mostly wanting to spend his time in the woods.

Soon they were back at the metal gate across the river from their house. Tye parked farther from the gate than he had previously and stepped out of the truck to examine the tire tracks in the mud.

"Looks like the fellows that were parked here before came back last night," Gary said as he loaded the shotgun.

"Yep," Tye said.

"Probably the same truck that pulled into Deborah and Vivian's house while you were lurking in the bushes."

"That's my guess," Tye said.

"Shame they didn't leave any tracks in the driveway," Gary said.

"It is." On the way, they'd stopped at Deborah and Vivian's house to check for tracks from the night before, with no luck.

"Onward?" Gary asked.

"Onward," Tye said.

It was pretty much a repeat of the day before. Tye tracked and looked for sign close by, while Gary kept an eye on the wider world around them. Yesterday, the sheriff's office had managed to track down someone with a key to the gate and had driven a truck down to remove the dead body, so most of the sign was obliterated. Tye still kept an eye out off to the sides of the track for anything he'd missed previously.

The sky was growing cloudier as they went. "Going to rain soon," Gary said when they took a quick break for a swig of water.

"It is," Tye agreed. "I'd like to get down to the bottom before it pours and washes away sign. I'm thinking we just need to speed up and get down there. I think the odds of us finding something we missed after the sheriff's department drove a one-ton truck down here are pretty low."

They covered the rest of the distance quickly, still staying alert but not stopping to investigate every potential track. Soon they were standing at the site where they had discovered the body.

The area was a trampled mess. Tye walked in an ever-widening circle, trying to get out of the zone where the crime scene techs had trampled all over everything.

Finally, he found what he was looking for. He dropped to one knee and motioned to Gary. "See here? Moccasin tracks."

Gary took a brief look, then went back to scanning the surrounding forest. Secure that his friend was watching his back, Tye took his time puzzling out the sign in front of him.

Someone had walked up to the base of a big Douglas fir tree, stood for a while, then walked back. The tracks were big, and the stride was long. They were looking for somebody well over six feet.

Tye started following the trail deeper into the woods. It was painstaking work. Despite their quarry's size and weight, the moccasins left little sign. It became a game of intuition. Tye had an idea of where the next footfall should land, and if he looked hard enough, he'd find a faint impression or a slightly bent piece of vegetation. Several times, they had to do a lost-track drill, where Gary stood beside the last definitive track, while Tye cast about for the next one.

They stopped for a break and stood shoulder to shoulder facing opposite directions.

"Whoever he is, he's good in the woods," Gary said.

"He's counter-tracking," Tye said. "Now and then he doubles back to watch his back trail, and he's deliberately putting his feet in places where he's less likely to leave sign."

"Kind of dangerous tracking a feller down who doesn't want to be found," Gary said. "If he wasn't in our backyard, I'd be inclined to live and let live. I hope it doesn't get western." Gary tapped the shotgun's receiver for emphasis.

"That's not the vibe I'm getting from him," Tye said. Tracking was a strange activity sometimes. Tye had been following the trail for over an hour now, and he'd gotten an intuitive sense of the person he was following. He couldn't explain why, but it felt like someone who just wanted to be left alone, not someone who was dangerous.

Gary seemed to accept that without question. He nodded and put his water bottle back in the pouch on his backpack's waist belt.

"Track on?" Gary asked.

"Track on," Tye said.

They moved through a stretch of mature hemlock forest. Now that their subject was farther from the crime scene, they seemed more confident and less worried about being followed. He was moving in a more or less straight line, walking quicker, and spending less time checking his back trail.

That continued for almost a mile, then the forest changed from big, old-growth hemlocks to a tangle of vine maple and red alder. Tye heard the burble of a stream.

They crossed the water by stepping from rock to rock. Tye went first, covered by Gary, then he stood with his hand on his revolver while Gary crossed. Only then did he look around for sign.

There by the water's edge were two clear moccasin impressions. They were deeper at the balls of the foot than the heels, and Tye figured it was the marks of someone squatting at the edge of the stream, either to drink or perhaps fill a water container.

The area was a tangle of vegetation. Tye guessed a landslide had moved down this gully at some point in the last fifty years or so, thus it was full of pioneer plants, like alder and vine maple.

He started passing multiple small trees that had been cut with a tool, ranging in thickness from the size of his thumb to his wrist. The marks were fresh, maybe a week or two old.

Ahead he saw bright light through the trees. He paused on the edge of the clearing, kneeling in a shadow until his eyes got used to the brighter light.

The clearing was small, maybe twenty yards across. First, he saw the ring of stones, and the breeze brought the smell of an old campfire to his nostrils. Then he realized that what he'd mistaken for a pile of broken wood from a fallen tree was a brush shelter made by a human.

He was looking at somebody's camp.

9

One of Tye's biggest strengths was his ability to wait. Once he was in the woods, his restlessness with modern life disappeared. He was a patient hunter, able to sit for hours in a bush blind until a deer walked by within range of an arrow.

Tye looked to Gary to make sure he'd seen the shelter, then tapped his watch. Gary nodded, and again stood next to him, facing the other way. Gary would wait as long as Tye felt they needed to.

Tye gave it a half-hour. That was longer than most people would wait. If there was someone in the hut, and they were unaware of Tye and Gary, it was almost certain they would make some kind of noise in thirty minutes. If they were aware, most people would feel a need to do something before a half-hour had passed.

No sound came from inside the hut. A flock of black-capped chickadees settled in the clearing and pecked at the ground, and a Douglas squirrel hopped from branch to branch at the edge of the clearing. It certainly seemed empty to Tye.

Finally, Tye glanced at his watch, pleased to see he'd estimated the passage of 30 minutes merely by the movement of the sun. He nodded at Gary, and they walked up slowly.

This was the tricky part. They were interlopers here, walking up to someone's camp while visibly armed. If Tye had misjudged things, he didn't want to startle the occupant into letting loose with a hail of gunfire, but he didn't want to walk into an ambush, either.

"Hello in the camp," Tye called loudly. The only response was from the Douglas squirrel, who skittered up to a higher branch and chattered at them.

Tye and Gary gave it a few seconds, then walked up to the hut. The camp was clean, with no trash. Tye held his hand over the fire pit. It was still warm, probably from the night before. The structure was well built, with a frame made of wrist-thick limbs lashed together with a kind of tarred string called bank line. The builder had woven smaller, finger-thick branches through the frame, making an effective windbreak. The roof was a brown tarp. The opening was just big enough to squeeze through and was covered by a woven door.

Tye pulled the door aside and stepped through. Instead of taking the time for his eyes to adjust to the light, he pulled his little flashlight out of a pocket. The little structure was almost small enough for him to stand in the middle and touch the opposing walls. There was a well-made bunk, covered with Douglas fir boughs and a rolled-up sleeping bag inside a trash bag. The boughs were freshly cut and filled the inside with their fragrance. Some cans were stacked in a corner: chili, pork and beans, and peaches. A nylon satchel hung from one of the rafters, up where a mouse couldn't chew at the contents. A pair of heavy Danner logging boots were tucked under the bed. They were huge. Tye picked one up. Size fourteen.

"Still clear out here," Gary whispered from outside. He was walking in circles outside.

"Another minute or two," Tye said. He pulled the satchel down and opened it on the bed. The first things he pulled out were some clothes—jeans and a t-shirt. He checked the pockets quickly and found nothing. Next, he pulled out a prescription pill bottle. It was full of something called quetiapine, which he didn't recognize.

The name on the bottle was Peter Etchells. Whoever he was, he was supposed to take 400mg every evening.

There was a thick sheaf of paperwork inside the satchel. Tye scanned it, seeing words like "Western State Hospital" and "involuntary commitment due to lack of mental competency."

"Tick-tock," Gary said from outside. They were on questionable legal ground here. They'd passed out of the land trust property and into state forest some time back. It was technically illegal to build a structure like this in the state forest, but Tye wasn't sure that meant it was okay to go rifling through somebody else's stuff. More to the point, there wasn't a cop within miles, and if the owner came back, they could register their objections ballistically.

Tye remembered the phone in his pocket. He pulled it out and snapped pictures of the pill bottle and the first few pages of the documents. Then he put everything back where he found it, under no illusion that the owner wouldn't know his belongings had been tampered with.

Putting the door back in place behind him, Tye stepped out into the light.

"What's the story?" Gary asked.

Tye opened his mouth to respond, then stopped. All the hair on the back of his neck was standing up. Everything around him had fallen silent. The black-capped chickadees had moved away from the shelter when Tye and Gary approached, but they'd still been hopping around in the trees. Now they were gone. The squirrel was still there, but it was still, crouched on a branch facing away from them.

Tye jerked his head toward the tree line, and they both moved into the trees and found a spot in the shadows. Gary didn't say anything. Tye knew he'd picked up on the same cues. The animals had grown accustomed to Tye and Gary's presence, and something new had caught their attention.

Again, they waited. Over the years, Tye had met numerous skilled outdoors people who were convinced they had a sixth sense about who and what was around them in the woods. In his early twenties, he'd dismissed it all as "woo-woo" stuff. But over the years, he'd learned to trust it. Many times, he'd felt intuitive that a particular patch of woods held a deer or an elk, then sneaked in and filled his freezer with a well-placed arrow. It had happened far too many times to be a coincidence.

Now he was certain there was someone on the other side of the clearing.

The silence in the woods became heavy, something he could almost feel. Just like he'd done earlier, Tye resolved to wait it out. The squirrel melted away, hopping from branch to branch, before it disappeared into the treetops without its usual chatter. The chickadees had vanished as well.

Tye felt a presence that wasn't malevolent, so much as disordered and broken. He couldn't quite put it into words, even in his mind. Lately, he'd been around some truly evil people, but that wasn't the sense he got here. Rather, he felt like he was in the presence of someone lost.

He gave it another half-hour. Whoever they were, they didn't budge. At times he was tempted to call out, but he didn't want to explain to someone why he'd invaded their camp and looked at their paperwork. Whoever Peter Etchells was, Tye preferred to meet him on different terms.

Finally, Tye broke. He moved first. But instead of moving out into the clearing, he pointed with his chin to the game trail behind them. He and Gary moved slowly for a couple hundred yards, going from tree to tree and pausing to look behind them. Now the roles were reversed. Tye tried to route them through patches of forest where they would leave minimal sign of their passage. A skilled tracker would be able to follow them. Tye's only hope was to move faster than the other person could follow.

It was still cool down here in the bottom of the river canyon, but Tye was sweating by the time they broke out into the openness of the overgrown road that would lead them back to his truck.

"That was interesting," Gary said.

"Yeah." Tye pulled out his phone and showed Gary the pictures he'd taken. Gary scrolled through them, zooming in on certain spots.

"I dislike trying to read things on these little screens. There's an awful lot of legal speak in here. It sounds like whoever this fellow is, they had him locked up against his will for quite a while."

Tye took a look at their back trail. The birds were flying from tree to tree like normal, plus he didn't have that overwhelming sense of pressure from behind him. He was still going to be careful, but he was reasonably sure they weren't being followed any longer.

"I guess the next step is to figure out who this guy is, and why he might be trying to break into Deborah and Vivian's house," Tye said.

"It is," Gary looked at his watch. "I think I've done enough amateur sleuthing for the day, unless there's some other thing you need to do. I can make it back to the house to meet May for lunch."

They walked back to the truck in companionable silence. Tye took a slow walk around the vehicle before getting in but found no sign anyone had tampered with it. He opened the back of the truck and removed a trail camera from a plastic tote.

He found a spot a few steps off the road where the camera wouldn't be too obvious and strapped it to a tree.

"Never too early to scout for deer season," Gary said as Tye fiddled with the camera settings.

"Nope," Tye said. "You never know what kind of wildlife you might see in a place like this."

Gary walked back and forth in front of the camera a few times to make sure it would trigger correctly. Tye erased the memory card and closed the camera housing.

"It will be interesting to check that," Gary said.

"It will. I wish I'd thought of it sooner."

As they drove up out of the valley onto the ridgeline, Tye's phone buzzed with a message from Kaity.

Call me.

He pulled off the road and dialed.

"I got a call from Detective Evans," Kaity said without preamble. "She wants to meet with us."

Tye felt a sinking feeling in his stomach. "At the police station? Should we get a lawyer?"

"Nope. She wants to meet for dinner. She said to bring red wine."

10

"I feel like bringing two bottles of wine for four people is reasonable," Kaity said as they walked across the parking lot. "One isn't enough, and three implies we're going to get drunk."

"Seems reasonable," Tye said.

"I'm nervous," Kaity said. "My therapist likes to point out that when I'm anxious about something, I tend to overanalyze a tangentially related detail."

"Oh?" Tye asked.

"That was a noncommittal response. I guess as my boyfriend, you'd be on shaky ground if you agreed."

"It does seem fraught with danger," Tye said.

Doyle's assisted-living community was like an apartment complex. Tye and Kaity were attracting stares as they walked across the lawn.

"I know we haven't done anything wrong, but talking to a police detective makes me nervous."

"Yep." Tye tried not to get irritated that, apparently, every old geezer they walked past was going to check out Kaity's legs. She rarely wore a skit, but today was one of those days.

They stopped in front of Doyle's door.

"Here goes," Kaity said as she knocked.

They heard the shuffle of footsteps from the other side of the door. When it opened, the aroma of Italian food wafted out.

Doyle was slender and a little stooped. He was well into his seventies and wore a nasal cannula hooked to an oxygen bottle at his waist.

"It's so good to see you two." He hugged Kaity and shook Tye's hand. They followed him into the apartment.

Doyle's place was sparsely decorated. His home had burned the summer before, courtesy of an arsonist. He'd told Tye that at his age, he had little interest in redecorating.

There were plenty of books, though, meticulously organized on a "to-be-read" shelf and an "already-read" shelf. Doyle didn't own a television. Instead, he spent his time reading everything, from Marcus Aurelius to the latest thrillers. Kaity had made it her mission to keep him well-supplied with books.

She walked over to the shelf and unloaded the tote she was carrying onto the "to-be-read" shelf and stowed the books he'd finished.

"That ought to keep you busy for a few days," she said.

Doyle beamed. "I appreciate it. It's like Christmas when you two come over."

Evans walked out of the kitchen. To Tye, it seemed weird to see her in a t-shirt and jeans and wearing a pair of oven mitts. "Thank you both for coming. I'm reheating Italian food from the place downtown."

Kaity thrust the two bottles forward. "We brought wine!" She seemed even more nervous than Tye for some reason.

They all busied themselves with setting the table, pouring wine, and serving food. Soon they were eating silently. Ordinarily, Tye was okay with silence, but now there was a tension around the table that was becoming unbearable.

"Okay," Evans said finally. "I guess this is the time when I say, 'I guess you're all wondering why I gathered you here.'"

"We were a bit curious," Tye said and took a drink of his wine.

Evans played with her food for a minute. "You two keep cropping up in my cases. I get a call about a dead body in the forest, and Tye Caine is standing there. You have to admit that's a little odd." She looked around the table.

Tye shrugged. "Can't argue with that."

"So, if you were in my shoes, you'd have to wonder what you were missing. Ordinary average people don't typically find dead bodies all that frequently. The very best outcome is that you're one of those amateurs that are into true crime podcasts and fancy themselves a wannabe cop."

"I'm not a fan of those," Kaity said. "I'm not even sure Tye knows how to find a podcast."

Tye felt like he should be at least mildly offended by that, but he really couldn't argue with it because it was true. There was a particular tension he could feel between Evans and Kaity he could feel but not quite explain.

Evans didn't answer her directly. "The other explanation in my suspicious cop brain is that you people are up to something that I haven't figured out yet." She pivoted to look at Doyle. "But Doyle here tells me I should trust you."

"Detectives working now are way smarter than my generation," Doyle said. "You've got access to all sorts of stuff. DNA. Cell phone tracking. Computer forensics. But us old geezers solved crimes by knowing people. Local people who knew things we didn't. Like how to track somebody through the forest."

Evans looked back at Tye. "We've got some guys on the SWAT team who think they are master trackers, and our K9s are pretty good at sniffing things out, but none of them put pieces together the way you do. I'm not sure I can use the things you find in court, but I can use them to guide investigations and find evidence I wouldn't find otherwise."

"Are you offering us a job?" Kaity asked.

"Nope," Evans said. "I don't have a budget to give you a consulting contract, and if I tried to get one, my brass would laugh me out of the room. I'm asking you for help. I'm not even sure what I can offer in return. The cop part of my brain wants to threaten you with violating state laws about operating as unlicensed private investigators, but I'm reluctant to do that, and Doyle told me I shouldn't."

"That's complete bullshit," Kaity said. Swearing was unusual for her, and Tye realized she was furious.

"It's a gray area," Evans shot back. "We've got perfectly good search-and-rescue teams that are sanctioned by the sheriff."

"Who often don't find people," Tye said. "We've never interfered in an active search. We only help when the search is officially declared inactive."

"Or there's no search because the sheriff refuses to take it seriously," Kaity said. She kept crumpling and uncrumpling her napkin.

Doyle held up his hands. "Let's all hold on a minute and remember, we're on the same side." He looked at Evans. "One of the things I always had to remember is just because somebody isn't a cop, it doesn't mean I have to talk to them like a suspect."

Evans let out a breath and visibly forced herself to relax. "I'm sorry. I guess what I'm trying to say in my ham-handed way is that you don't have to worry about any issues around investigative work from me. I can't guarantee that it won't come up from somebody else in the future, though.

"I'm asking you to help," she said, looking at Tye. "We've gotten off to a bad start, so maybe we could just reset a bit."

Tye's gut instinct was to agree to help Evans, but he held his tongue. Evans was primarily talking to him, but he'd heard Kaity emphasize the word "us" loud and clear. Being in a partnership where his romantic life and professional life overlapped was new territory for Tye.

Kaity dropped her napkin on the table and turned to look at Tye.

"We could help more people this way," Tye said softly. They'd spent more than one night in the bed in Tye's yurt, staring at the ceiling and talking about what they wanted to do. One of their previous adventures had left Tye with a paid-off mortgage, and he scraped by well enough to meet his expenses. Kaity's librarian job would never make her rich, but she got by. They'd mutually agreed that their consulting business was to help people first and make money second.

"Okay," she said, reaching over to touch his face for a second before turning to Evans. "You need to remember you're working with both of us, though."

"And my friend Gary," Tye added before Evans could answer. "He's an integral part of the operation as well."

"You mean your friend that killed somebody in West Virginia?" Evans asked.

"The man was trying to rape his sister," Tye said. "He needed killing. I'd imagine that was something a cop would understand. The sheriff didn't quite pin a medal on him, but he didn't put him in jail either."

"Fair enough," Evans said.

"What do you want us to do?" Kaity asked. She was sitting there with her arms folded across her chest, not touching her food.

Evans looked away. She stared at an empty corner of the room for an uncomfortably long time.

"You both realize that becoming a detective is a promotion, right? You work as a uniformed deputy for a long time, then eventually you can apply to be a detective."

Kaity and Tye both nodded.

"Then when you become a detective, you start out working mostly property crimes. Retail theft, residential burglaries, and things like that. Then you sort of graduate to working violent crimes, serious assaults, rape cases, murders."

She looked at both of them to make sure they were following. Tye realized that one of the reasons he was uneasy about Evans was she seemed to feel like everybody else was either an idiot or up to something.

"My first major crimes case wasn't a murder, exactly. It was a disappearance. Hannah Malley, eighteen years old. She vanished just a few days after she graduated from high school. She lived with her grandfather, who waited almost a week to call it in. He was a piece of work himself. He was an ex-con who did time for smuggling heroin across the Canadian border in his horse trailer."

"Nobody ever found her?" Tye asked.

Evans shook her head. "Nope. She never turned up. We never found a body either. We zeroed in on two suspects: the grandfather and one of her classmates."

"What does this have to do with us?" Kaity asked.

"The house your trigger-happy friend Deborah lives in is Hannah's old house."

Tye's nostrils were filled with the floral scent from his dream, and he remembered the teenage girl's bedroom he'd seen. The pasta he'd just eaten suddenly felt like a rock in his stomach.

"The grandfather disappeared a week into the investigation. We had a deputy drive by the house a couple of times a day, just to keep tabs on him. One day, his truck was parked in the driveway, the next day it wasn't. We never found him either."

"What about the classmate? The other suspect," Tye said. "You looked like you recognized the dead guy we found in the woods. Was that him?"

Evans shook her head. "You're right. I recognized him. His name was Cody Weber. He was a classmate of Hannah, the missing girl, but he was never officially a suspect. He was a witness. He was one of the last people to see Hannah alive, at a party out in the woods."

"And now, ten years later, he's shot to death across the river from Hannah's old house," Tye said. "That's a hell of a coincidence."

"I'm a cop. I don't believe in coincidences. It gets weirder."

"It usually does," Tye said. "Who was the other classmate, the suspect?"

"He was a weird kid. We found a hoodie that belonged to Hannah in his car. It had a few drops of blood on it. Her blood. We matched it to DNA from her hairbrush. The kid insisted it was planted. He also insisted he knew Hannah was dead because she appeared to him in visions. We could never build a criminal case on him, but he was involuntarily committed to the Western State Hospital. At least he was until last week when he was released."

Tye gave an involuntary laugh, which earned him an odd look from everyone at the table. Lately, it seemed like he had little control over his life. Events conspired to steer him in a certain direction, and sometimes he felt like a pinball in a pinball machine.

"Let me guess," he said as he pulled his phone from his pocket. "His name was Peter Etchells."

11

"That's him," Evans said as she scrolled through the photos on Tye's phone. "Where did you get these?"

Tye described following the trail to the hut in the forest and finding the paperwork inside. He left out the part where he'd been certain they were being watched, and he certainly didn't mention the dream he'd had of Hannah's bedroom. All his life, Tye had seen people that weren't there, people who were dead, and he'd often had vivid dreams that sometimes came true. He'd lived in fear of being labeled crazy and locked up somewhere for his own good so he could be pumped full of drugs, just like Peter Etchells.

"So you were already playing junior detective," Evans said.

"Somebody had to. All this happened near my home. Deborah and Vivian are my neighbors."

Evans put her hands flat on the table, with Tye's phone between them. "This fits with Etchells. He spent a bunch of time alone in the woods. It wasn't a happy home life. Single mom, all that. He and Hannah were close. They were pretty much social outcasts in high school."

"So that was it?" Kaity asked. "She disappears. Her grandfather disappears. This Peter kid gets locked up in the state mental hospital, and that's it?"

Evans took another long pause, staring at Tye's phone between her hands. "I wasn't happy," she said finally. "She disappeared from a party thrown by the football team out in the woods. There were lots of people there who all seemed to have the same story. It was almost too perfect."

Tye thought back to his high school days. "What was the weird social outcast girl doing at a party thrown by the football team?"

Evans gave him a look that made him feel like a rabbit caught in the sights of a diving hawk. "Exactly. Nobody had an explanation for that one. Nobody seemed to know how she'd gotten there or who she left with."

"Did anybody care?" Tye asked. "Weird kid with an ex-con grandfather."

"I cared," Evans said. "But let's just say there wasn't much enthusiasm on the part of my department to pursue it. Officially, we suspended the case due to a lack of evidence. Unofficially, I think there was an even split in the department between people who thought her grandfather killed her, and the people who thought Peter Etchells killed her."

Evans shoved Tye's phone across the table at him. "There's another thing that bothers me, though. It's tough to get somebody civilly committed. I've dealt with mentally ill people who think they are Jesus Christ reincarnated and live in a filthy apartment with no water or electricity. The best we can usually do is get them in for a seventy-two-hour hold and then discharged with a bag of prescriptions. We never even indicted Peter Etchells for a crime. He lived in his mom's trailer home. Didn't bother anybody, but his civil commitment sailed through the courts because he thinks he sees visions of dead people?"

"Yeah, it seems like that shouldn't be enough to lock somebody up," Tye said as he slid his phone back into his pocket.

"What now?" Kaity said. "What do you want us to do?"

Evans drummed her fingers on the table. "I'd like to see this hut you found in the woods. Maybe we can talk to Peter Etchells."

"He's not gonna be there," Tye said. "I'd bet the farm on that. He knows we were there. I'm guessing he'll be long gone."

Evans shrugged. "I have to try."

"Fair enough. In the morning?"

She nodded. "In the morning. I'll meet you at the gate."

"I don't have to work tomorrow," Kaity said. "I'll come along."

Evans opened her mouth to say something, but Tye cut her off. "Sounds good to me."

Doyle looked at all of them. "I told you this was a good idea," he said and patted Evans's arm.

She relaxed and laughed. "Yeah, I should have listened to you sooner." Her tone was completely different when she talked to Doyle.

The rest of the dinner passed in slightly-less-awkward silence. Kaity didn't say much, and Tye found himself trying to guess what she was thinking, something he found maddening. Doyle tried to keep the conversation going. He wanted everyone to get along. Tye knew the old man had two daughters, but he rarely talked about them.

Kaity helped clean up in silence, and they made their farewells. Evans stayed behind. Tye had the impression there was more she wanted to say to Doyle in privacy.

As they rode home, Kaity was quiet until they passed the outskirts of town.

"I don't trust her," Kaity said. "I feel like there's more she isn't telling us."

That snapped him out of the reverie he'd been in. He'd been trying to make all the pieces fit together. The dead man in the woods, the camp in the forest, the dreams, the missing woman, the tracks on his property—it all had to add up to something.

"I think that's a safe bet," Tye said as he turned onto the road that would take them closer to home. The farther they got from the city, the more relaxed he felt.

"I also don't like the way she talks to people. It's like she thinks they're idiots or lying."

"Or both," Tye said. "If you don't think we should do this, we can punch out."

"And then what? She makes good on her threat about needing a license to run our consulting company? We've talked to two lawyers and they both think we don't need a PI license to consult on cold search-and-rescue cases. I think we'd win, but we don't need the hassle."

"I have to agree with that." Tye had a long-standing belief that it was best to have no dealings with the police at all.

They rode in silence for a while. The days were getting longer after the long, dark winter, and Tye was glad for the sunshine. Just a month ago, it would have been dark this time of day. Now he was wondering if he would have time to go for a walk after they got home. Maybe Kaity would come with him.

"But there's the girl," Kaity said.

"Yeah. The girl," Tye agreed. "Plus, all of this is happening just down the road from our home."

"I can't believe they just dropped the investigation into her disappearance like that."

"I can," Tye said. "You saw the state of that house before Deborah and Vivian moved in. Calling it a fixer-upper was pretty charitable. It was a dump. She was a weird kid from a poor family who lived with her grandfather, the ex-con. Evans didn't say why she lived with him instead of her parents, but I bet it isn't a happy story."

"I guess I grew up thinking the police would look out for people like that," Kaity said.

"I guess I grew up knowing they wouldn't."

"It reminds me of Natalie," Kaity said. "The night she disappeared, the sheriff's deputy didn't even take her mom seriously."

"Yep. That little girl would have died in the cold if you hadn't been out looking for her."

She reached over and took his hand. "Well, it wasn't going so hot for me either until you showed up."

"So, I guess we're in," he said. "For the sake of the girl."

"Yeah. For the sake of the girl. Also, there's this guy they had locked up for ten years."

"The guy who sees visions of dead people? That hit a little close to home."

"I thought it might have."

He pulled in behind her Jeep and stepped out. The sun was low in the western sky, but there was still a little daylight left.

"I was thinking about a walk up around the property, maybe check the trail camera and such."

She yawned. "Fine. But after that, I think I want an early bedtime. It's been a long week, and we have an early start tomorrow."

They walked up the hill hand in hand until the trail narrowed, and Kaity took the lead, pausing here and there to examine deer tracks.

"I think it's the same doe that hung out here all winter. The one that looks like she's pregnant on the trail camera pictures."

"Yep. I think those are her tracks."

"You're not allowed to shoot her in the fall."

"I promise," he said. They continued up the trail. During the long, gray days of winter, it seemed like nothing changed from day to day here on the property. Now that spring had started, there was something new every time he went outside.

As soon as they were at the top of the ridgeline, he made a beeline for his trail camera. He checked the muddy spot where he'd seen the boot print the day before. Tye had brushed the print away, and he was relieved to find no new track in its place.

He pulled the card out of the trail camera and stuck it into the reader attached to his phone. As he scrolled through the pictures, Kaity looked over his shoulder.

"There she is," she said as he scrolled to a picture of a deer. "She looks pretty rotund to me."

"Yep. Gonna have a baby deer walking around here in another month or so." He went through the rest of the pictures, relieved to find no sign of a human.

"Nothing more from your mysterious intruder?" Kaity asked.

"Nope."

"Maybe it was just somebody that walked in from the private timberland and stumbled on your camera by accident."

"Maybe." He wanted to believe that. They turned and started walking down the hill. In ten more minutes, it would be dark enough to need flashlights. The birds were calling back and forth in their evening chorus, and the temperature was already dropping.

As they walked toward the yurt, Kaity moved next to him. Her hip bumped his.

"It's getting cold," she said. "I think we still need a fire at night."

"Yep."

"So, yesterday, we got interrupted at a critical moment. I'm pretty tired, but I think I could pick up where we left off."

"I reckon I could too."

She stopped him at the door to the yurt and gave him a good, long kiss, which seemed like the perfect antidote for the stressors of the day. After a while, they came up for air.

"Whew," she said. "I'm still not tired of that."

"Me neither. Let me grab some wood and we'll continue this inside."

Distracted as he was, he didn't see the footprint in the mud until he was on his way back from the woodshed.

"Dammit," he said. He set the wood down and kneeled by the track.

"What's wrong?" Kaity asked. She started walking toward him, but he motioned for her to stop.

"Somebody's been here," he said. "Hang on, I don't want us to walk over any sign." He pulled his flashlight from his pocket and illuminated the print.

"Same guy," he said. "Same track as the one from the top of the hill yesterday." Like before, it looked like this print and been deliberately placed in a soft spot of bare dirt, just so he could find it. With his light, he could see bent-over grass. One trail led from the trees, and the other led back. Someone had walked out from the tree line, stomped on the muddy ground, then walked back.

"How old?" Kaity asked.

"Not very. The grass is still springing back up."

Leaving the wood in the wet grass, he grabbed Kaity's hand and pulled her inside the yurt with him. He flipped on the electric lantern and unlocked his gun cabinet. He pulled out his gun belt and started buckling it on.

"What are you doing?" Kaity asked.

"Going after him."

She put her hands on her hips. "It's getting dark."

"I'm getting tired of this cat-and-mouse game with this guy."

"Can we think this through for a minute? If this guy wanted to hurt us, he could have ambushed us from the trees on our way in. For that matter, you don't even lock the yurt. He could have been waiting inside for us."

He stood there with his hand on the door handle. "Fair point."

"You're sure it's not the same guy as the one from over by Deborah and Vivian's house?"

He shook his head. "Nope. They're different tracks."

"So, could you not go charging off into the woods alone with a gun? First, we'll have to argue about whether I'm going to go with you or not, and you know I'm going to win that one."

He sighed.

"And second, I'm not sure you need to. He didn't try to hurt us, and nothing is broken or stolen that I can see."

He took his hand off the door handle and sat down on the bed.

"Let's just make a fire," she said.

Grateful for something to do, he squatted in front of the little stove and lit the tinder and kindling that were already in the firebox. Soon the inside of the little yurt was warming from the flames. Tye unbuckled his gun belt, but instead of locking it away, he coiled it up on the top of his workbench within easy reach.

He kicked off his boots, and Kaity reached for him. They lay there in silence for a few minutes, arms wrapped around each other.

"You've been a little jumpy lately," she said.

"Up until last summer, the worst I had to deal with was some redneck trying to beat me up in a bar because I had long hair. Now everywhere I look I see evil. That's an old-fashioned word people don't like to use anymore, but I think it fits."

She didn't say anything for a while. A piece of wood popped in the stove.

"I think it fits too," she said. "A year ago, I would have smirked at that word, given you some pat answer about how people do things because of their early-childhood trauma or something. Now I'm not so sure."

"I don't feel safe," he said. "I used to love living in this yurt. Now all I can think about is how easy it would be for somebody to slit the wall open with a knife and come in here and hurt you."

"You're not knife-proof yourself, buster," she said, tracing the outline of the scar on his ribs. "You worry more about something happening to me than you worry about something happening to you. You're the one who got stabbed. And let's not forget the part where you had to swim naked across Puget Sound."

"It was only from one island to another," he said. "And we had a float. I do worry about you. I got you kidnapped."

"I seem to remember you being locked in the back of that truck with me."

He shrugged, not knowing what to say. She nudged him with an elbow.

"Stop being such a dude and pretending like you're the only one who has to solve this problem. I appreciate you wanting to protect me, but I'm a grown woman."

"Okay."

She kissed him on the cheek. "Let's get ready for bed. We have an early start tomorrow."

Soon they were snuggled up under the covers, with the fire banked down to burn all night long. Kaity was soon asleep, but Tye stared at the ceiling for a long time, listening to the night sounds outside.

12

———

"Well, so much for my camera," Tye said. The cover of the trail camera he'd strapped to the tree beside the land trust gate was hanging open.

"They took the card?" Kaity asked. She stood next to him, dressed in a puffy outer layer and wearing her backpack. The sun was just up, and it was still cold.

"Yep. Smashed it up pretty good, too. I'm glad I erased the pictures of Gary yesterday."

"You're sure it's the same people?" Evans asked as she walked up.

"I'm sure," Tye said. "Same tire tracks as before. Same boot prints from the same two men."

He walked over to a nearby tree and pointed. "See that? It's the mark from the butt of a rifle. The guy that smashed the camera leaned his rifle against the tree so his hands would be free."

"You think they're gone now?" Evans asked.

"Yeah. The tracks showed they drove in and drove out."

"Good," she said. "I don't want to haul a rifle through the woods with me." She was wearing her police gun belt buckled over her khaki pants and a sheriff's department waterproof jacket.

As they walked down the road on the other side of the gate, Tye wished he did have a rifle. They hadn't discussed the subject of him being armed with Evans, but he was pretty sure the answer would be "no." Kaity had watched him slip the little revolver into his pocket without comment.

"So, tell us some more about the dead guy," Kaity said to Evans.

For a minute, Tye thought Evans was going to refuse, but finally, she started talking like every word she said was costing her money.

"Cody Weber was a classmate of Hannah Malley, the missing girl, and Peter Etchells, the guy we're hoping to find out here. We interviewed him, and he told the same story as everybody else. He had a vague memory of Hannah at the party but didn't know who she came with or who she left with."

"What about the years since then?" Kaity asked.

"That's the interesting part. We checked the address on his driver's license, an apartment in downtown Vancouver. He hasn't lived there in a couple of years. It's the same address used to register his motorcycle, which we still haven't found. I'm still trying to find next of kin to even notify them he's dead."

"How often does that sort of thing happen?" Tye asked.

Evans shrugged. "With somebody homeless, it can be pretty hard to track down next of kin and almost impossible if there's no ID on the body. But this guy is clean and well-fed. We know exactly who he is, but it's like he just decided to drop off the map at some point. I'm trying to pull his state tax returns and see if I can identify an employer."

She turned to Tye. "You were right, by the way. Your neighbor didn't shoot him. The bullet that killed him wasn't from her gun. At the autopsy, they dug out fragments from a .30 caliber projectile. That's the size bullet a .300 Blackout uses. They think it's something called a Controlled Fracturing bullet, designed to break up as it passes through the body. It turned his lungs into pulp."

Tye grimaced. "That sounds pretty nasty. Also, I'm finding it hard to believe Peter Etchells got his hands on something like that after being out of the state hospital for only a few days."

"You're likely right, but guns get stolen out of cars and homes all the time. I've been looking for reports of a recent theft, but people sometimes don't report them, or even realize the gun is gone for a while."

"Is that crime scene tape up there?" Kaity asked.

She was right. Up ahead was the place where they'd found Cody Weber's body.

"Looks like some of it is torn down," Evans said. Where before a giant square of tape had surrounded the site, strung from tree to tree, it now hung loose, fluttering in the wind blowing down the river valley.

"Maybe an animal?" Evans asked.

"Nope," Tye said. The tracks of the two men they'd been following went straight through to where the tape had been torn down.

"Well, I'm glad we did a comprehensive sweep of the scene before we left," Evans said. "Although we like to keep people out for as long as we can, in case we develop new leads."

"What's that?" Kaity asked and pointed at a tree.

Tye walked over. Carved in the smooth white bark of a red alder tree were four letters. WOTN, in all capitals. True to its name, the wood of the tree had turned a vibrant red where it had been gouged.

"What does that mean?" Kaity asked.

Evans swore under her breath. She pulled off her backpack and pulled out an evidence camera. "That wasn't here the last time," she said.

"Nope," Tye said. "You're standing on the tracks of the two fellows we've been following. They walked down here, tore down the tape, carved up the tree, and walked back."

"Why?" Kaity asked. "What does it mean?"

Evans snapped a couple of photos, then handed Tye a photographic ruler so he could hold it up to the letters and took a few more.

"I don't know what it means," she said as she snapped the lens cover back on the camera. "But there's something I need to show you."

She put the camera away and pulled out her phone. She scrolled through some pictures and held them out for them to see. They were looking at a close-up photo of the pallid skin of a man's bare chest. There on the sternum were the same letters, WOTN.

"Please tell me that's not an autopsy photo," Kaity asked.

"It's an autopsy photo," Evans said. "It's Cody Weber's chest. It's not a tattoo. It's a brand, made with hot metal."

"Ugh," Kaity said. "So, is that some kind of gang sign or something?"

Evans shook her head. "Not that we know of. I asked our gang guys to look into it some more."

Tye walked around the area in a circle, looking for more sign. He didn't see anything, but he was filled with a sense of unease. Maybe it was his imagination, but it felt like the air was colder in the area immediately around the area where Cody Weber's body had been.

He saw Kaity watching him and shook his head. "I don't see anything else. Let's head on up to the camp we found." He started walking, figuring Kaity would follow and leaving it up to Evans whether she wanted to come or not. Tye wanted out of the area. He felt a little nauseous and a familiar pounding was starting in his head. He'd suffered from migraines most of his life, and he didn't want one right now.

Evans had apparently had enough too, as she followed without comment. Kaity walked beside him, shooting him occasional "Are you okay?" glances. He reached over and squeezed her hand.

Tye picked up the track where he and Gary had walked back and forth to the campsite the day before. He spent most of his time looking up, watching out for danger, and took the occasional glance down to verify that he was on the right path.

As they moved through a soft patch of bare ground, Tye stopped and dropped to a knee.

"What is it?" Kaity asked as she squatted beside him.

He pointed at a big moccasin track.

"Oh. He followed you."

"Yep," he said. "How big is Peter Etchells?"

"Six-foot-five," Evans said from memory. "Two hundred and twenty pounds."

"Got to be him," Tye said. "The foot size. The stride length. It all fits."

Tye pressed on, and soon they were standing at the edge of the clearing, behind the same tree he and Gary had hidden behind yesterday. The same chickadees as before were hopping around in the grass. In his gut, Tye felt like the place was empty, but he thought it would be smart to be cautious.

He was about to open his mouth and say, "Let's wait a minute," when Evans cupped her hands to her mouth and yelled. "Peter Etchells, this is the Clark County Sheriff's Department. Come out where we can see you!"

Evans unsnapped her holster, pulled out her gun, and held it down by her leg. Tye fought the urge to swear and put his hand in his pocket on the grip of his revolver. He tried to look everywhere at once. Just because Etchells wasn't in the debris shelter didn't mean he wasn't somewhere nearby.

The chickadees all bolted from the ground, taking refuge in the treetops where they gave their distinctive alarm call, but there was no other sound.

"I think there's nobody home," Evans said.

"You're probably right," Tye said.

"Let's go check it out. Do me a favor. If you whip that gun out of your pocket, don't point it in my direction."

"Fair enough."

She walked slowly up to the door, gun held out in front of her, and Tye and Kaity followed. Evans peeked her head into the opening, then holstered her gun.

"Empty," she said and walked inside.

Tye followed her in. Not only was no one inside but all the gear was gone, too. Tye saw a scrap of paper on the bed. It looked like half a page of notebook paper.

Evans moved in front of him, donned a glove from the thigh pocket of her cargo pants, and picked it up. She showed it to Tye.

I didn't do it. The wolves killed her. The handwriting was shaky and spidery, like something a young kid would make.

"Wolves?" Kaity said. "There aren't any wolves in this part of Washington."

"He's been in a psych ward for a long time," Evans said. She pulled an evidence bag out of another pocket and deposited the note inside.

Tye walked outside and started circling the hut. He easily picked up the trail of a set of heavy boots headed east, away from the clearing.

"Yesterday there was a pair of Danner logging boots under the bed," Tye said as he pointed at the tracks with a stick. "He's carrying his gear and wants to move quickly, so he changed out of the moccasins."

"What's in that direction?" Evans asked, jerking her chin in the direction of the tracks.

"Nothing but trees," Tye said. "If he keeps headed east, he'll walk out of the state forest and into the national forest, federal land. There's nothing in that direction for miles. Plenty of room to hide."

Evans stood there for a minute, arms crossed over her chest.

"How far ahead of us is he?"

Tye walked over to where the trail went between two trees. "See his footprint? There's a deer track on top of it. So a deer walked past the debris hut and walked right over the top of his tracks. Deer usually move around at first and last light this time of year. It could be that he cleared out this morning, and a deer followed the trail just a little later. What I think is most likely is that he left last evening, and the deer came through this morning, after his scent had dissipated."

"So, we are way behind him," Evans said.

"I'm guessing about eighteen hours, twelve at least. He knew we came here and found his shelter. I'm guessing he packed his stuff and lit out right after."

"Could you find him?" Evans asked.

"Maybe," Tye said. "Given enough time. I'd want to have more gear with me, and no offense, but I'd want Gary with me too. I'd need another tracker."

Kaity gave him a sidelong glance, and he figured he'd have some explaining to do later.

"Well, this has been a fun nature hike, but I think I need to regroup and come up with a plan," Evans said. "I can't justify calling out an all-out search for this guy. I'm not even sure he's a suspect."

"I don't think Peter Etchells killed Cody Weber," Tye said. "The sign isn't right. All the tracks point toward whoever followed Weber. They got out of their truck, followed him, shot him, then loaded his motorcycle up and drove away."

"Etchells was still in the area," Evans said. "So he's a person of interest."

"But who walked down here to carve up that tree, and why?" Kaity asked.

"I'm pretty sure it was the same people in the same truck," Tye said. "As to why, that's a great question."

Evans turned and looked behind them. "I guess we have to hike back up that ridge."

"I guess we do. Might as well get started."

They were all quiet on the way back. Tye could tell Kaity was lost in thought, but she didn't say anything until they had parted company with Evans and were on their way back.

"So, when do I get to be your backup when it's time to trail somebody through the woods?" she asked.

"That's a great question. Please don't be offended. Just remember that Gary and I have been doing this since we were teenagers. Also, I don't know if Peter Etchells is dangerous or not, and Gary can work a 12-gauge shotgun like nobody's business."

"I guess that's fair. They didn't cover that in librarian school."

He reached over and squeezed her hand. "Still glad you're with me, though."

"I have ideas," she said.

"I figured you would."

"So, WOTN is carved on the tree. Then Etchells said, 'The wolves killed her.' I guess he means Hannah?"

"Fair guess."

"But we don't even know for sure she's dead."

"Sounds like Etchells knows some things we don't."

"Wolves starts with 'W.' Is that part of WOTN?"

He paused at the end of the gravel state forest road for another truck to pass, then pulled onto Dole Valley Road. "Seems like a reasonable guess."

"But what does the rest stand for? I feel the need to do research."

"Evans didn't ask us to do that."

"She didn't say not to, either."

Tye laughed. "I guess that's a fair point. We can look into it when we get home."

"I'm tempted to drive into town rather than use your painfully slow internet connection, but if you make me coffee, I'll stay."

"Deal." A second cup of coffee sounded like a good idea to Tye as well. It was still before noon, but he felt like he'd packed in a full day already.

He gunned the truck to build up enough speed to carry them up the steep driveway. As he came around the corner, he saw someone sitting on the front steps of the yurt. At first, he assumed it was Gary, then as they drew closer, he saw that it was a shorter, broader man. By the time all this registered, the truck was already coming to a stop just a few feet away from the front of the yurt.

The man set aside the book he was reading and stood, holding both hands in front of him in an open-fingered wave. He was of medium height and broad-shouldered, with dark skin and jet-black hair in a braid down his back. He wore jeans, an old fatigue jacket, and boots.

"Who's that?" Kaity asked.

"Great question," Tye said. Part of him wondered if he should back the truck up the driveway and open up some distance between them and the stranger. Instead, he stepped out, hand in his pocket on the grip of the revolver. Tye saw the man's boots looked like a pretty good match for the tracks he'd been finding on his property.

"Howdy," the man said. "I take it you're Tye Caine. I'm Jean Fiddler. Hattie sent me."

"Oh," Tye said, and stood there, his mind completely blank for anything to say next.

Kaity looked back and forth from Tye to Fiddler.

"We were just about to have some coffee," she said. "Want some?"

13

———

"Nice place you've got here," Jean said and blew on his mug of steaming coffee. "Simple."

Tye held his mug and took a sip. "Thanks."

Once again, he regretted his lack of furniture. Tye and Kaity sat on the edge of the bed while Fiddler perched on the stool in front of Tye's workbench. He studied Fiddler. At first, he'd assumed the man was about forty, but now he realized he was probably on the other side of sixty.

"So..." Kaity said. "Where are you from?"

Fiddler took another sip. "Canada."

"That's a long drive," she said. "I didn't see your car."

"Didn't drive. Hitchhiked some. Walked the rest."

"Wow."

"Why have you been walking around my property?" Tye said. The question had been in his mind since he'd seen Fiddler standing there, and now it forced its way out unbidden.

"We could have a great discussion about whether anybody has a right to call land 'their property,'" Fiddler said as he looked at Tye over the rim of his cup. "But for now, let's just say I had to make sure you were the kind of man I thought would be smart to get involved with."

"What do you mean?" Tye asked.

"Cousin Hattie says you see visions. You see dead people in dreams. Sometimes the things you see come true. Is that right?"

"Yes." Tye gritted his teeth as he said it. It was hard to admit it to a stranger.

"She also says you have put yourself in harm's way to help people. A little girl. A wife missing her husband. A mother missing her son."

"Yes," Tye said. He looked at Kaity. "Her too."

Fiddler nodded. "It is good you do these things together."

"That's not an answer to his question," Kaity said. "Why have you been lurking around here? It's creepy."

"I've learned to be careful," Fiddler said. "Sometimes people aren't what they seem. They look good on the surface, but underneath, they are not so good."

"So, we passed the test?" Kaity asked. There was an edge to her voice Tye had come to recognize.

"I see someone who lives simply. When I watch you walk on the land, you do it with respect. These are good signs." He looked at Tye with a gaze that made him feel like a deer caught in headlights. "People like you are capable of great harm. Or great good."

"Why me?" Tye asked.

Fiddler nodded at his backpack over in the corner. A battered copy of Tolkien's *The Return of the King* sat on top. "If we were living one of your white people's stories, it would be because you are special, that your grandaddy was a king or a wizard or something. Your people tell good stories, but you need to get over yourselves sometimes. What you can do used to be not so special. Lots of people could do it. But nowadays, you all spend time looking at computer screens and numbing your minds. You're lucky to walk down a path and not trip over a rock, never mind see into the other worlds."

"Are they real?" Tye asked. "The things I see. It's not just in my head?"

Fiddler shrugged. "Do they tell you things that are true?"

"Yes." Tye didn't want to say it, but he did.

"Then that is your answer."

"I have some things I want to show you," Tye said. Suddenly, the air inside the yurt seemed too hot and too stuffy. He wanted to be outside and moving.

"Let's go," Fiddler said. He picked up his backpack.

Tye looked at Kaity. She raised an eyebrow at him. "If you think you're okay, I could stay here and research. Or I might go into town for the internet."

Tye and Kaity had been together long enough that he knew her raised eyebrow meant, *Are you safe without me, or do you want me to come?*

"I think I'm good," he said. Fiddler was intimidating in his way, but Tye didn't feel like he was in danger.

Kaity stood up and gave him a peck on the lips. "Catch you tonight?"

Tye nodded. He felt supercharged with energy, like he was about to take the long-overdue next step. Wordlessly, Fiddler followed him to the truck and climbed in the passenger seat.

"She cares very much for you," Fiddler said as Tye backed down the driveway. "You should be careful and not mess that up."

"That's the second time I've gotten that advice in as many days," Tye said.

They rode silently for several miles. There was a stillness to Fiddler that Tye recognized. It was rare these days to find someone comfortable being still and quiet. Fiddler clearly felt no need for small talk.

Tye wound his way through back roads, climbing higher into the foothills of the Cascade Mountains until he came to a locked gate. The road beyond was little more than two tire ruts covered with dead leaves and fallen branches.

"We have to walk from here," Tye said. "I don't have a key."

Fiddler nodded. "I am no stranger to walking."

"This is the old McCaslan place," Tye said. "You know the story?"

"Yes," Fiddler said. "He stole boys. Not for their bodies but for their life energy. My Uncle Remy died fighting him."

The surrounding trees were gnarled and twisted. Usually, Tye felt safer in the woods than he did anywhere else. But this property had always filled him with an urge to leave as soon as he crossed the boundary line.

"One of those boys grew up and went bad," Tye said. "He called himself Bodhi. He took a child himself, a little girl."

Fiddler's eyes never stopped moving. "That is often the way. It's like a poison that goes from one to another."

"I have your Uncle Remy's knife," Tye said. "Bodhi had it."

"The killing knife," Jean said. "I should like to see it."

They rounded the corner, and there was the house. Tye felt a shiver when he saw it. The empty windows were like eyes staring at him.

"It is empty still," Fiddler said.

"I guess the legal situation is complicated," Tye said. "Bodhi died with no heirs, no executor or anything. I guess he had some money squirreled away, and there's a big legal mess."

"Bad men are often rich. And rich men are often bad. This is what you brought me here to show me?"

"Not just this. Over here." Tye gestured to the side of the house. Fiddler followed him. Just before noon on a spring morning, there should have been life here: birds flitting about, squirrels calling, and maybe even deer bedded in the overgrown grass around the house. But there was nothing. Tye didn't even see any sign of animals passing close to the house. Even the old, abandoned apple orchard was full of rotten apples from last fall. Normally, a place like that would be a magnet for deer and bears. But not here.

The old shed was still standing. Tye stopped outside the closed door.

"This is a bad place," Fiddler said. "I think this is where my Uncle Remy died."

"I think so too," Tye said. "We don't have to go in."

"I have been to bad places before. Show me what you must show me, Tyrell Orrin Caine."

Tye didn't ask how Jean knew his full name. Instead of questioning it, he pushed the old door open. The inside of the old shed smelled musty, and something small skittered away from the light with a squeak. Nothing was inside but a trapdoor on the floor with a ring in the center. Part of him wanted to turn around and walk back to the truck, but instead, Tye walked over and jerked up on the ring. The sour odor of damp earth wafted out.

"He kept them in here," Tye said. "The boys." He pulled the flashlight out of his pocket and clicked it on. There it was in the center of the beam: the outline of a dark figure, drawn by a child's finger, rubbed in the dirt.

"That's what I see in my dreams," Tye said. "That's what Natalie draws in her pictures." He took out his phone and snapped a picture of the drawing.

Jean knelt down to see it better, then grunted. "Which one of the boys drew it? Bodhi? Or your friend Brian?"

Tye hadn't told Jean he knew Brian, but he wasn't surprised Jean knew it either. "Brian says he doesn't remember. I think he's blocked out a bunch of what happened to him."

"That is often the way." Jean rose and dusted off the knees of his jeans. "This place should be burned down."

Tye blinked. Jean had said it in a matter-of-fact tone, like he was discussing going to the store.

Jean looked at him. "But maybe not today, and not by us. What else did you want to show me?"

"I was kind of hoping you could answer some questions about all this," Tye said.

"Patience, Tye Caine. You've waited a long time for answers. You can wait a little longer. There is more I need to see."

Tye rubbed his temples. He felt a pounding behind his eyes. "There's another place I want to show you, but it's a bit of a drive, then a walk after that."

"Then let us drive and walk."

14

Tye wanted to ask questions as they walked back to the truck, but the pain in his head was keeping him from forming coherent thoughts. The migraines had plagued him on and off his whole life, but over the last year, they'd been especially bad.

By the time they were back at the truck, the pain was so bad he felt nauseous. He did what he always did at times like this: gritted his teeth and worked through the pain. Jean was silent as Tye wound his way through back roads until he was on State Highway 503. Fiddler leaned his head against the door and fell asleep as they passed Lake Merwin, where the once-wild Lewis River had been dammed to provide hydropower. They passed Yale Lake and Swift Reservoir, each with its dam, before turning east toward Wind River Road. The farther they got from the McCaslin house, the more the pressure in Tye's head eased. Fiddler snored on, until Tye turned onto a rutted forest service road on the edge of the Indian Heaven Wilderness Area.

Fiddler woke and stretched. "This road is terrible."

"I wish I could say it kept the riffraff out," Tye said as they passed a trashed campsite. Now that he was awake, Jean looked around, his face impassive. Tye was a little surprised he hadn't asked any questions about where they were or where they were going. He seemed content just to let Tye drive and take him deep into the forest.

Tye found the spot he was looking for and pulled the truck off the road. "About an hour's walk from here," he said and got out to fetch his pack and an electric lantern from the bed of the truck. Jean settled his pack on his shoulders, and they set out.

The narrow game trail led up a narrow valley, about halfway up the slope from the creek at the bottom. In places, the trail all but disappeared, but Tye kept steadily onward, knowing he'd pick it up again. The forest here was old and had inexplicably escaped the saw during the timber-hungry days when vast swaths of the Gifford Pinchot National Forest had been extensively clear-cut. Now it was inside the designated Indian Heaven Wilderness area and would hopefully be protected from logging forever.

The farther they walked up the valley, the bigger the Douglas fir trees became and the fewer animal sign Tye saw. The giant fir trees kept the ground below in perpetual shade, so very few low-growing plants that were the favored diet of deer and elk could exist here. This kind of environment was one of the few places in a Pacific Northwest forest where it was possible to see farther than twenty-five yards among the trees. Tye loved it here. It reminded him of a cathedral.

Tye had been worried that he wouldn't be able to find the place again and that he would look like a fool in front of Jean. He'd spent a single exhausted night here with Kaity in the fall, on the run and hypothermic, with little equipment. But his feet took him right to the place he was looking for. He stopped and looked back at Jean.

"A cave," Jean said, looking at the crack of the rock face in front of him. "That is unusual here, is it not?"

Tye nodded. "Something about the rock in this part of the forest. There aren't many caves."

Unlike when they'd been back at the McCaslin house, Tye found himself wanting to go in here. He'd often thought of returning, but the roads had been impassible under snow until recently. He'd also felt somehow that the time wasn't right, that he should wait for something to happen.

A slight cool breeze blew out of the cave opening. Tye pulled the lantern from his backpack and switched it on before stepping inside. The crack narrowed, forcing him to turn sideways, then opened into a chamber big enough for him to stand.

It was just as he remembered. The burnt remains of a campfire under a crack in the wall filled the air with the smell of old charred wood. A bough bed sat in the corner.

He lifted the lantern high, and then they could both see the drawings. Figures covered the walls, drawn in charcoal and ochre. Tye heard Jean's sharp inhale as the light hit the drawings. Jean turned in a slow circle, his head tilted back.

"How did you find it?" Jean asked.

"A dead man led me here," Tye said. "I was awake at the time, so I guess it wasn't a dream."

Jean shrugged. "That difference isn't as big as some people like to think."

Tye stepped closer to the side of the cave that held the fire pit. "This is the one I keep thinking about." He held the lantern close to a picture of that same dark figure that had been drawn on the side of the pit under McCaslin's shed. He pulled out his phone and scrolled to the picture he'd taken earlier.

They were identical. He showed the phone to Jean.

"They are the same," Jean said.

"How?" Tye asked. "The picture from under the shed at the McCaslin place is twenty years old. The pictures in this cave have to be hundreds of years old."

"Older than that, I think," Jean said. "I think these pictures were drawn by the people who came before my people. That would be thousands of years. What did you see when you were here?"

Tye didn't answer for a while. He listened to the breeze rustle the trees outside, and realized there was a constant drip of water somewhere in the cave, regular as a heartbeat. He'd been hearing it since they walked in but hadn't noticed it.

"I dreamed of someone who called himself the First Man," Tye said. "It was brief. Only a few minutes."

Jean's eyes seemed to glitter in the light of the lantern, and for a moment, Tye had the feeling that the man had somehow grown to fill more space.

"The First Man. You have seen him. What did he tell you?"

"He told me to watch out for people who always want more," Tye said. "People who take."

"And you haven't been back since?"

"No. I've thought about it. I want some answers, but it doesn't seem like the right time."

"And what will you do with those answers?"

"Help people," Tye said. The words slipped out of his mouth before he had a chance to think about his answer.

"But if you found the right answers, you could be rich," Jean said. "You could make people do what you want."

Tye shook his head. "I've got enough. Kaity and I are going to build a little cabin, which will be nice. But I'd be happy with what I have."

Jean seemed to shrink, to fill less of the cave. It must have been a trick of the light, because before, Tye hadn't been able to see the light filtering in from the opening, but now he could.

It was then that he realized Jean had been holding a long-bladed, bone-handled knife, a virtual twin to the one locked up in Tye's safe at the yurt. Jean slid it back into a sheath Tye hadn't even seen under Jean's coat. Tye's mouth went dry.

"What was that about?" Tye asked.

Just like he'd done back at the yurt, Jean held his hands in front of him and showed his palms. "You are dangerous, Tye Caine. Very few people can access what you see. Has it ever occurred to you that you might have money? Fame? Women?"

Tye blinked. "What am I going to do? Have seances where I try to contact people's dead relatives? No, thanks."

Jean threw his head back and laughed. He clapped Tye on the shoulder. "It's never even occurred to you, all the ways you could enrich yourself, has it?"

"Not really."

Jean shook his head. "This is a good place, but it's not the kind of place you want to spend too much time unprepared. You should fast for a few days and meditate for a while before you enter here." He took one last look around the cave. "Let us step into the light."

It was painfully bright outside after being in the cave. Even though it seemed like they'd only been inside for a few minutes, the sun looked like it had traveled across the horizon. Tye looked at his watch and was surprised to see over an hour had passed.

Jean sat down on a rock and pulled an apple from his backpack. Tye found a rock and took out some elk jerky and tortillas.

"So, what now?" Tye asked after they'd been eating for a while.

"You need to find a teacher," Jean said around a mouthful of apple.

Tye blinked. "I thought that would be you."

"No," Jean said, shaking his head. "Hattie thought you would think this. It is not right for me to be your teacher. We are not of the same people. I do not understand your life, and you do not understand mine. I'm one of the few people in Canada raised traditionally. My people have been renegades in the forest for decades. You live pretty well, with your yurt and your bow and arrow, but you are still a product of this culture. Our practices are closed. I can only teach them to my people."

"How the hell am I supposed to find somebody to help me with this?" Tye asked. "I can't just go look up a shaman on the internet."

"Actually, you can. They are all fakes, plastic shamans, white people playing Indian. Take your time and be patient, Tye Caine, and a teacher will appear." Jean finished his apple and fastidiously stashed it away in his pack. He stood and stretched.

"Now, let us return to your truck. Hattie has promised to cook me dinner and I don't want to miss it." He started walking.

Jean walked unerringly back to the truck, not saying anything the whole time, while Tye followed along and stewed.

Back at the truck, Tye stowed his pack in the back of the truck while Jean climbed in. Tye slid behind the wheel but paused before he started the engine.

"The First Man," Tye said. "What has he said to you?"

Jean crossed his arms over his chest. "I have journeyed into the other worlds hundreds of times. I have never seen him."

"Oh," Tye said. It was all he could think of to say.

Jean reclined his seat and shut his eyes.

15

Jean had Tye drop him off at the end of Hattie's road, leaving him with a mile or two walk, but he insisted he wanted to stretch his legs before dinner. Tye watched him walk down the narrow two-track until he was out of sight. Jean had left with a vague promise to be in touch, but Tye wondered if he'd ever see him again.

Tye felt like answers were tantalizingly within reach, but still not quite within his grasp.

He checked his phone. No messages from Kaity. He wasn't sure if that was because she hadn't tried to contact him, or if he just didn't have enough of a signal out here in the hills to receive anything.

Tye was so lost in thought he almost didn't remember the drive home. He was on autopilot the whole way, listening to music and thinking, so he almost didn't notice the pickup truck parked in Deborah and Vivian's driveway until he drove past.

Tye's truck fishtailed a bit as he slammed on the brakes. With a quick glance in the rearview mirror, he backed up to a point where he could see the other truck and stopped.

It was a black three-quarter-ton truck, riding on a jacked-up suspension and oversized tires. Tye figured it probably got horrible gas mileage and would flip over if you took a corner too fast.

Despite the voice in the back of his head that said this wasn't a good idea, Tye pulled the truck into a spot where he wasn't blocking the road, and the driver of the giant pickup in the driveway could get out if they wanted to. He unlocked the center console of the truck, pulled out his revolver, and stuck it in his pocket. His phone had no signal, typical down here in the valley. If he wanted to make a call, he'd have to drive up his driveway to the top of the ridge.

The jacked-up truck was empty. As he walked past, Tye noted the bumper sticker with a picture of a gun that said, "I don't dial 911," and another that said, "Ditch the bitch, let's go hunting." On the one hand, Tye found things like that distasteful, but on the other, he was always glad to know exactly who he was dealing with.

Tye paused for a second to look at the tires. They were the same tread pattern that he'd seen up at the land trust gate. He memorized the license plate.

There was no one in the front of the house. Tye avoided the gravel of the driveway. His footsteps were nearly silent on the grass strip beside the driveway. He walked with his hand in his pocket on the grip of the revolver.

When he peeked around the back corner of the house, he saw a man sitting on the deck. He was stocky and wide-shouldered, with a long unkempt beard. He wore stained work clothes and heavy leather boots. Tye itched for a chance to get a look at the tread pattern.

The man took a long pull from a whiskey bottle and wiped his mouth with the back of his hand. Tye took another step around the corner, deliberately showing himself.

"What the fuck do you want?" the man said. His voice was deep and gravelly. Tye was sure it was the voice he'd heard the other night.

"I'm a neighbor," Tye said. "Just saw the truck and wondered what was up."

The man tossed the empty whiskey bottle into the grass and stood up, swaying on his feet. As he turned to face Tye, he realized the man was wearing a black semi-automatic pistol in a belt holster.

"Why don't you mind your own business, neighbor?" the man half-snarled, half-slurred. Tye realized he was quite drunk.

"Just trying to help out," Tye said, his stomach going cold. "What's your name?"

"'What's your name?'" the other man repeated in a high-pitched, mocking falsetto. He staggered forward toward Tye. He could barely walk, but at this range, Tye figured the man could still hit him with a pistol.

In the last few months, Tye had been stabbed, shot at, and kidnapped. All of that had left behind a hot ball of anger in his belly, and now it rose to the surface.

"Stop." He said it so loud, Tye surprised himself. He was even more surprised when the other man halted in his tracks.

It only lasted for a second, but Tye saw an expression he recognized pass across the other man's face. All his life, Tye had dealt with bullies who didn't know what to do when someone stood up to them.

"You talk big," the other man slurred. "But it looks like you brought your mouth to a gunfight."

An icy calm settled over Tye, and he shifted his focus from the other man's face to his hands. If they started moving toward the gun, Tye planned to draw his pistol, step to the side, and start shooting.

"Eddie, what's going on?" Tye turned just enough to see two other men had walked up.

There was no doubt they were father and son. The older man was tall and thin, with an aquiline nose and a full head of silver hair. He wore dark slacks, a white button-down shirt, and dress shoes. A pistol rode in a holster on his side.

The younger man was a virtual carbon copy of his father. He was heavier, more muscled, with a fuller face, but there was no mistaking the relationship. He was around thirty and wore a pair of cargo pants and a too-tight t-shirt chosen to show off his chest and arm muscles. There were combat boots on his feet, and like the other man, he was armed with a handgun. Tye could see his forearms were covered in tattoos but from this distance couldn't quite make out the designs.

"Jared. Mr. Bauman," the bearded man slurred, and he took a half-stumbling step toward them.

"Let's get you home, Eddie," the older man said. There was no tenderness in his voice, just a tone of command.

"Hold on a second," Tye heard himself say. "I want to know exactly what this guy is doing here."

Jared, the younger one, turned to him. "And what business of that is yours?" Unlike Eddie, who was full of bluster, his voice was flat. Tye felt like he was being measured for a coffin when this guy looked at him.

The smart thing would probably have been to back down. But that had never been Tye's strong suit. "This is my neighbor's house. Somebody tried to break in the other night, and now I find this guy sitting on the porch drinking whiskey. I want to know what's going on. Who are you people?"

"Are you accusing Eddie of a crime?" the older Bauman asked. His tone was mild, but there was an edge to his voice that Tye didn't like.

Tye didn't answer. The three of them were arrayed in front of him in a line, and the Baumans were between him and his truck. Tye could maybe shoot one, at most two of them, before being shot to pieces. Suddenly the little five-shot revolver in his pocket didn't seem like that big of an asset.

Jared smirked. "Awful convenient, the way we're so close to the national forest like this. Lots of places to cover up a problem."

Tye was starting to think he should just go for it, draw his pistol, and start shooting. If he managed to get a bullet into one or two of them, that would at least be a place for the cops to start looking after he disappeared.

Jared opened his mouth to say something else but was interrupted by the sound of a pump shotgun racking.

"Well, this is quite the little party." Gary stepped from around the corner of the house. Tye's battered old Mossberg shotgun was in his hands, not quite pointed at the Baumans, but not exactly pointed away either.

"I was a mite curious about the gaggle of trucks parked at this supposedly empty house, so I thought I'd stop and investigate," Gary said. He nodded at Tye. "Evening, Tye."

"Gary. Good to see you," Tye managed to say, even though his mouth seemed entirely devoid of moisture. He was suddenly very glad that his friend carried a spare key to the lock box in the back of Tye's truck.

"This situation is creating all sorts of questions in my mind," Gary said. "But it's hard to have a reasonable dialogue with all these guns around. So why don't the three of you just mosey on out of here, and we'll all go our separate ways?"

"There's still three of us and two of you," Eddie said. "And dumbass over there doesn't even have a gun."

"Oh, you never know with old Tye," Gary said. "It's kind of like Schrödinger's gun. You don't know what he's got in his pockets until he shows you."

Eddie's brow furrowed. He wasn't getting the reference to Schrödinger's cat. Leave it to Gary to throw in a reference to quantum mechanics in the middle of an armed standoff.

"Besides," Gary said as he flicked off the Mossberg's safety. "If this gets western, I don't think anybody is going to win. I think some of us are just going to have bigger holes in them than others."

Before Eddie could answer back, the older Bauman turned to him. "Eddie, get your bottle. Jared will drive you in your truck. You're in no condition to drive."

"Yep. Wouldn't want to break the law by littering," Tye said. *Or leave evidence with fingerprints and DNA behind,* he added in his mind.

Gary stepped aside as the Baumans and Eddie all marched out toward their trucks. It was quite the gaggle of vehicles Tye saw. There was another jacked-up pickup parked behind Tye's. Presumably, it belonged to the Baumans. Behind that was Gary's battered old International Scout.

"I see you have the Scout running," Tye said as Jared helped Eddie into the passenger side of his truck.

"For the moment," Gary said. "I expect it's going to be time to say goodbye soon and buy a different vehicle, although it pains me to admit it. I'll probably be forced to buy something made in this century."

"It will be the end of an era," Tye said. "I don't suppose you managed to get the license plate number of the truck the elder Mr. Bauman is climbing into?"

Holding the shotgun in one hand, Gary tapped his temple with the index finger of the other. "Yep. Got it right here."

"Excellent," Tye said. "I appreciate the assist. I thought that was gonna get ugly for a minute."

"Yep. Not sure I see the point of those fellows walking around carrying pistols like that all the time, in this day and age."

"Makes you wonder if they're up to something," Tye said.

"Or compensating for some inadequacy they perceive of themselves. Come to think of it, you have that little five-shot Smith and Wesson in your pocket?"

"I do."

"Polite of you, not to go around flaunting your gun like that. Those fellows are carrying their guns at people, like they want to make a point."

Both of the big trucks pulled out with a burble of aftermarket exhaust. As they vanished down the road, Tye let himself relax. He realized his hands were shaking.

"The plot thickens," Gary said as the engine noise faded into the distance.

"Yep."

"You got your work cut out for you now," Gary said as they walked toward their vehicles. He ejected the shell from the chamber of the Mossberg into his hand as they walked.

"How so?"

"You gotta choose between explaining to Kaity how you got into a confrontation with three armed knuckleheads, or just find a way not to mention it to her."

Tye sighed. "Well, seeing as how it's germane to recent events, I can't just not mention it to her."

"Well. Good luck," Gary said.

16

—————

"I feel like all I'm doing is driving," Kaity said as she sat the bag of takeout Thai food on Tye's workbench.

"I could stay at your place sometimes," Tye said.

"Yeah, it's always fun watching you tense up when a car drives by on the street outside," she said. "Besides, I like it out here. It'll be nice to get the house built so we can have an actual kitchen.

"So," she said over a forkful of Pad Thai. "What did you find out?"

He tried to condense his day into a few minutes. He was glad he had a few minutes to think about it first because it had been a bizarre day.

Kaity listened in silence, eating her dinner thoughtfully.

"Wow," she said finally. "I'm really glad Gary showed up when he did. Have you talked to Evans yet?"

"I was just about to," Tye said, waving his cell phone.

Kaity nodded, and he dialed. Evans sounded irritated when she answered the phone. Tye put her on speakerphone and told the story again, doing a better job of telling it concisely this time. When he finished, there was a long pause.

"The Baumans," Evans said finally.

"You know them?"

"Yes. They are kind of a big deal in the part of the county where you live. They run the Church of the Sword and Spirit."

"Are they the ones that require every male member of the congregation to pack a gun at Sunday services?"

"That would be them."

"What about the boots and the tires? They are a perfect match for the ones at the scene where Cody Weber was murdered."

There was another long pause.

"Tracks," Evans said finally. "I need more than that. The first question the DA is going to ask me if I talk about tracks is if you are a certified expert witness. You're going to have to explain every step from the gate to Cody Weber's body, and a defense attorney will try to tear you to pieces."

There was another long pause.

"I need more than that," she said again. "Especially against the Baumans."

"Let me guess," Tye asked. "They're special."

"They have money," Evans said. "And they spend it on political donations. I've heard rumors that nobody wants to go up against them. Child Protective Services won't touch them. Some driving-under-the-influence and domestic-violence cases just went away, like magic."

"I guess this place isn't that different from West Virginia after all," Tye said.

"Keep the information coming," Evans said. "Now that I have the Baumans on my radar, I can work the case from other angles. We need to be careful, though. Very careful."

"Will do," Tye said.

"Good luck." Evans ended the call.

"We've dealt with the Church of the Sword and Spirit at work," Kaity said. "They challenge books all the time, trying to get them removed from the library."

"What do they challenge?"

"Pretty much anything that isn't the bible. King James Version, specifically."

"That would get a bit old," Tye said. "I suppose it would make shelving easier." He opened his food and started eating.

"I have some news," Kaity said. "I have an address for Cody Weber."

"How?" Tye asked.

"He had a library card. He verified his address six weeks ago to renew the card."

"Why didn't you tell Evans?"

"Because I'm breaking the rules by looking him up at all. I don't want to get fired for being a rogue librarian. The funny thing is, the address is another church. It's kind of the opposite of the Sword and Spirit, though. It's called the Church of the Open Heart. We deal with them at work too. They politely suggest lists of books about civil rights leaders and liberation theology and offer to donate money for us to buy them."

"Churches," Tye said. "I didn't see that coming. What books did he check out?"

"Can't tell you. Our system doesn't keep track of what books you've read. That's private."

"Well, that's good to know."

"But I can see a record of what is currently checked out. He has three titles about redemption and overcoming guilt. All currently overdue."

Kaity stood and stretched. Tye found himself momentarily distracted by the way her shirt rode up, exposing a band of skin on her belly.

She noticed him looking and laughed, then tugged her shirt down. "Try to stay focused, nature boy. I think tomorrow we could visit the Church of the Open Heart."

"It's been a while since I've been in a church," Tye said.

"Me too. I guess we've never talked much about religion."

"Nope."

She yawned. "I'm too tired for that tonight, though."

"Me too."

17

The town of Vancouver, Washington was only an hour's drive from Tye's house, but it felt like a different world. Just across the Columbia River from Portland, Oregon, the town was growing rapidly as people fled Portland's high real estate prices for more affordable homes.

Tye and Kaity drove separately, meeting in a supermarket parking lot where Tye left his truck and climbed into her Jeep. Their destination was in the older part of Vancouver, where the streets were narrow and his full-size pickup would be a tight fit.

"The logistics of this relationship are getting complicated," Kaity said as she shifted through the Jeep's gears.

"I feel like you're doing way more than your fair share of driving," Tye said. "Burning lots of gas."

She shrugged. "You're worth it. It's nice to spend time out of the city, too."

"We've got the last meeting with the tiny house contractor next week," Tye said.

"Yes. Finally."

What Tye hadn't mentioned was that their final payment was due that day as well. He had his half of the money, barely. His money from being on the reality TV show was long gone, spent on purchasing the land he lived on. Now he was subsisting on income from their search-and-rescue consulting business, which was irregular at best.

Kaity had been adamant that she was keeping her house in town. Somehow on her librarian salary, she was affording to share half of the construction costs of the tiny home on his land. After some initial hesitation, their relationship had proceeded at breakneck speed. They'd been very open with each other about a great many things, but Tye found that Kaity played her cards very close to the vest when it came to money. She seemed to have plenty of it, more than he'd expect somebody on a librarian's salary to have.

"There it is, up there," Kaity said.

This was an older, quieter part of the city. Here there were small homes, most of them built during the post-World War II economic boom. Many of them didn't have driveways, leaving the streets crowded with parked cars.

The church was simple, a plain white square box of a chapel, with another smaller building that looked more modern on the other side of a parking lot. Kaity parked next to a van with faded paint and "Church of the Open Heart" on the side in peeling letters.

A woman wearing jeans and a flannel shirt stood on a ladder, driving long spikes into a sagging gutter. She waved as Tye and Kaity walked up.

"I'll be down in just a minute," she said.

Tye looked around as they waited. The building was old. Quite a bit of effort was being put into upkeep, but it still needed a new roof, and in places, the trim around the windows was rotten. Pacific Northwest winters were hell on wood structures.

"Look out below," the woman said. After Tye and Kaity stepped well back, she dropped the heavy framing hammer into the grass with a thud, then climbed down the ladder.

"Jacqueline Elliott," she said, sticking out a hand. Tye guessed she was in her late forties. She was tall, with straight gray hair and a scar over her right eyebrow. "I'm the reverend here. And the maintenance person and the groundskeeper."

Tye and Kaity shook hands with her, and Kaity produced a business card. "We're wondering if you can help us out with something," Kaity said.

Jacqueline handed the card back and looked at Tye. "I thought I recognized you. You were on that TV show. How can I help?"

"We're here about Cody Weber," Kaity said.

Jacqueline looked from Kaity to Tye. "I haven't seen him in days. His motorcycle is here, but I don't think he's been in his room."

"Wait," Tye said. "His motorcycle is here?"

"Yes. This way." She led them behind the smaller building. A Honda dual-sport motorcycle on its kickstand sat on a concrete patio.

"Weird," Kaity said.

"Yeah." Tye squatted beside the bike. There were fine scratches all over the right side. Tye guessed this was from being on its side in a pickup truck bed.

"You mentioned Cody's room," Kaity said. "He stays here?"

"We have several rooms downstairs in this building. We help people out from time to time."

"Who else is staying here now?" Tye asked as he stood.

"Cody is the only one presently. Can I ask what this is about?"

Kaity and Tye looked at each other.

"I saw an article in the news," Jacqueline said. "A man's body was found in the state forest. That's where Cody likes to ride. Was it Cody?"

Tye and Kaity looked at each other again. Tye realized they could have done a better job planning this.

"We have to be very careful to maintain client confidentiality," Kaity said. "But we really are trying to help."

"I normally don't talk about the people who stay here," Jacqueline said. "Sometimes they're hiding from husbands or boyfriends, or abusive parents."

"Who was Cody hiding from?" Tye asked.

Jacqueline stared at Cody's motorcycle. "Come up to the office. I'll make tea."

The upstairs of the little building held Jacqueline's office. The walls were lined with self-help books and theological texts. Through an open doorway, Tye saw a sparse room with a single bed and little else.

"I live here too," Jacqueline said as she poured hot water from the electric kettle. "It saves on rent."

She put two cups of herbal tea in front of Tye and Kaity, then made another for herself.

"Cody first started staying here three or four months ago. He was semi-homeless. I got the impression he would stay a few nights at a friend's or relative's, then maybe a few nights on the street. We have services and a meal almost every night. He would show up, eat, and help clean up. He started offering to help with some of the upkeep on this place, so I eventually started letting him stay here."

She nodded toward the bedroom. "There are a couple of doors with locks between here and the rooms downstairs, but I'm pretty careful about who I let in. Most of them are women."

"Did he say why he was on the streets?" Kaity asked.

Jacqueline took a sip of tea and shook her head. "He asked a bunch more questions than he gave answers. I don't pry. I just try to meet people where they're at."

"What did he ask about?" Tye asked.

"Forgiveness. He asked lots of questions about atonement, about how people could be forgiven for their sins. Frankly, that's not our focus here. We don't preach hellfire and damnation as a central part of our message. We believe everyone is worthy of love and respect, not that you're going to hell for being an imperfect person. But I tried to answer him the best I could."

"I wonder what he was atoning for?" Kaity asked.

"Sometimes, I did too. I think it would have done him some good just to spit it out and tell somebody what was on his mind. But that has to happen at the right time, and it can't be forced."

She looked from Tye to Kaity. "And now I get the feeling it's too late."

"Can we see his room?" Tye asked. "It might help us figure out what's going on?"

Jacqueline drummed her fingers on the desk for a moment, staring into her teacup. Then she opened a desk drawer, pulled out a key, and stood.

"This way."

She led them downstairs, to a corridor that ran the length of the building with doors on either side. At the last door on the right, she tried a couple of keys before finding the one that fit.

The room was small, just big enough for a single bed, a small desk, and some shelves. Weak light came from a window high up on the wall. An empty backpack sat in a corner, and neatly folded clothes filled the shelves next to a pile of books.

He tilted his neck to read the book spines: *The Power of Forgiveness, Starting Over, Healing Trauma.* They were self-help books about overcoming the past.

"Check this out," Kaity said. She'd opened a desk drawer and Tye saw she had another book in front of her. "It fell open to this page."

Tye realized it was a high school yearbook. Kaity tapped a picture. It was a young woman with dark curly hair, smiling into the camera. The name under the picture read "Hannah Malley."

"Huh," Tye said.

Kaity thumbed through the rest of the book, finding Jared Bauman and Cody Weber's pictures. "They were all seniors. Same graduating class."

"Wait," Tye said as she flipped through more pages. "There." He recognized a younger version of Eddie. Eddie Guff. That was his full name.

"Also a senior. Cody didn't own more than a backpack full of clothes, but he kept this?"

Jacqueline looked sharply at Kaity at the use of the past tense. "So it was him?"

Tye looked at Kaity. "We're going to have to tell Evans."

Kaity nodded, then looked at Jacqueline. "It would help if you could call the sheriff's office and wonder if the body found in the forest is related to your missing resident here. They'll put you in touch with a Detective Evans, who will ask you the same questions three or four times."

"I've dealt with the cops before," Jacqueline said, then touched the scar over her eyebrow. She jerked her hand away when she realized what she was doing. "Did Cody have a family?"

"I don't know," Tye said. "We're still trying to figure things out."

Jacqueline let them see themselves out. She sat at her desk, staring into her cup of tea.

On the way back to the car, Tye took one last look at the motorcycle.

"There's a little black paint transfer," he said, pointing at the bike's frame. "See it there. That's the same color as Eddie Guff's pickup truck."

"Why bring it back here?" Kaity asked.

"To confuse things, I guess."

"Will you drive?" Kaity asked as they walked back to the car. "There's stuff I want to do."

Tye drove while Kaity dialed Evans and put her on speakerphone. The detective listened silently while Kaity explained everything they'd found out.

"Well, that's all excellent," Evans said. "Now I just have to figure out how to explain how a pair of civilians led me to the big break in the case."

"Any minute now, Jacqueline Elliot will call the sheriff's non-emergency number and say she read a news story about a body being found in the forest and she's concerned it might be her missing tenant."

"That will be convenient," Evans said. "Do you two super-sleuths have any more ideas? I'm just going to prop my feet up and drink coffee while you two solve the case."

"Have you had any more luck with the initials carved into the tree? WOTN?"

"Haven't even started, but it's on my list," Evans said.

"Well, keep us posted," Kaity said. She clicked off the phone. "I get the feeling there are things she's not telling us."

"Most likely," Tye said. "That's the cops for you. Now what?"

"I want to go do some research at the downtown library, so unless you want to come with me, let's go back to where we parked your truck."

He drummed his fingers on the wheel, trying to decide what to do.

"I would probably be able to research more quickly if you weren't in the background, looking over my shoulder and trying to help," Kaity said.

"Is that a subtle hint?" Tye asked.

"If you want to call it subtle, I can go along with that," Kaity said.

They made their goodbyes next to Tye's truck. She gave him a distracted peck on the lips and drove away. He could tell she was deep in thought, and the best thing he could do was stay out of her way. After the first few weeks of their relationship, when they'd spent almost all their time together, the intensity had cooled off a little, and they each found ways to spend time by themselves.

Part of him wasn't surprised to find Jean sitting on the steps outside his yurt. Just like before, Jean put aside his book, stood, and stretched. Tye got out of the truck, wondering what would happen next.

"Hello, Tye Caine," Jean said. "It is time for you to show me the killing knife."

18

Inside the yurt, Tye felt a strange reluctance to open his gun locker. Fiddler stood next to him, passive and silent, while Tye's fingers hovered over the keypad. Finally, he punched in the numbers. Fiddler was polite enough to look away while he entered the combination and opened the door.

The Bowie knife was nearly as long as Tye's forearm. The elk-antler handle, yellowed with age, always felt slightly warm. It rested on the top shelf of the gun locker, above his rifles. He pulled it out with both hands.

He felt another moment of reluctance when he handed it to Fiddler. Tye didn't particularly care for the knife. For use in the woods, he favored a knife with a blade barely longer than the palm of his hand, and he often made fun of men who showed up in the woods with knives that were the size of a small sword. This knife was a killing knife, long enough to reach a man's heart with a thrust, and heavy enough to lop off a hand with a slash.

Fiddler drew the blade halfway out of the sheath. Tye realized the other man was breathing deeply.

"I have heard of this knife from my father. My Uncle Remy bore the burden for a long time."

"Why do you call it a burden?"

"It was Remy's job to deal with people who were possessed by the Wendigo, those overcome by greed and hunger that could never be satisfied. It is a sickness that has always been with us, since the beginning of time, but when your people came to our country, it exploded. Books have been written about smallpox and other diseases that scientists can see under a microscope, but no one speaks of this other madness. I guess when it is all around you, you can no longer see it."

"So, he killed people? The ones infected by the Wendigo?"

Fiddler nodded. "Yes. Sometimes our people would feel it coming over them and disappear into the forest, to let the cold take them before they became a threat to others. Others would beg for release. In the old days, they would be strangled with a cord. But when your people came, too many people caught the sickness."

He handed the knife back to Tye. "Thank you for showing me this."

"But don't you want it?" Tye asked, confused. "It belongs to your family."

Fiddler shook his head. "It belongs to whoever has found it. Right now, that person is you. I do not need it. The people I live among have found their way back to the right path. You are the one who lives among the Wendigo. I suspect that you will need the knife someday. I am sorry for you, Tye Caine. The only thing worse than becoming a Wendigo is fighting them. Keep your friends close to you and remember to enjoy the small things in life. The smell of a spring flower. The warmth of the summer sun. The colors of the leaves in fall. The touch of the woman who loves you in winter."

"I don't want this," Tye said. "I don't want this knife or this job."

"One of the many differences between your people and mine is that you think that what you want matters." Fiddler nodded at the knife in Tye's hands. "It is best to put that away." From the knapsack at his feet, Fiddler drew out a bag of coffee. "My time here is short. There are things I must do. But in return for showing me the knife, I thought we might brew ourselves some coffee and enjoy it."

Tye realized his hands were shaking a little as he put the knife away. They grew steadier as he performed the familiar ritual of making coffee with his hand-cranked grinder, gas backpacking stove, and French press.

The coffee came out dark, hot, and bitter. Like Tye, Fiddler preferred it without cream or sugar.

Fiddler took a few inhales of the steam coming off the cup, seeming to enjoy the coffee as much as a man drinking fine wine. Finally, he closed his eyes and took a sip.

"Ahh," he said. "Such an excellent thing, coffee."

"I'm fond of it, myself," Tye said. They were sitting out in front of Tye's yurt in folding camp chairs, looking out into the valley through a narrow gap in the trees.

"I have thought very hard about what to do about you, Tye Caine," Fiddler said.

"That's not the first time somebody has said that about me," Tye said.

"It is not the right thing for me to instruct you, as I have said before," Fiddler said, then took a sip of coffee. "You are not of my people. Even if you were, I am not yet a teacher. I must grow a bit more before I am ready to take on students."

Tye blinked. Fiddler had an incredible gravitas about him. Sometimes the man was downright scary. Tye wondered what his teacher was like.

"But I have looked into your eyes, and I have decided you are a good man," Fiddler said. "So I will put the word out to people I know, to see if any of them can help you."

"Who?" Tye asked.

Fiddler shrugged. "It is not my place to say their names to you. If they decide it is the right thing, you will hear from them."

"I feel like I'm just a puppet on a string sometimes," Tye said. "I feel like I'm being jerked around by... something. The universe? Fate?"

Fiddler smiled at him. "And the sooner you stop fighting it, the easier your life will become." Fiddler looked around, his gaze encompassing the surrounding woods. "It seems that if you wish to live like this, the universe is going to expect certain things from you. If you don't want to do those things, maybe try moving into town. Get a job selling insurance during the day, then go home and play video games at night. I'm sure it will all fade away, eventually."

He stood, placing his coffee cup carefully on the little folding table between them. "Thank you for brewing me an excellent cup of coffee, Tye Caine. There are things I must do."

"Do you want a ride?"

Fiddler shook his head. "I prefer to walk. I see more that way." He shouldered his pack, gave Tye a wave, and walked down the driveway.

Tye sat there, watching him go and drinking the last couple swallows of coffee. Fiddler had given him more questions than answers, and Tye knew if he sat here and stewed, he'd go crazy. After sitting in the car all day, then sitting more and talking to Fiddler, his body craved action.

His mind had decided to shove the things Fiddler had told him aside, and he found himself chewing over the things they'd learned today. If he stood at the base of a big maple tree, he could get enough of a signal on his phone to use the internet. He searched for the Church of the Sword and Spirit and found the address.

From the seat pocket of his truck, he pulled out a Washington State Gazetteer. He spread it out on the tailgate and located the church.

It wasn't that far away. Tye had heard of the church before and had a vague idea that it was to the north of his house. Now his finger traced a route to the church. He realized it was in a valley below a big stretch of private timberland. Tye and Gary had both kicked in to buy a yearly permit from the timber company, in the hopes the hunting would be better behind locked gates.

Tye turned at the sound of a boot scuffing on gravel. Gary was being polite as he walked up, making a little noise so as not to startle Tye while he was poring over the map.

"Was your new friend just here? I saw a fellow matching his description hoofing it down the road," Gary said. Tye had filled him in about Fiddler's visit over a glass of bourbon.

"Yeah, he declined a ride."

Gary looked at the map. "What are you plotting?"

"Something rash," Tye said.

"Well, it's been at least a couple of months since we did something ill-advised and dangerous. Fill me in."

Tye explained everything he and Kaity had discovered today. Gary looked at the map.

"So, if I'm following your train of thought, it seems like a person ought to be able to drive through the timberland and park right about here." He put his finger down on the map. "Then we could walk out this here ridgeline and have an unobstructed view of the Church of the Sword and Spirit."

"You're using the word 'we,'" Tye said.

"That's because I've done all the homesteading chores I have a mind to do for the day, and I rather like the idea of gallivanting around the woods and spying on the local weirdos."

"It's been a while since we've had a good gallivant," Tye said as he folded up the map.

"I'll fetch my pack. Meet me at the driveway split in ten minutes."

When Gary climbed into the passenger seat of the truck, he dropped his gun belt, with his worn old Smith and Wesson in the holster into the footwell in front of him.

"Just in case," Gary said.

"Yep," Tye said. "Just in case."

19

The private timberland wasn't a forest. It was a tree farm. Douglas fir trees grew in orderly rows, so close together that nothing could grow underneath them, and in spots, a person would be hard-pressed to thread their way in between the trunks. As soon as Tye and Gary took their first trip up here, they'd regretted spending several hundred dollars on the permit. Tye found the whole idea of a manufactured, manicured forest creepy, and in the large stretches of cultivated trees, they'd found little sign of deer or elk. They took some consolation from the areas close to streams that had been allowed to grow unmanaged. There they found an abundance of animal sign.

Tye and Gary talked about inconsequential things as they traveled. Tye knew his friend was curious about what he'd discussed with Fiddler, but right now, Tye couldn't even articulate his thoughts about it to himself, much less to Gary. So he left it alone and was glad to just pass the time. Gary had been busy with projects of his own, and Tye had been spending much of his time with Kaity these last few months, so he and Gary had spent less time with each other than they had in years. The two had grown up together and were practically brothers. Tye could sense an impending pivot in their relationship as they grew into their adult lives, and it sometimes made him sad.

"Right about here," Gary said, looking up from the map unfolded across his lap. Tye pulled the truck off to the side of the road, and for a few minutes, both men busied themselves getting their gear ready. Tye wondered how many times they'd done this, left a vehicle parked in some lonely place and geared up for some adventure in the forest. Sometimes at night, Tye would worry about money and the future, and wonder if he should have taken a different path in life, but at moments like this, he was grateful he wasn't stuck in an office somewhere.

Tye led the way through the trees, pausing infrequently to consult the GPS attached to one of his backpack straps. They fell into an easy rhythm, walking for ten minutes or so, then pausing for a couple to observe the surrounding woods. The long rows of trees surrounded them with geometric precision, and this stretch of timber was dead quiet, save for the occasional flutter of a ruby-crowned kinglet far above them in the tree canopy. The little birds were so small that Tye couldn't see them if he looked at them directly. He would just catch the impression of movement out of the corner of his eye as they darted from branch to branch.

After about an hour of walking, the land began to slope down, and ahead past the rows of gray-brown Douglas fir trunks, Tye could see a riot of green vegetation. This was the border of the timberland, and in the valley below them, Tye saw buildings and the thin ribbon of a road.

A large fallen log lay just past the tree line. Tye nodded at it, and Gary mouthed the word "perfect." They crept up and squatted behind the log.

"Right on the money. We're directly over the church compound," Gary whispered. There was no one nearby to hear them, but Gary often said that stealth was a state of mind. They were both in the habit of talking quietly while in the woods. Most of the animals worked hard to stay quiet, so it only seemed polite.

Gary hadn't used the term "compound" casually. The church

property was several acres of flat land at the bottom of the valley, with an eight-foot-tall chain-link fence surrounding the perimeter. Tye focused his binoculars on the fence and realized it was topped with three strands of barbed wire.

The buildings were modern construction with flat roofs. There was one long, low building Tye assumed housed the sanctuary and two other two-story buildings. Tye didn't know what they were for, but it seemed like an awful lot of space for a church. The parking lot was mostly empty but for two trucks Tye recognized. One was Eddie Guff's, the other Jared Bauman's.

On the east side of the compound, Tye saw a low, three-sided shed. The open side faced a dirt berm a hundred yards away.

"Is that what I think it is?" Tye whispered.

As if in response, Tye heard a muffled crack, and dirt puffed up from the berm. It was followed by several more in rapid succession.

"Yep," Tye said. "That's a shooting range."

"If the Second Reformed Baptist Church back home had a shooting range, I would have been more inclined to let Mom drag me to services on a Sunday morning," Gary said.

"The shots sound funny," Tye said.

"I think they're using a suppressor," Gary said. "In the movies, they make the gun almost silent, but in real life, if the bullet is going faster than the speed of sound, you still hear that crack."

"Still pretty quiet, though," Tye said.

"It is. I've often thought it would be nice to have one for hunting. Wouldn't spook the other animals so badly. The paperwork is a mite onerous, though, unless you build one in your garage by yourself, and then you run the risk of going to prison."

A man came out from under the shed roof. Tye focused his binoculars and recognized Eddie. He was holding a five-gallon-sized plastic jar with a screw-top lid in front of him, and there was a stubbly little black gun slung around his neck.

"What kind of gun is that? It looks like some kind of machine gun," Tye said.

Gary was looking through his binoculars. "It's a cut-down rifle.

Technically, it's a pistol, because the thing on the end that looks like a stock is actually a brace. Jared is carrying one just like it."

"Huh," Tye said. He'd accumulated several firearms over the years, suitable for hunting and backcountry survival. It seemed like every time he walked into a sporting goods store, he saw an increasing variety of black plastic guns that looked more suitable for rescuing hostages from terrorists than they were for shooting deer or keeping someone from breaking into your house.

"You know the interesting thing about that gun," Gary said. "It's commonly chambered in .300 Blackout." Gary was one of those people who seemed to absorb information like that by osmosis. Tye had known him long enough not to be surprised when Gary whipped out some random fact like that.

"The round that killed Cody Weber," Tye said. "Seems awful stupid to shoot somebody, then hang on to the gun."

"I'm not sure these boys have any expectations that they will be held accountable for their actions," Gary said.

As they watched, Eddie placed the plastic jar against the berm, then walked back to the firing line.

"What's in the jar?"

"If it's what I expect, you'll want to watch your ears."

A single shot came from the firing line, and a puff of dirt appeared right next to the jar. Rough laughter sounded from below.

There was a second shot, then instantly a giant boom and dust cloud as the jar exploded.

"What the hell?" Tye asked.

"Exploding target," Gary said. "You mix two chemicals, and the shock of the impact sets them off."

The blast echoed down the valley, and Tye heard the cattle on the land next door mooing. They were all running away from the fence line toward a stand of trees.

"That must make them popular with the neighbors," Tye said. Below them, Eddie and Jared opened up on the berm in a fusillade of rapid fire. They didn't seem to be aiming at anything in particular.

They were just jerking triggers as fast as they could, making the dust fly on the berm. Tye heard a ricochet sail off into the distance.

Both guns ran dry at the same time, and Tye could hear both men talking excitedly, although he couldn't make out what they were saying. They sat their guns on shooting benches and bent over, picking up their spent brass and pitching it into buckets.

"I bet they don't find every piece of brass," Gary said. "Sure would be interesting to pick one up and see if it's a match for the one we found by Cody Weber's dead body."

"It would." Tye started scanning the fence line with his binoculars. "There's a gate on this side of the fence. I guess so they can come out and mow the strip of land between the fence and the trees. The gate is locked. I wonder if we could contrive a way to get over that barbed wire without getting all sliced up."

"That's the least of our worries," Gary said. "Focus on the southeast corner of the building, right under the eave of the roof."

Tye shifted his binoculars and saw the round eye of a video camera mounted on the side of the building.

"Well, so much for that."

"Yep," Gary said. "I doubt somebody is sitting there watching the cameras all the time, but I can pretty much guarantee they're being recorded."

Jared and Eddie walked over to their trucks. Eddie took both buckets of spent brass and put them in the bed of his pickup.

"I wonder if he reloads those," Gary said. "And I wonder if there's another way to get our hands on a piece of brass."

They watched as Jared and Eddie made their goodbyes. Jared turned left, headed west, and Eddie went the other way. Tye rubbed his chin as the gate rolled closed automatically.

"You thinking what I'm thinking?" Gary asked.

"If I'm remembering my geography correctly, there aren't too many houses to the east," Tye said. "That road dead ends in a gate that enters this exact private timberland."

"So, if we were to drive out that gate and mosey down the road, paying attention, we might see where Eddie lives," Gary said. "If his house is on the south side of the road, we could drive back into the timberland, find a place to park, and walk up behind it just like we did with the church here."

"We could. Assuming his house is that way, we've got at least a fifty-fifty chance."

They walked back to the truck, moving much quicker than on the trip in. After stowing their gear in the back, they consulted the map to make sure their assumptions were correct. Tye and Gary had entered the private timberland from a gate on the south side. If they exited via the north gate, they would drive right past the church. Assuming Eddie lived between the church and the gate, they'd drive right past his place. There were no side roads.

Just as Gary hopped out of the truck to open the gate, Tye's phone started buzzing with incoming messages. They'd driven into a pocket of cell phone reception.

Where are you? Kaity asked.

North side of the private timberland, Tye typed back. *By the Sword and Spirit Church.*

Are you up there doing something dangerous? Alone?

Gary is with me. He figured he could probably get away with answering half the question.

That makes me feel better, but don't think for a minute I didn't notice that you didn't answer the first part. I found out some stuff. Too long to type.

Tye looked at his phone.

I have one bar. Can I talk to you later?

Yes. I'm about to leave for your place. More driving. What exactly are you doing?

His fingers hovered over the keyboard for a minute. Gary got back in the truck and looked at him quizzically.

We are going to see if we can figure out where Eddie Guff lives. That was true in the sense that it was the first thing they were going to do.

I already have his address. She sent it in the chat. Tye saw it was between the church and the gate, on the south side of the road. *I think that's close to where you are?*

Yes. Going to check it out.

Be careful. Love you.

Will do. Love you. Tye put the phone away.

"Well, that's convenient," Gary said. He'd been reading over Tye's shoulder.

"Guess we don't even need to drive by," Tye said. "We can just drive back in, pick a spot, and sneak up from behind."

"We can." Gary opened the truck door. "She's right handy to have around. Let's go get this done before it gets too late."

20

———————

Tye dropped a waypoint on his GPS right over Eddie's address. Once again, they parked the truck in the private timberland and set out on foot. They had maybe an hour until nightfall. Technically, they were supposed to be out of the private timberland an hour after dark, but the roads were rarely patrolled, and if they happened to be caught, Tye planned to fake an ankle injury and say they'd been delayed hiking back to the truck.

Tye and Gary moved at what they called their hunting pace. They would walk ten to fifteen steps, quietly and slowly, to avoid stepping on branches and making other noises, then they would stop and listen for a few seconds. It was nearly impossible to walk through a forest making zero noise, but it was possible to walk through the woods and not sound like a human. Humans tended to walk at a steady, metronome pace, their footsteps clomping through the leaves and brush for long periods. No other animal moved like that. Animals moved in a broken rhythm with lots of pauses in between to feed or observe.

They were almost at the edge of the private timberland when the evening breeze brought the smell of frying bacon to them. Tye took a knee and double-checked his GPS. They were almost there.

"Smells like he's cooking dinner," Gary whispered.

"Yep. Let's see the lay of the land."

They crept forward, moving a dozen feet or so at the time. They crossed a well-trod footpath that led off to the east in one direction, and straight to Eddie's trailer in the other. They followed it to the edge of the tree line.

Soon they were looking at the back of a single-wide trailer. A covered porch extended for part of its length, sheltering a weight bench and fire pit. A small shed sat in the backyard, and through the window, Tye could see a workbench with an ammunition reloading press bolted to the top. Eddie's truck was parked right next to the trailer.

As they watched, Eddie passed in front of the window of the trailer, beer in hand.

"Those shell casings are likely either still in the back of the truck or in that little shed," Gary said. "I don't see a way to creep our way in there without getting spotted. I think our only option would be to hunker down here until he goes to bed. I'd want to give it a couple of hours after that to make sure he's good and asleep."

Tye thought about it. The smell of frying bacon was making his stomach rumble. It wouldn't be the first time the two of them had spent unexpected time in the woods. He and Gary could retreat a couple of hundred yards back into the trees, eat some of the food bars they both carried in their pack, and wait until Eddie had turned in for the night.

"If he stays up late playing video games or something, we could be here a long time," Tye said. "I'm not sure it's worth all that effort to steal something Evans can't use as evidence, anyway."

Gary nodded. "Maybe the smart thing to do is just ease out of here and let Evans take it from here. She's bound to be interested in the fact that both Eddie and Jared own guns that are similar to the one that killed Cody Weber."

"Yep," Tye said. "Let's ease on out of here. We can check out the other end of that trail on the way."

Tye gave one last look inside the trailer. He could see Eddie's back as the man worked at the stove. He retraced their steps up the footpath, passing the point where they'd entered from the woods, and continued to the east. The path saw a bunch of traffic. Tye wasn't sure if they were still on Eddie's property or the private timberland at this point. The sun was just setting, and it was that period of half-light where his eyes struggled, as they hadn't adapted from daytime vision to night just yet, so he didn't want to fool with his GPS.

The path ended in a clearing. Four tall stakes made a circle, one at each of the cardinal directions. In the dim twilight, Tye saw a white blob atop the one on the north side. He realized he was looking at an animal skull.

"What the hell?" Gary whispered.

They crept forward, into the circle. In the middle was a fire pit full of burned charcoal, just in front of a mound of rocks with a single flat stone on top. The slab was covered in old candle wax. A cold shiver ran down Tye's spine, and a spike of pain shot through his temples. For a second, his nostrils filled with the stench of death, and the taste of dirt filled his mouth.

Nauseous, Tye walked to the north side of the circle. The skull was massive, with a heavy sagittal crest and huge canines. There was little doubt in his mind it was a wolf skull. It was bleached perfectly white, and the lower jaw was wired in place.

Something was carved into the pole. Tye pulled his little red LED light from his pocket and shielded it with his hand.

WOTN was carved on the pole.

"Just like where we found Cody Weber," Gary said. He reached out to trace the letters with his fingers but drew his hand back rather than touch the pole. "This is some creepy shit. Is that a wolf skull?"

"Pretty sure it is. This is a bad place," Tye said, realizing as he said it that he was echoing Jean Fiddler's words from the day before.

"Time to go," Gary said. "I'm not a fan of the cops, but they get paid to deal with stuff like that."

Tye nodded, his mouth dry. In the distance, they heard the screen door of Eddie's trailer slam. Tye didn't think the man would carry his dinner out here, but you never knew.

They moved off through the woods, both of them moving faster than they usually did. Tye was willing to accept a little noise in return for getting the hell away from the circle and skull. He still had a bad taste in his mouth and wanted a shower.

It was a relief to break out onto the timber company's gravel road about fifty yards from the truck. Tye relaxed and headed toward the vehicle, already thinking about what he was going to do next.

Gary grabbed his shoulder and pulled him back. "There's somebody over there." He shone his flashlight at the truck.

In the glare of the light stood a tall lanky man wearing an old green Army coat, fatigue pants, and a backpack. He raised his hand to shield his eyes from the light, but not before Tye got a glimpse of his face.

"That's Peter Etchells," Tye said. "Hey, Peter! We want to talk to you."

Etchells ran. He slid in the gravel, nearly taking a spill, then ran around the truck and into the woods. Tye heard him crashing through branches.

"We want to help!" Tye yelled. He took a step forward, then stopped.

"I'm not sure how enthusiastic we should be about charging into the woods after that fellow," Gary said.

"Yeah. Good point. Great way to get ambushed," Tye said. Still, he was frustrated. Etchells likely had the key to what they were trying to figure out.

"I'm more concerned about what he was doing to the truck," Gary said. "It's a long walk home."

They walked over and found one of the windshield wiper arms was propped up. A scrap of paper that looked like it had been torn from a notebook and a stub of a pencil sat on the hood.

"Was he leaving a note?" Tye asked.

"Looks like it. Shame we didn't arrive a few minutes later so we could find out what was on his mind."

Tye looked the truck over carefully. His vehicle had been tampered with before out in the woods, and he didn't want to build up a bunch of speed only to find out his brake lines had been cut. He found nothing amiss.

"Tonight just keeps getting weirder," Gary said. "My vote is we head for home while we're still in one piece and we haven't had to commit any felonies."

Tye sighed. Part of him still wanted to start tracking Peter Etchells. Once he started solving a problem that was important to him, he was like a dog worrying at a bone. It was hard to give up.

"Kaity's probably back at your place by now," Gary said. "Sounds like she had some info she wanted to share."

"Yeah, good point." Tye unlocked the truck and climbed in.

"I figured the allure of your favorite librarian would be enough to bring you out of the woods," Gary said.

Tye started the truck and pointed them toward home. He still felt queasy and much colder than he should have, given the temperature of the night air. Now and then he thought he smelled a whiff of death and dirt.

"That skull on a stick was pretty weird," Gary said. "Made my hair stand up on end. I was kinda wondering how you felt about it?"

Tye drove for a while without answering, telling himself it was late and he had to watch out for deer. He'd started to open up more about this sort of thing lately, but it was still difficult to talk about.

"It made me feel kind of sick," Tye said finally. "Still do, a little. I think something bad happened there. Did you smell anything while we were there?"

"You mean other than Eddie's bacon frying? Nope."

"I did. I smelled something rotten. And dirt."

Gary considered that for a few moments. "Kind of makes me reconsider your great-aunt Enid sometimes."

Tye's great-aunt had been the family member nobody liked to talk about. She'd been diagnosed as schizophrenic in her early twenties and had been institutionalized and subjected to electroshock therapy off and on all through her adult life. After a while, electroshock had fallen out of favor, and she'd been on and off medications until her early death when Tye was in his late teens.

Enid had lived her life convinced she could see ghosts and receive communications from the spirit world in her dreams. The not-so-subtle message through Tye's childhood had been not to reveal any odd behaviors, lest he wind up like Enid.

"Yeah," he said. "I've been thinking about Enid a bunch these last few years."

They came up over a rise, and both Tye and Gary's phones dinged with incoming messages.

"Got a message from May," Gary said. "She said somebody was lurking around your yurt. She's positive it wasn't Jean Fiddler."

He picked up Tye's phone. "You got a message from Kaity saying pretty much the same thing. Says there's a note and to call her as soon as you get a chance. I'll call May."

Gary swapped Tye's phone for his own and tried to dial. "Nope. I guess I won't. We're out of signal again. I reckon we could turn around and go back to that rise, or just press on."

"We're ten minutes to the gate," Tye said.

"On we go then."

Tye mashed down on the accelerator and fishtailed in the gravel around a curve.

21

They made it home in record time. Kaity's Jeep was parked in front of Gary and May's trailer, instead of the yurt. Every light in the trailer was burning and the porch lights were on.

May stepped out onto the porch as they rolled up. She was wearing Gary's spare pistol belt around her waist and held an old Stevens Fox double-barrel shotgun.

"Looks like she has things well in hand," Gary said as he climbed out.

"Kaity's inside," May said to the unspoken question in Tye's eyes.

He and Gary followed her into the trailer. May leaned the shotgun in a corner so she could hug Gary. Kaity appeared from the kitchen with a mug of tea in her hand. Tye took a step toward her, but there was something in her body language that held him back.

"I drove up to the yurt and saw a guy standing there," Kaity said. "Not the same guy as before, the Fiddler guy. I'm pretty sure it was Peter Etchells."

"What time was it?" Tye asked.

She looked at her phone. "Just over four hours ago. I left town right after I texted you Eddie Guff's address."

"Pretty sure you're right then," Tye said. "We saw him walking through the timberland. The spot where we saw him is ten or so miles away. On those roads, a person could easily walk two and a half, three miles an hour."

"I saw him lurking around right before Kaity rolled up," May said. "By the time I got over there with the shotgun, he was gone."

"We've been sitting here with guns and the lights on ever since," Kaity said. "Well, May's had a gun."

"If he'd just walked up and politely introduced himself, he could have just waited for you two to come back," May said.

"I'm not sure everything is firing right in that guy's head," Gary said.

"He left a note," May said, pointing at a piece of paper sitting on the coffee table. "He was slipping it under the door right as I rolled up."

Tye picked up the note. It was hard to read.

"It's barely legible," Kaity said. She moved close to Tye. Her hip bumped his, and he put an arm around her. She leaned into him.

"I wonder if he has dysgraphia," Tye said. The handwriting resembled his own. He'd struggled with penmanship all through school and had been dismissed as stupid more than once. It wasn't until he was well into his twenties that he'd even heard of dysgraphia.

"I wondered about that," Kaity said.

"'I'm writing to tell you I didn't do anything wrong,'" Tye read aloud. "'They locked me up for something I didn't even do and gave me pills that made me a zombie. It wasn't until I stopped taking them that I could think again. They took years of my life. I didn't kill Hannah. I loved her. Eddie Guff is a wolf of the north, and he's not the only one. The cops won't believe me, but you are a good man. I watched your TV show when I was locked up. It was one of the only things they let me watch. I know you are a woodsman like me. I hope you will help me get justice for Hannah. I will contact you again.'"

"Sounds like your TV show made you famous even in mental institutions," Gary said.

"What the hell am I supposed to do about this?" Tye asked. "And what the hell is this 'wolf of the north' business?"

Kaity opened her laptop and plopped it down on the table in front of them. "The Wolves of the North are either a hate group or a neopagan brotherhood of men, depending on who you ask. They have a social media page."

"Of course they do," Tye said.

Kaity pressed "play" on a video she'd bookmarked. Heavy metal music started playing through the tinny speakers of the laptop, and slow-motion black-and-white video of a bunch of tattooed, shirtless, muscled men dancing around a fire started playing. As the song progressed, the video cut from still shot to still shot rapidly. The men's faces were always obscured, but it showed them throwing axes, butchering a goat, and chopping down trees.

"It's like a motorcycle gang without the Harleys," May said.

"It gets better," Kaity said. The song faded out over a final still shot of a very familiar wolf skull on a stick.

"Wait a minute," Tye said. "That's the circle behind Eddie's house."

Kaity opened another tab in her browser. "Here's a picture of Jared Bauman on his trophy wolf hunt in Montana two years ago."

In the picture, Bauman stood with his arms wrapped around the carcass of a black wolf. It was almost as long as he was tall.

"Asshole," Tye said through clenched teeth. Tye hunted deer and elk so he could eat. People hunted wolves just as a trophy.

"But wait a minute," May said. "You just said the Wolves of the North group is a neopagan group, but Bauman is hooked up with this Church of the Sword and Spirit."

"It seems a little out of sync, doesn't it," Kaity asked. "They claim to worship Odin, the Norse god. Another way of saying his name is Wodin. The abbreviation WOTN is a kind of play on words."

"We've known plenty of pagan people over the years," Tye said. "None of them were like this."

"The Southern Policy Law Center calls them a hate group. Here's why."

She queued up another video. This one showed a couple of dozen men around a bonfire. It was lit in a way Tye couldn't definitively make out faces, but they all seemed to be dressed in combinations of animal skins and black leather. One man was standing in the center of the circle with his back to the fire so he could only be seen in silhouette.

"It's time to stand up for what we believe in," he said. "Do we believe in the supremacy of men?"

"Yes!" the rest shouted in unison.

"Do we believe in the supremacy of the white race?"

"Yes!"

"It's time for us to stop being apologetic for who we are. It's time for women to stop telling us what to do. It's time for us to seize our power!"

"Yes!"

The video cut away to historical footage of people rioting in the streets and burning buildings.

"Gross," May said.

"Yeah," Tye agreed. "This is getting weirder all the time. Now what?"

Kaity waved her phone in the air. "Let's call Evans."

Gary grunted and walked over to the sink to fill the tea kettle. Tye knew Gary had even less of an affinity for the police than him, but Kaity had a point.

"The cops are different here," Tye said to Gary's back. "We're not in West Virginia anymore."

Gary shrugged. "Cops are cops. I guess all this is more their business than ours, but just remember, they are playing their own game."

Kaity looked from Tye to Gary. Tye gave her a nod, and she dialed Evans. She picked up on the first ring.

"What have you got?" she said by way of answering.

Tye outlined what they'd seen and read her the note from Peter Etchells.

"So you saw him?" Evans asked when he finished.

"Yeah. I'm pretty sure it was him. I don't understand why he ran away. He's leaving me notes, so he must want to talk to me."

"Peter is an odd duck," Evans said. There was a familiarity about the way he said it that piqued his interest.

"What do you want us to do now?" Tye asked.

"Nothing. I've been following along behind you all day long. Now it's time for me to take the lead. We seized Cody Weber's motorcycle from the church parking lot. That pastor made us get a warrant for his room. I don't think she likes the police."

"I got that same impression," Tye said. "Can you get a search warrant for Eddie Guff's trailer?"

"Based on you seeing him shooting a gun? No. But I can drive out there tomorrow and have a chat with him. He might tell me to go to hell, or he might say something interesting. We'll see. Either way, I want you and Kaity to stay out of this for the time being."

"Fair enough," Tye said. "Any chance you can call us with an update? I'm getting a little tired of looking over my shoulder, wondering who is going to show up outside my yurt."

"I'll do what I can," Evans said and clicked off.

"That wasn't much of an answer," Tye said.

"Nope," Gary said as he handed May a cup of tea.

Kaity shut her laptop and put it in her bag. "Well, I've got an early start in the morning."

"Me too," May said. She'd been mostly quiet through the discussion. Tye found her hard to read, and sometimes he got the impression she wasn't thrilled about the situations that Gary became involved in on Tye's behalf.

Kaity moved close to him on the walk to the yurt. He reached down, and she slipped her hand into his.

"I was pretty scared when I saw Peter Etchells," she said. "Since last summer, so much has happened. I've never really had to deal with physical danger before. It's all been social stuff, the fear of being rejected, snarky comments from people I knew, and stuff like that. After you've dealt with people dying, none of that seems important."

"I'm sorry you were scared," he said, for lack of anything better to say.

"May started running around, locking doors and grabbing guns, while I just stood there. I don't feel my background has prepared me for all this."

"You're pretty good in a pinch. That time we got kidnapped and locked in the back of a box truck, we wouldn't have made it out if not for your ideas."

"Yeah, I've been thinking about that a bunch."

Tye had been walking with his flashlight in his left hand. As they walked up to the yurt, he shone it around.

"Looks all clear," he said.

"Good. I'll still be glad when we get a house with actual walls. I don't like not feeling safe."

"Me neither," he said.

22

Tye woke to the sound of his phone buzzing on the stand next to the bed. He reached over to feel a warm spot next to him, but no Kaity. It was then that he remembered she was already gone. She'd kissed him while he was half awake, before heading to work.

"Hello?" His voice was thick with sleep and his throat felt scratchy.

"Tell me again what time you were at Eddie's house?" Evans asked without preamble.

Tye sat up in bed and rubbed the sleep out of his eyes with the hand that wasn't holding the phone. "We backed out a little after nine. Maybe half an hour after sunset."

"Good to know, helps me narrow down what time he died," Evans said.

"Huh?" Tye asked. "Died?"

"When I went to talk to him this morning, I found him dead on his kitchen floor."

"How?"

"Looks like somebody shot him in the back of the head. This puts me in an awkward situation, though, because I'm going to have to explain how I know two guys who just happened to be hanging out in the bushes at Eddie's house right before he was killed."

"Wow," Tye said.

"That's sort of what we said when we looked through the window and saw the mess. When you saw Peter Etchells, he wasn't carrying a gun was he?"

"Not that I saw. We would have mentioned it."

"Well, right now he's suspect number one."

"Are you sure?" Somehow that wasn't sitting right with Tye.

"Well, I'm not sure of anything. But he left that creepy note at your place, then you saw him not far from Eddie's house. In our business, we call those things 'clues.'"

"Yeah, I guess."

"How soon can you get here? I've explained things to my supervisor, mostly, and he's agreed to an experiment where we use a volunteer tracker on some of our rural cases. I want you to take a look around and tell me what you see."

"I can be on my way in ten minutes," Tye said. He would have said five, but he desperately needed coffee.

"I'll tell the deputy at the perimeter that you're coming."

There was no time for his usual French press routine, so Tye settled on freeze-dried coffee in water heated on his backpacking stove. Normally he reserved the freeze-dried for long backpacking trips. He found the longer he'd been in the backcountry, the better it tasted.

This morning, it was terrible, but it served to kickstart his foggy brain. As he walked to his truck, travel mug in hand, he saw a white piece of paper fluttering under the windshield wiper of his truck.

"This is getting old," Tye said. He stopped and took a careful look around, transferring the coffee cup into his left hand and putting his right on the grip of the revolver in his pocket. He didn't see anybody, but that didn't mean anything. The woods around the yurt were so thick there could have been a dozen people crouched in the bushes. He did see the chickadees and juncos and spotted towhees going about their normal morning routine. They acted unconcerned, so

Tye figured there was probably no one around. They were used to him, so they barely reacted to his presence.

He walked over to his truck and put the coffee mug on the hood. The note was written on the same paper as the night before, and it was the same terrible handwriting.

"The other wolves got Eddie last night. They will probably try to blame it on me again. But I didn't do it. I don't want to go back to the hospital. I'm not going to prison. I need to find what Hannah hid, but I don't know where it is. Tell Darla I didn't do it."

"Darla," Tye said. It had taken him a moment to remember Evans's first name. "That sounds awful friendly." He folded the note up and put it in his pocket.

Gary's Scout and May's car were gone from their parking places as he drove past the split in the driveway. He texted Kaity but didn't get a response before he drove out of cell reception. He took a long way around to Eddie's house, on county roads instead of through the private timberland. Going through during weekday work hours would run the risk of being detoured around logging equipment.

A sheriff's department SUV blocked the driveway at Eddie's house. Behind it were two unmarked units and a plain white van. As Tye drove up, several people pushed a gurney holding a black plastic bag into the back of the van.

The deputy scrutinized Tye's driver's license and peered inside the truck like he was looking for a reason to arrest him, but finally, he let Tye through after the white van pulled out. Tye parked in the spot the van had occupied and got out.

Evans walked around the corner from the back of the trailer and saw him.

"Oh good, let's start inside first." From the back of her SUV, she pulled nitrile gloves and a pair of plastic booties for him to wear over his shoes. "Don't touch anything without asking me first."

He followed her wordlessly into the trailer. The inside smelled like blood, and faintly of the bacon Eddie had cooked last night. A crime scene technician in a Tyvek suit was taking pictures in the kitchen as they walked in. Blood spatter covered the kitchen cabinets, and there was a puddle on the floor by the sink. One of the cabinets was open, and Tye could see a bottle of bourbon, its label flecked with blood.

"We think he was standing right in front of the cabinet when somebody shot him."

"What kind of gun?" Tye asked.

"I'm pretty sure it was a nine-millimeter pistol. We found a mangled expanded bullet stuck in the wooden frame of the cabinets."

"So, different than the gun that killed Cody Weber."

"Yeah. Still pretty messy, though."

"Shell casing?"

Evans shook her head. "We haven't found one. We looked everywhere. They tend to roll under furniture and such, but we think the shooter took it with him. That's unusual. Whoever shot Cody Weber left their brass right there in the forest. Makes you wonder if it was the same person."

"So, Eddie was comfortable enough with whoever shot him to invite them in and turn his back to them."

"I think he was getting ready to pour some drinks. Look on the counter."

Two shot glasses sat on the counter in front of where Eddie had died.

"I'm having trouble with the idea that Eddie would be so welcoming to Peter Etchells."

"Maybe," Evans said.

"What do you want me to do?"

"Look around in here. See if there is anything different from last night. Then have a look outside."

The smell in the kitchen was nauseating. Tye stepped into the living room to get away from it and turned in a circle. He'd only seen this room through the narrow window the night before; now he got a close-up look. There was a threadbare couch along one wall, facing a giant television. A battered coffee table stood between them, holding a remote control and nothing else.

Tye looked around the room, but there was no sign of any books anywhere. He walked down the hallway, Evans following. He passed a bathroom in desperate need of a cleaning. There were no books inside. Nor were there any in the tiny room beside it. It held a futon and some dusty boxes that hadn't been moved in a long time. The master bedroom at the end of the trailer was also devoid of any books, containing only a queen-sized bed and dresser.

"We couldn't see in here last night, the shades were drawn," Tye said. "Where did the books go?" The mirrored sliding door to the closet was open. Tye shone his flashlight inside, seeing only clothes on hangers and shoes and boots on the floor.

There was a gap between the hangers. Fortunately, the smell from the kitchen hadn't drifted back here. He smelled something else, though. He stuck his face in the closet and took a whiff.

"What?" Evans asked.

"Leather. I smell tanned leather." He shone his light back and forth along the clothes hanging from the rod. "But there's nothing made of leather in the closet." He pointed at a gap where clothes had been shoved to either side. "I bet it was right there."

"What's your point?" Evans asked.

"Whoever killed Eddie Guff took something leather out of the closet. In the Wolves of the North video we watched, they were all wearing matching leather vests. Kind of like bikers."

A metal gun cabinet was bolted to the wall in one corner, its door standing open. There were spots for eight long guns and a shelf on top for pistols. It was empty. Tye looked at the lock. There was no sign of any damage, and the door hadn't been pried open. A plastic tote sat on the floor beside the gun cabinet. It held holsters and empty magazines, but no guns or ammo.

He looked around the room. On the wall opposite the south-facing window, there was a bare nail. The sun had faded the cheap wall paneling, but there was a darker spot around the nail.

"They took something off the wall too, maybe. A picture?"

She stood there looking at him, her hands on her hips, then turned and walked toward the door. "Let's check out the shed."

He followed wordlessly. The shed was ten feet by ten feet. Tye looked around, shining his light into nooks and crannies.

"Did you find a bucket of fired brass casings in the bed of his pickup?" Tye asked.

"Nope."

"There's not a single round of loaded ammo in here or in the house," Tye said.

"Or the interior of the truck," Evans said. "We checked."

Tye looked at the dies screwed into the top of the reloading press. They reformed the fired case to the proper dimensions and seated the new bullet.

"Those are .300 Blackout dies. It says so right there on the side. Somebody cleaned him out."

"They did. I'm a little skeptical about the leather and the picture, to be honest with you, but there should be a whole bunch of guns and ammo in this house and shed."

Tye clicked off his light. "How about the woods behind the house?"

"Follow me."

He followed her to the clearing where they'd found the circle of wooden poles. Three of them were still there, albeit lying on the ground. The one with the word "WOTN" on it was gone, as was the wolf skull.

"Would you mind staying here, at the edge of the clearing?" Tye asked. Evans nodded and stayed put.

There was a line of footprints going from pole to pole. Now that he was closer, Tye could see the bare poles had been jerked out of the ground and then thrown down hard enough they had left an impression on the ground. The tracks were from a booted foot. He compared it to all the tracks he'd found so far. It was a new pattern.

Whoever left the tracks had walked around the clearing, pulling the poles out, and presumably had walked off with the carved pole and wolf skull. Tye walked in an ever-widening circle around the clearing until he found what he was looking for.

"Here," he said and motioned Evans over.

He pointed at the track in the ground. There behind a Douglas fir tree were two plus-sized moccasin tracks.

"Those are Peter Etchells's tracks."

"He has big feet," Evans said with a nod.

He followed the tracks a hundred yards back toward the private timberland. Peter had followed a route very close to the one Tye and Gary had taken.

"See this spot here?" Tye asked and pointed. "He sat on the fallen log and switched his shoes. Boot tracks coming in. Then moccasin tracks leading back and forth from the circle, then more boot tracks coming out. See those crushed ferns? That's where he dropped his backpack while he snuck up to the house."

Evans was taking pictures of it all and making notes.

"You realize Peter didn't kill him, right?"

Evans let the camera hang on the strap around her neck. "Talk me through your reasoning."

"First, his tracks never approach the trailer. There were spots where it looked like he probably paused to look in the windows, but he never went inside. And whoever shot Eddie shot him from inside the house, not through a window."

Evans nodded. "I'm with you so far."

"Also, there's no way Peter could have hauled off all the guns, ammo, a carved pole, and a wolf skull." Tye walked over to a muddy spot in the ground. "See the track coming in, then the track heading out? They're the same depth. If he was carrying more stuff on the way out, they would be deeper."

Evans crossed her arms over her chest. "I don't know how any of this would work in court."

"I can explain it, as long as somebody is willing to listen."

"That's the real trick, isn't it?" She sighed and pulled her notebook back out of her cargo pocket. "Walk me through it again. I want to make sure I get it right."

23

"I just don't know what this guy wants," Deborah said as she leaned on her cane and gestured around the living room. "Nothing valuable was taken."

Tye had given Deborah and Vivian a ride back to their house to retrieve some more clothing and other items. Their Subaru still wasn't fixed.

Tye stood there, listening to the sound of the river outside. He looked again at the back door. It had been pried open very carefully, to minimize the damage. A familiar muddy footprint, from a size-fourteen moccasin, marred the hardwood floor just inside the door.

"Nothing at all?" Tye asked.

Vivian came down the stairs. "I've checked," she said. "My jewelry is still there. Deborah's shotgun she got from her dad is still in the corner of the closet."

Deborah breathed a sigh of relief. "I love his old Browning."

"He trashed the junk room upstairs, though," Vivian said. "The one we haven't remodeled yet."

"Can I see?" Tye asked.

"Of course."

Kaity and Tye followed her up the stairs, following a trail of muddy footprints as they went.

Tye stopped in the hallway at the top of the stairs. It was just like his dream. The upstairs was all one room, with hardwood floors and ceilings that sloped almost to the floor. The rock band posters from his dream were missing, but he thought he could see faint outlines on the walls where they had been.

The room was full of boxes, all of Deborah and Vivian's stuff they hadn't gotten around to organizing yet. Tye felt the vague unease he always had when he was in a cluttered, disordered space. One box was half-open, with clothes sticking out the top. Another had tipped over, and old vinyl records spilled out across the floor.

"All these boxes were lined up over there," Vivian said and pointed at the narrow space where the ceiling met the floor along the west side of the house. "I don't know why he moved them."

Tye walked the length of the floor, right where the ceiling sloped low enough to brush his head. There were streaks of mud here and there from Peter's moccasins, but he couldn't make out any kind of pattern. There were marks in the dust where boxes had been shoved out of the way.

The other wall was the same, boxes moved away toward the center of the room. Most of the boxes were still sealed up with tape. The only open ones had not been taped. The flaps had been folded over instead, and Tye got the impression they were open just because they'd fallen over, not because Peter had sorted through them.

"What does he want with boxes of old clothes and knickknacks?" Vivian wondered.

"I don't think it's the boxes," Tye said." I think he's looking for something in the house."

"Like a secret compartment?" Kaity asked.

"Oh! That's like something out of a movie," Vivian said. "That doesn't happen in real life."

"I don't know," Kaity said. "In the last few months, I've seen quite a few things that I thought only happened in movies."

Tye stooped over, looking at the floorboards to see if one was loose. They were worn a weathered gray color, with decades' worth of scuffs and scratches. Nothing unusual stood out to him.

"There was nothing up here when you moved in?" Tye asked. "Nothing left behind?"

Vivian shook her head. "No. Nothing. The room was empty."

Tye walked to the center of the room and looked around, hands on hips. Except for the lack of furniture and posters, it was just like his dream, something he tried to ignore for right now because he didn't want to consider the implications. For a moment, it was like his vision of the room from his dream was superimposed on what it looked like now, and his nose was flooded with that familiar floral scent. Honeysuckle. He was sure of it now.

"There's something in here," he said. "Something left behind."

"Or Peter thinks there is, anyway," Kaity said. "He could be wrong. We do have to consider that the guy was locked up in a mental hospital for a long time."

Tye nodded. "Maybe."

Vivian looked at her watch. "It's almost time to leave for Deborah's physical therapy appointment. I don't know if I should call the sheriff or what. Nothing was taken."

"It's up to you," Tye said. "But we're liable to wait for hours for a deputy to show up."

Vivian sighed and headed for the stairs. "Sometimes I think we shouldn't have moved here, because this terrible man keeps trying to break into our house. But you are all such wonderful neighbors, which somehow balances it all out."

"I'm glad we can help," Tye said with a backward glance before he followed her and Kaity down the stairs.

The rest of the day was spent in a blur of errands and appointments. George was sharing his truck, and Marsha and Brian were sharing their car, but with so many people needing to be in different places at once, two vehicles just weren't enough.

By the time they dropped Deborah and Vivian back at the trailer parked on George's property, it was dinner time, and Tye didn't know where the day had gone.

They drove down the road from Tye's place into the Gifford Pinchot National Forest. There was a little spot by the river with a fire ring. Tye parked the truck so they could unload folding chairs and a cooler full of groceries.

"I think they all know each other," Tye said.

"Huh?" Kaity said as she looked up from the fire she was building.

"In Peter's note, he called her Darla. And she already knew that Peter had big feet. She also called Eddie by his first name. Cops always use last names." He opened the cooler, moved the container of steaks and the foil-wrapped potatoes aside, and pulled out two bottles of beer.

"Hmmm…" Kaity scraped a ferrocerium rod against the spine of her LT Wright bushcraft knife, and a shower of sparks fell into the tinder bundle she'd prepared. The knife was expensive, easily twice the cost of the knife Tye owned. She'd just shown up with it one day and started using it, without so much as a "Hey! Look at my new knife." Most of the time Tye felt close to Kaity, but there were other times he felt like there were things she wasn't sharing.

"So, I started thinking. How old do you figure Evans is, anyway?" Tye asked.

"Maybe thirty-five? A few years older than us, at least. Which seems young to be a detective." The flames were growing nicely. She pulled her phone out of her pocket and hit a button. "Hah. Knee-high flames in six minutes. I'm getting better."

"Impressive," Tye said. He wasn't patronizing. In less than a year, Kaity had gone from being new to the woods to becoming a fair hand with fire-making, navigation, and tracking. Sometimes she'd be gone for a weekend and come back with a higher level of skill. He suspected she'd been taking classes, but she'd never been forthcoming about it.

"So she's too old to have gone to high school with Peter Etchells, Hannah, Eddie, and Jared Bauman."

"Yeah, by a few years." Kaity sat in the folding camp chair next to him and started rooting around in her shoulder bag. "And she's probably too old to have even been in high school as a senior when they were freshmen, but I have another idea."

She opened her tablet and started scrolling through files. He craned his head to see. "What are you looking for?"

"I downloaded a digital scan of the high school yearbook," she said. "Here we go, Evans. Neal Evans. Same class as all the rest."

She tilted the tablet toward him and zoomed in on a picture of an awkward-looking young man with a shock of dark hair. "I think he looks like her. I bet they're related," she said.

"I've never been very good at that, telling when people are related, unless it's really obvious," Tye said.

"Something about the nose and the set of the eyes. Once we get back into cell service, I'll see if I can put the pieces together." She put the tablet away, and Tye handed her a bottle of beer.

She clinked the neck of her bottle against his. "To being home-owners," she said. "All goes well, we'll be sleeping in the tiny home at the end of the week."

"Yeah," he said and took a drink. He sat there for a while, watching the river roll by and picking at the label on his beer bottle as the fire burned. Periodically, Kaity would get out of her chair and stack bigger pieces of wood.

"A little bit longer and we should have a good bed of coals," Kaity said. "We'll put the potatoes on first, then the meat a little later. Should all get done at about the same time?"

"Yep," Tye said.

"Six months ago, I was vegan, and now I'm getting ready to grill elk steaks on an open flame. I'm not sure if that makes you a good influence or a bad one," she said.

"Well, at least it's not store-bought meat."

The sun was just starting to go down, and Tye felt the first hint of the evening breeze. The river ran from high on the mountain's crest, three thousand feet above them. As the air up there cooled, it would spill down the river canyon.

"You're quiet tonight," Kaity said. "What's on your mind?"

He took a deep breath, then finally said what had been on the tip of his tongue for so long. "I'm worried about money."

Kaity took a drink. "Not what I was expecting. I figured you were worried about the two recent homicides and the fact that at least one killer is roaming around the vicinity, never mind the fact that nobody has solved the disappearances of Hannah Malley and her grandfather from ten years ago."

"We've been dealing with stuff like that so much recently that it almost feels normal. But what's on my mind right now is money."

"Why?"

"I'm just about tapped out after making the last payment on the trailer. You made your part of the payment without blinking an eye. I feel like I'm overstepping my bounds here, but you burn through a bunch of gas driving back and forth out here, buy us both dinner on the regular, and every so often, you show up with a pretty expensive piece of outdoor gear. I guess I'm wondering how that happens on a librarian's salary."

It came out harsher than he meant for it to sound. He felt a twist in his gut. Ever since he and Kaity had seriously started dating, he'd been afraid of saying or doing something that would blow it up, and he wondered if this was that moment.

"Are you trying to figure out if I'm living on credit cards or something like that?" There was an edge to her voice he'd only heard a couple of times before.

"Maybe that's part of it. But it's more than that. We've been pretty open with each other, talked about old relationships and stuff like that. But I feel like there are certain things you always deflect and dodge around, and money is one of them. We're going together on a pretty big deal here, sharing a house."

A log popped on the fire, sending a shower of sparks skyward. In his mind's eye, Tye pictured her gathering up her stuff and driving off, but instead, she sat there, the firelight reflecting off her glasses in the growing dark.

"I have a trust fund," she said so softly he barely heard her over the sound of the river.

"Huh?" The words had entered his ears, but they weren't making sense.

"Trust fund," she said a little louder. "Where a rich relative leaves a bunch of money, then you get to live off the investment income. Mine kicked in when I turned thirty."

"Oh."

She looked at him and laughed. "Oh my God, I wish you could see your face."

He didn't know whether to laugh along with her or be mad. Finally, he wound up doing a little bit of both.

"You never did an internet search on me or my family?"

"Right after we met, I found your staff bio on the library website."

"I hate that picture. Bad hair day. But seriously? You never did it? It's not that hard to figure out on Google. The spelling of my first name is a little unusual."

"Nope."

She sighed, then laughed a little more. "I swear, you're like a throwback to the past." She looked at him. "I mean that in a good way."

"Thanks. I think."

"So, you've never heard of the Rollins Collection?"

"No." But as he said it, something tickled his memory.

"Order this limited edition from the Rollins Collection," Kaity said, affecting a deep voice. "Please be ready with a credit card, check, or money order. Allow four to six weeks for delivery."

Then it clicked. "Oh. The plates. They would advertise them on TV when I was a kid."

"Yep. That's us. My family made their fortune selling collector plates for twenty-nine ninety-nine. Airbrushed portraits of Elvis, Marylin Monroe, and professional wrestlers, they've all graced the walls of middle America for decades, thanks to my family."

"I think one of my aunts had some of those in her trailer. They were nice."

She looked at him. "Oh, come on. They were hideous."

He didn't say anything for a bit. "Okay. Yeah. I thought they were pretty lame, even when I was a kid."

She took a pull off her beer. "Yep. I'm set for life thanks to kitschy pop art. It's a dying industry. I bet the whole thing goes belly up in ten more years. But my trust fund is separate from that."

"So you just get money?"

"Yep. Grandpa Rollins set it up before he died. I was required to get a four-year degree at an accredited institution and live to the age of thirty before it kicked in."

He just blinked, trying to wrap his head around the idea.

"You want to ask me how much, don't you?"

"I kind of do but feel like I shouldn't."

"It's about double what I make at the library."

"Oh. That much."

"Yep. That much. Some of the people I grew up with would sneer at that amount. But Grandpa Rollins wanted to leave us kids enough money to do anything, but not enough to do nothing." She reached into the cooler and handed him a second beer. "Do you need to sit there and let that sink in for a minute? I'll be the designated driver."

He sat there and drank half of the beer while she put the potatoes on the fire.

"You seriously never Googled me?"

"Nope."

"I was 99% certain you weren't after me for money. Now I'm 100%. I just didn't know how to tell you."

He took another pull of his beer and sat there, feeling equally frustrated and relieved.

"I think I was more concerned that you wouldn't want to be with me because of the money," she said, staring into the fire and not looking at him.

"Why is that?"

"You haven't exactly had complimentary things to say about wealthy people. I'm not sure if a triple librarian salary qualifies me as wealthy or not."

"I spent quite a few years living out of the back of my truck, so it seems like a lot to me."

"When I brought up the idea of the tiny house, I almost just offered to buy it, but I kind of felt like you wouldn't have liked that."

"It probably would have bothered me."

"But if you'd had the money to buy the house on your own, and just invited me to live there, you would have been fine with it."

He sat there watching the fire pop and crackle.

"Yeah. I probably would have," he said after a while.

"Double standard much?" She got up and put the foil-wrapped steaks in the hot coals.

"I reckon that's a fair point. I've got a question for you. When we first met, you said you took the job at the library out here because you could get your student loans paid off if you took a rural librarian job. But now you're telling me you've got a trust fund."

"When I moved here, it was true," she said as she adjusted the position of the steaks with a stick. "I wasn't getting my trust fund payments yet. I was thinking about not taking them. I don't care for my family or what they stand for."

"But after you started getting the money, you stayed."

She stood and dusted off the knees of her pants. "I like it here. I like the work I do. And then I met you." She walked back over to sit beside him. "I wish this wouldn't be an issue between us, but I think at times it probably will. You've got a pretty strong prideful streak. But please don't let it come between us too much."

She held out her hand to him, and he took it.

"So, you can go anywhere you want but you're gonna stay here and work at the library?"

"Yes. And look for lost people. With you."

The night settled in around them, and the cool wind blew down from the mountains, making the flames flicker back and forth. He could just hear the hiss of their cooking food over the murmur of the river.

"I love you, Kaity."

"I love you too."

24

———

Back at the yurt, they called Evans and filled her in on the break-in at Deborah and Vivian's house. They both sat cross-legged on the bed, listening to the detective's voice come through the tinny speaker of Kaity's cellphone.

"They're sure nothing was taken?" Evans asked.

"They were positive," Tye said. "There were all sorts of valuable objects sitting in plain sight. He didn't touch them."

"And you're sure it was Peter?"

"Either that or another tall man wearing size-fourteen moccasins."

"That's a fair point. He must have broken into their house before he walked through the timberland to Eddie's place. The autopsy on Eddie's body won't be done for a few days, but we did find something on the initial examination. Here, I'll send you a file."

Tye's phone dinged with an incoming message, and he put it on the bedspread next to Kaity's. He opened a picture that showed the letters "WOTN" branded into pallid skin.

"Ewww," Kaity said. "More dead-guy pictures. Can we get a trigger warning next time?"

"Sorry," Evans said. "Our gang guys had never heard of the

Wolves of the North before. I guess it's mostly an east coast thing. I've got a call into my contact at the FBI to see what they can tell me."

"Maybe Eddie was starting a west coast chapter," Tye said. "Any theories on who killed Eddie?"

"The consensus around here is Peter Etchells. I tried to talk about the tracks you discovered, and my boss looked at me like I had a third eye growing out of my forehead."

"I'm pretty much used to that," Tye said. "What else do you need from us?"

"Hang on a second." There was a long pause, a rustle, and Evans said something unintelligible. Tye wondered, not for the first time, if Evans lived by herself or if she was with somebody. She kept such a distance from everyone that it was hard to imagine her as a person, with an ordinary day-to-day life, and not just a cop.

"Sorry. Right now, I think I just need you to stand down. I'm going to do some research into court cases where expert witness testimony from trackers has been used, and try to have another talk with my boss about bringing you on board as a consultant."

Tye knew she'd get mixed results when it came to tracking evidence used in court. There was an infamous case from New Jersey where tracking evidence from a famous tracker had been used to charge a man with burglary and rape. Later the charges were dropped, and debate still raged about whether he'd been the correct suspect or not.

"Well, let me know how that goes," Tye said.

"I'll be in touch. I have to go now," Evans said and ended the call.

"Wow," Kaity said. "An official consultant for the cops."

"Yeah, the folks from back home would be shocked to hear about that."

Kaity stifled a yawn.

"Yeah. Me too," Tye said.

"Bedtime," Kaity said. "I don't have to work tomorrow, so we can play amateur sleuths in the morning. Right now, I need sleep."

She gave him a long kiss. "I'm glad we talked tonight. About the money."

"Me too." The full implications of what she'd told him hadn't sunk in yet. There were just too many other things going on. But he wasn't worried about it. In his gut, it just felt like something he would need to adjust to, not something that would bring things to an end.

She was asleep in minutes, but it took him longer. He sat up in bed for a long time, his hand on the warm skin of her hip, listening to the night noises of the forest outside the yurt. He was finally able to name the deep-seated fear that had been hounding him for months: he was afraid he wouldn't be able to protect Kaity.

She was competent and able to take care of herself, but lately, they'd had some close calls. They'd been kidnapped and nearly killed. There had been a few moments when a bad man named Isaac had made it clear he could do anything he wanted to Kaity, and all Tye would be able to do was watch. It hadn't worked out that way in the end, more because of luck than anything else, and those moments bothered him every day.

All his life, Tye had dealt with other people's bad behavior. He'd been the odd kid at school, picked on and ostracized. In his young adulthood, he'd wandered the West, never staying long at jobs and feeling like a failure at everything he did. Only in the year or so before he met Kaity, he felt like he'd hit his stride. The modest amount of money he'd earned from the TV show had bought him this place, and he finally found like he had a cushion between himself and the modern world that didn't have any place for him.

It was like his life was on two parallel tracks. At the same time as he was settling into owning a home and having a life with Kaity, he was dealing with madness and evil. It was like death was following him at every turn.

He wasn't used to feeling afraid. Usually, lying in bed listening to the sounds of the forest was comforting. Now he found himself focusing on every sound, wondering if it was someone coming for them.

Finally, he slept, but it brought little relief. He found himself in the attic bedroom of Deborah and Vivian's house. This time it was both Hannah's bedroom and Deborah and Vivian's junk room. It was like both places existed at the same time in the same place.

That familiar floral scent filled his nose, then the smell of dirt made him gag. A cold wind blew through the attic as if a window had been left open, while he turned in a circle.

"Show me what you want to show me so I can get out of here."

A picture frame fell off a dresser with a thump, and Tye walked over to it. Inside was a snapshot of Hannah and a younger Peter mugging for the camera.

He set it back on the dresser and turned another circle.

"Well, Peter's not here right now."

As if in answer, he heard the heavy tread of a boot from downstairs and shivered like an electric shock ran down his spine. For a moment he stood frozen in place, then he made himself walk on shaky legs to the top of the stairs and look down.

A familiar featureless black silhouette stood at the bottom of the stairs. It wasn't a shadow so much as the complete absence of light. Tye's mouth went dry, and his tongue stuck to the top of his mouth. With more heavy steps, the Dark Man started climbing the stairs. It was like Tye's legs had grown roots, locking him in place.

For some reason, his appointment with Kaity at the end of the week came to mind. If the figure at the bottom of the stairs killed him, he'd miss seeing their house delivered.

"To hell with that," he said out loud. He stuck his hand in his pocket, grasping for the little revolver.

He came up empty. The gun wasn't there, even though he knew good and well that he'd left it in his pants when he'd folded them up on top of his workbench before climbing into bed.

Instead, his arm brushed something on his belt, Remy Fiddler's big bone-handled Bowie knife. As far as Tye knew it was still locked up in his safe, but long ago, he'd learned not to argue with the logic of dreams. He yanked the knife out of the sheath and held it in front of him. His fear was replaced with hot fury. If he was about to die, he was going to lop off some parts from the figure climbing the stairs.

It stopped, and Tye felt a queasy sensation of being watched and evaluated, like a shark might size up some fish that it was considering eating, weighing the energy it would expend hunting it down, versus the calories gained.

"I won't make it easy," Tye said, waving the knife back and forth. Gary had studied Filipino knife fighting for six months while they were working a job out of Grand Junction, Colorado. Tye had never had an interest in formal martial arts practice, but now he found himself wishing he'd shown up for a few lessons.

The figure climbed the stairs slowly, and Tye steeled himself.

He jumped at a hand coming down on his shoulder.

"Tye?" It was Kaity's voice in his ear, and suddenly he was in a different place, in his bed, with her warm skin pressed against his.

"Bad dream," he said. His tongue felt too thick for his mouth.

"I thought so. You were shouting."

"What was I saying?"

"I'm not sure. I just woke up. Something about making it easy."

"Or not," he said. "I'm sorry I woke you up."

"It's okay." She kissed his cheek. "I was dreaming I was in our new house, but the walls were covered with country music singer commemorative plates, so I was kind of glad you woke me up."

"Wow. That might be worse than my dream."

"Maybe. I'll be the little spoon. You be the big spoon." She rolled over and pulled his arms around her. She was asleep again in minutes.

He felt his heart rate slowing down as he lay there, with the scent of Kaity's hair in his nostrils and the feel of her skin against his. He listened to the noises of the night, while he fought the temptation to get the killing knife out of his safe and put it on the nightstand next to the bed.

25

"I think finding Peter Etchells is the key," Tye said the next morning as he made coffee.

Kaity grunted from underneath the covers. The inside of the yurt was cold. The fire in the wood stove had burned down the night before. He'd just put in fresh wood and blown it back to life. Tye found the morning cold invigorating, but Kaity clearly felt otherwise.

He looked at his watch and realized the coffee had steeped long enough. He pushed down the plunger on the French press.

"Here," he said. "You can have the first cup."

An arm appeared from under the covers, and he put the cup in her hand. She sat up and stuck her head out from under the covers just enough to take a sip.

"It's ridiculously cold in here," she said.

"I forgot to put wood in the stove before I fell asleep."

"Well, we were occupied with other things."

"We were," he said with a smile.

He readied his cup of coffee, and while it steeped, he pulled out a paper map of the area.

"You said something about Peter Etchells," she said.

"I think he's the key. We need to find him."

"How?"

"Just like any other search. Go to the point last seen and start looking."

"Isn't that a needle in a haystack?"

"As far as we know, he doesn't have a vehicle. For every mile a person walks, their feet hit the ground two thousand times. All we have to do is find the signs and follow them."

With a groan, she crawled out from under the covers. "I'll get my stuff."

To her credit, Kaity was ready to go in fifteen minutes. She nursed her coffee in between bumps in the road while Tye drove them through the private timberland.

"So, I found out a little more about Peter," she said as Tye stopped to let a herd of elk cross the road in front of them. "He lived with his grandmother on a rural property not far from the Baumans. Not long after he was committed, her house burned, with her in it."

"Arson?" Tye asked, putting the truck back into gear as the last elk calf disappeared into the trees with a backward glance.

"I found one newspaper article that said the cause of the fire was under investigation, but no follow-up after that. Her obit listed Peter as her sole next of kin. That's the only way I found it."

"Huh. There are an awful lot of dead people connected with this mess."

"I was thinking that same thing. I was also wondering why Evans hadn't mentioned that little fact to us."

"Maybe it didn't cross her mind," Tye said.

He stopped a little short of where they'd seen Peter lurking around the truck before heading off into the woods.

"Well, that's interesting," Tye said as he walked in a circle where the truck had been parked. "We're not the only ones with this same idea."

He almost explained further, then stopped to see if Kaity would figure it out.

She craned her head to one side, coffee cup still in hand, and looked at the marks in the grass and pea gravel.

"Those really big footprints must be Peter Etchells's," she said.

"Yep."

"And these two. Is that you and Gary?"

He nodded.

"But there are more tracks. Two more people?"

"I think so."

"Coming up out of the woods, circling the spot where your truck was parked, and then going in the same direction as Peter."

"Yep."

"Somebody is following Peter." She squatted by one track that was more clear than the rest. "I don't think these tracks are that old."

"This morning I'm guessing," Tye said. "Only a couple hours ahead of us at most."

"Now what?"

"I think I still want to follow, just to see what's going on. But I want to do it carefully, and we'll back out at the first sign of trouble."

"Good plan. Can we catch up to them?"

"I bet we can track two people tracking Peter quicker than they can track him."

He moved the truck out of the middle of the road, then they started getting their gear together. They were both dressed in shades of green, brown, and gray. Tye found muted tones like that almost as effective as camouflage, but he didn't feel like a clown wearing them in town.

They both had Hill People Gear backpacks. Tye also had a Hill People Gear chest pack. He unzipped the main compartment of the chest pack and slid his big .357 Magnum revolver inside. He already had his little five-shot Smith and Wesson in his pocket. He usually didn't carry two guns, but he figured if things got bad, he could hand one of them to Kaity.

She watched him check the load on the big revolver and stow it without comment. Guns had been a sore subject between the two of them in the beginning, and at first, the fact that he was carrying one would have prompted a snarky comment. Tye guessed that getting shot at was changing Kaity's thinking.

Kaity took the lead. The two men following Peter had bulldozed through the woods, taking little care to hide their sign. Kaity did a good job of staying on track. She focused on the ground in front of her while Tye kept a lookout for things in the distance, a pattern he had followed for years with Gary. It seemed strange at times to be doing the same thing with Kaity.

The people following Peter were mediocre trackers at best. They frequently lost his trail, circling in confusion until they picked up the trail again.

It was hard to age sign precisely, and Tye was immensely skeptical of anyone who claimed to be able to age tracks as being two hours old as opposed to four. But the farther they went, the more he became convinced they were gaining on the people ahead of them. It made sense since their trail was so obvious that Tye and Kaity were moving at almost a normal walking pace, while they were wasting ten minutes at a time dithering around trying to find Peter's trail.

The trail led through a muddy spot, and Kaity knelt, then motioned to him. Tye took a slow, careful look around them and listened for sounds. Only when he was satisfied that they were in the clear did he focus his attention on the ground in front of him. He put a finger in front of his lips.

"Quiet," he said. "I think we're getting closer."

"Me too. These tracks look super crisp.

"I think they are both men," Kaity said, pointing at the muddy spot. "They're all pretty big. I don't think they're good trackers."

Tye shook his head. "I don't think they are either. I don't think Peter expected to be tracked from here, or if he did, he didn't care." Tye checked the GPS attached to his pack strap. "We've gone in a big arc, toward the west and then north. The road isn't far, over that way." He jerked his chin toward the north, the direction they were heading.

The wind shifted, and Tye heard a faint snatch of conversation, rough male voices, then it was gone. He looked at Kaity.

"If you want to take the lead, I'm not going to argue with you," she said.

"We have to go super slow."

Tye knew from his search-and-rescue training that the distance a human voice could travel was highly variable. In the southwest deserts, he'd heard people having normal conversations from as far as a mile away, even though the words weren't distinguishable. He was betting the people they were following were much closer now, though. The dense forests of the Pacific Northwest swallowed sound. In meadows and ridges of the Rocky Mountains, he'd heard elk bugle from miles away. Here in the foothills of the Cascades, their calls only traveled a few hundred yards.

He moved from tree to tree, and Kaity followed. They spent more time looking and listening than moving, usually only taking a few steps at a time. Tye was willing to let the gap between them and their quarry increase rather than risk running into them.

Finally, Tye saw movement through the trees. He stood behind the trunk of a big fir and peeked around. He saw indistinct figures ahead through the tangle of trees. From the waist belt of his pack, he pulled a little low-powered monocular. It was perfect for conditions such as this.

It was Jared and Samuel Bauman. They looked like some kind of mercenary hit squad, with tactical clothing and boots. Each man wore a stubby little black carbine slung around his neck, and a pistol worn low on the hips.

They stood at the edge of the road, apparently not caring if a car drove by and saw them all decked out like they were ready to go on a commando raid. Tye handed Kaity the monocular, and she slowly leaned out to look at the pair. From behind the tree trunk, Tye checked his GPS. Just as he suspected, they were directly across the road from an old, abandoned sawmill. Tye had often driven past it and thought what a forlorn, ugly place it was. The place was surrounded by a high fence with plastic slats woven through the chain link, but through the gaps, he could see dilapidated buildings and broken-down machinery surrounded by weeds.

The wind shifted, carrying with it the sound of voices.

"I told you he was going here," Samuel said. "We could have saved a bunch of time."

"Let's just go and see if we can find him. Nobody kills my friend and fucking gets away with it." Tye recognized this voice as Jared Bauman.

Tye and Kaity traded a look, then she went back to looking through the monocular. Tye peeked around the other side of the tree trunk and saw them crossing the road toward the gate of the old mill.

Kaity handed him the monocular and started to move forward. Tye put a hand on her shoulder.

"Hold on," he whispered in her ear. "They've got guns, and Jared sounds a little wound up. We can see well enough from here."

She nodded, and they both peeked back around the tree. Both men were standing in front of the gate. Jared Bauman dug around in his pocket and produced a key. The gate opened with the squeal of rusty hinges, and they went through the gate.

"Jared thinks Peter killed Eddie," Kaity whispered in his ear.

"Yep. And here I was kind of wondering if he'd done it," Tye said. "Sort of interesting that they have a key to that place."

"I wonder who owns it." She pulled out her phone. "No signal. Now what?"

"I don't think following them in there would be a good idea, seeing as how we'd be trespassing and they have all those guns."

From across the road, someone yelled, "There he is!" and there was the rattle of gunfire. The shots were suppressed and sounded more like some kind of pneumatic tool than a gun. A bullet passed close to them with a hiss before smacking into the trees behind them, and Tye pulled Kaity behind the tree.

"Are they shooting at us?" Kaity asked.

"I don't think so, but it'll still hurt if they hit us."

There was another burst of fire, but this time no bullets passed their way.

"Do you see him?" Jared called from across the road.

Tye heard the rattle of chain link and risked a peek around the tree trunk in time to see Peter Etchells running out the gate. At first, Tye thought he was going to run across the road straight at them, but he turned to his left instead. His long, lanky legs carried him at a dead run along the fence line.

"Should we call out to him?" Kaity asked.

"No," Tye said, as Jared Bauman appeared at the gate. Just as Peter hit the end of the fence line and turned left, to the north, Bauman raised his carbine and fired a couple of shots. One sparked off a fence post. Tye saw Peter stumble before he vanished from view.

"Over here, he ran out the gate," Bauman yelled and took off after Peter. He vanished around the corner, then the other two came boiling out of the gate.

"What do we do?" Kaity asked and checked her phone again. Tye could see she still didn't have a signal.

"Just wait until they're around the corner, then we need to ease out of here," Tye said. "I'm not going to get into a shootout with those two to save Peter Etchells."

Kaity opened her mouth like she was going to say something, then apparently thought better of it. Tye waited until a couple of minutes passed. He didn't hear any more gunshots, although he wasn't sure how far the sound of the suppressed guns would carry.

He stood and looked at Kaity. "Let's get out of here."

"I agree. This is a little bit over our heads."

"Yep. Time to call the cops."

26

"Jared Bauman says he and his friend were shooting at coyotes," Evans said. She had a cup of coffee in her hand and a sour expression on her face.

"Kind of hard to mistake Peter Etchells for a coyote," Tye said and took a sip of his coffee. They'd met Evans in the parking lot of a US Forest Service regional headquarters a couple of miles from Eddie's trailer and the abandoned mill where they had last seen Peter.

"I could hear him smirking on the phone," Evans said.

"Who owns the old mill?" Kaity asked. "I looked it up last night, and it's registered to a limited liability corporation with a generic name. Acme Enterprises or something like that."

"The Baumans own it," Evans said.

"Oh. I thought they were in the religion business."

"In addition to being the head of the Sword and Spirit Church, the elder Bauman owns the old mill, has a half interest in a construction company, and is a partner in the rock quarry up here in this part of the county."

"I hate that place," Tye said. "Every time they blow up some rocks, it makes everything shake. Why does he own an old, abandoned mill?"

"Parts," Evans said. "Bauman buys old logging and sawmill machinery and sells the parts. Some of that machinery hasn't been made in 40 years. Small independent mills depend on people like Bauman to keep their machinery running."

"Can you get a search warrant for the mill site?" Kaity asked.

Evans pulled a sour face. "Based on what? Reports from two anonymous witnesses saying they saw Jared Bauman and his buddies shoot at Peter Etchells, who then ran off into the woods?"

"I think they hit him," Tye said. "He sort of stumbled, then kept running. So I don't think it was a solid hit, maybe just a graze or something. What if I went over there and found blood?"

"So you want to trespass on private property and run the serious risk of Jared Bauman shooting you, so you can find blood that Bauman will say is from a coyote?"

"Can't the blood be tested?"

Evans sighed. "I don't think you two watch as many TV cop shows as most people, but you have to understand, I can't just whistle up fancy lab tests on a whim. We have a budget."

"There would be tracks," Tye said. "Peter's tracks. Not coyote tracks."

"Again, that's a hard sell," Evans said.

"It sounds like you have all sorts of reasons why you can't do anything," Kaity said.

Evans shot her a hard look. "I have to deal with the reality of police work. This isn't like some mystery novel you shelve at the library."

Normally, Kaity wore her emotions on her sleeve. It wasn't hard to tell if she was angry. But Tye had learned that when she was deeply, truly angry, her expression became flat, and she went quiet.

"Did your brother Neal know them?" Kaity asked. "Did he know Jared, Eddie, Peter, and Hannah?"

Evans's nostrils flared, and for a second, Tye thought maybe this wasn't such a good idea. "Yes," she hissed finally.

"I can't find anything about Neal," Kaity said. "He was in the high school yearbook along with the rest of them, but after that, nothing. I can't find social media profiles. An online search finds nothing."

Evans looked away and stared at two Forest Service workers who were loading construction materials in the back of a flatbed truck. "You must not have tried an inmate search."

"He's in prison?" Kaity asked.

"Walla Walla State Penitentiary," Evans said, still not looking at them.

That hung in the air between them for a while. He waited for Kaity to ask the obvious question, but she didn't.

"Rape," Evans said finally after a while. "He raped a girl. His freshman year of college. It was bad. He videoed it on his phone. There wasn't much of a defense after the cops found that."

"Oh," Kaity said. "I'm sorry."

Evans still wasn't looking at them. She was blinking behind her sunglasses. "I guess the danger of asking people to help you find things out is that sometimes they find things out."

"So he knew them? Jared and the rest?"

"Neal was a kid that never seemed to fit in anywhere. He wasn't athletic. He wasn't good at school. I made straight A's, and my other brother was a football player. My parents just didn't know what to do with Neal."

She drained the rest of her coffee cup and turned toward them. "When he started going to church with Jared and Eddie, it was a big relief for them. We'd never been churchgoers, but it just seemed nice he'd found a place to fit in. It wasn't called the Church of the Sword and Spirit then. It was just a regular old church. This was before the gun range and all that."

"They've gotten more radical over time," Kaity said. "At least that's what the other librarians say."

"They have. Neal… changed. He started working out and got buff. Looking back now, I think he was probably doing steroids. He started treating my mom terribly, talking down to her and yelling at her. I was out of the house by then. I'd been working for the sheriff's department for a couple of years."

"Was he with Eddie and Jared the night Hannah disappeared?" Kaity asked.

"Yes," Evans said. She stuffed her hands in the pocket of her coat and finally turned to face them. "I think my parents were relieved to send him off to college. He was halfway through his freshman year at Washington State University out in Pullman when it happened."

"That was almost ten years ago," Kaity said. "He's still in prison?"

"He's still in prison," Evans said. "It was... bad."

"And he videoed it?"

"He did. They didn't offer him much of a plea bargain. He will be eligible for release in a couple of years. We'll see."

Nobody said anything for a while, and the only sound was a group of crows squabbling in a tree overlooking the parking lot. Finally, Tye asked the question.

"Do you think your brother had anything to do with Hannah Malley's disappearance?"

Evans looked away from them again. "I'd like to say I'm hoping to find evidence that he didn't. But I'm afraid I'm going to find the opposite."

"Then what?" Tye asked.

"Then I do my job," Evans said. "I'm a cop."

"Even if it puts your brother in prison for longer?" Tye asked.

Evans met his eyes for the first time since she started talking. "Neal sat through his sentencing and smirked. He never offered a word of remorse for what he did. He refused to say where he got the drugs he gave her. Right after it happened, he emailed the video to a couple of email addresses the Pullman police were never able to trace. It's all over the internet for any creep to download."

She took a deep breath. "I'm not sure my brother deserves to get out."

"I'm sorry this happened," Tye said. He wasn't sure it was the right thing to say, but he said it anyway.

She shrugged. "I never meant to tell you any of this. I guess it was dumb to expect you wouldn't find out."

"I did a pretty exhaustive search on your brother and didn't find any of this," Kaity said.

"You didn't look in the right places then," Evans said. "The girl's family and the college both wanted to keep it out of the news, and they mostly succeeded. The sheriff's office didn't try to intervene in his prosecution or sentencing, but they did what they could to keep it out of the news."

"Where's the victim now?" Kaity said.

"She killed herself. There's no way to get the video off the internet. It's like whack-a-mole. One server full of that sort of stuff gets taken down, and two more pop up."

"Wow," Tye said.

"There's more," Evans said. She took a deep breath. "My boss? Derrick Crown? I think he knows more than he's letting on. His wife is related to the Baumans. He doesn't know that I know that." She said it all in a rush, like if she didn't spit it all out quickly, she'd have second thoughts.

"They didn't look very hard for Hannah back then," Tye said.

"No. They didn't."

Tye felt like a hole was opening up beneath his feet, and for a moment, he regretted getting involved in any of this. He wondered if it was too late to just get in his truck with Kaity and drive away. Going up against the Baumans was bad enough. The thought of crossing a dirty cop was something else entirely. In the back of his mind, Tye saw himself standing behind a jail cell door while it slammed shut.

"I guess we'll have to do the job for them now," Kaity said. There was a look of determination on her face that made Tye feel suddenly ashamed of his urge to run away.

"I guess we will," Evans said. Something had shifted between Evans and Kaity that Tye couldn't quite put his finger on. He was suddenly less afraid the two were going to get into a fistfight.

"What now?" Kaity asked.

"We need to find Peter Etchells. Ten years ago, nobody took him seriously. I think he knows things, and he might be willing to talk to the right person."

"He liked Tye's TV show," Kaity said.

"Maybe that's our in with him," Evans said and looked at Tye. "Will you talk to him if we find him?"

"Yep."

"Do you think you can pick up his trail without getting shot by Jared Bauman?"

"Assuming he's not dead in the bushes somewhere, I ought to be able to do it. I've been working on a plan."

Evans looked at the time on her phone. "I have an investigation progress meeting in an hour. If I leave now, I can make it back to the office in time. Keep me posted."

She headed toward her SUV. Halfway there, she turned. "Thanks." It sounded like it cost her something to say the word.

Tye and Kaity both nodded and watched as she drove off.

"Wow," Kaity said. "Her brother."

"Yeah. You mind driving while I look for tracks?"

"I can do that. There are some things I want to research, but there's no cell signal out here, so it will have to wait."

Tye studied the map for a moment before they drove out. Eddie's trailer, the old mill, and the Church of the Sword and Spirit all sat on Haley Road, which ran roughly from east to west. Peter had run off to the north, into the tract of woods between Haley Road and the north fork of the Lewis River. The woods were bounded on the west by Highway 503 and Canyon Creek to the east. The houses were few and far between along the roads, and the center of the area was rugged, wooded terrain. Tye wasn't sure who owned it, and in some ways, it didn't matter because he'd have to cross private property to get there, and people out here were not too keen on letting strangers traipse around on their land.

They settled for driving the length of Haley Road slowly while Tye looked for any sign along the shoulder that Peter had doubled back and crossed the road. It was still midday, and most people were at work, but when they tried the same thing on the two-lane Highway

503, they just irritated other drivers by going so slow. When Kaity sped up enough to keep them from getting rear-ended, they were going too fast for Tye to see details.

"This isn't working," Kaity said.

"Yeah, and we're attracting attention," Tye said. "People are going to start wondering if we're burglars casing houses for later tonight."

"What now?" Kaity asked as they waited to cross the single-lane Yale Bridge.

"I'm out of ideas. If I could just walk over to that fence line, I could pick up Peter's trail easily enough. But there's no telling if Jared Bauman is sitting in there with a rifle, waiting to plug me."

"And we have no idea where Peter's gone to ground," Kaity said.

"No. I doubt he's going to return to his bush shelter on the other side of the river from our house, either. Let's head back to the yurt so you can do your research, and I'll do my best not to get in your way."

She fiddled with the radio, trying to tune in to a station, but thanks to the ridges and valleys, all she could get was talk radio and country and western. Finally, she turned it off in exasperation. "You need to get a satellite radio receiver like a normal person."

"I think I'd have to buy a satellite radio receiver and slide a whole new truck in under it. Something made this century. Which reminds me, we've been talking about whether we want to put some kind of audio system in the new house."

"I think we should just get one of those sound bar things. I had one, but it's broken. Will you be offended if I drive into town instead of hanging out with you? I want to use my internet."

Unspoken in what she asked was that it seemed like sometimes Kaity just needed some alone time. Tye didn't mind because he often felt that way himself.

"Nope. I won't be offended at all. I've got some arrows to fletch and whatnot, so I've got plenty to keep me busy. I'll probably spend some time fruitlessly poring over maps too, trying to come up with a way to find Peter Etchells."

She nodded. "Promise you won't do anything stupid without me?"

"Promise."

27

Back at the yurt, Tye puttered around, tidying the place up. It didn't take long. When a person lived in three hundred square feet and owned few possessions, it kept the housework to a minimum. Tye had always been fastidious about keeping his living space uncluttered, and fortunately, Kaity was the same. She had a couple of duffle bags of clothes under the bed, and there were two locks and a set of picks on the workbench.

Tye leaned the broom in its spot by the doorway and looked around. When he'd bought the yurt two years ago, it had felt like a major step up in the world, compared to living out of the back of his truck more often than not. Now he was looking at full-blown home ownership.

Over on the nightstand, his phone buzzed. Assuming it was Kaity, he answered it without looking at the display and stepped over to the wall opposite the door, where the cell reception was better.

"That was quick. What did you find out?" he asked.

"Tye, it's Jean Fiddler." Tye blinked. It took him a second to realize who he was talking to.

"What can I do for you?"

"Peter Etchells is here with me. He's hurt, but not too bad. Do you want to talk to him?"

Tye stood there in silence for a moment, phone to his ear, unsure of what to do. "Yeah. Put him on," he said finally.

"Mr. Caine?" His voice sounded younger than Tye expected.

"You can call me Tye."

"I didn't kill Hannah."

"I know. I believe you."

"I still see her sometimes. Do you?"

Tye felt a wave of dizziness pass over him at the question, and he sat down on the bed. There was a rush of static, and he stood back up again, fearing he would lose the connection.

"I haven't seen her. Not exactly. But I've dreamed about her room. And I smell honeysuckles."

Peter gave a little laugh. "That was her. She dressed like a skateboard chick, but she always smelled like honeysuckle. I miss her."

"I bet you do."

"I didn't kill Eddie either. But I'm afraid people will think I did, just like the last time. I'm not going back to the hospital. That place isn't a hospital where they try to take care of you. It's just another prison."

"I believe you about Eddie. And I don't blame you for not wanting to go back there. Jean said you're hurt?"

"Bullet in the leg. I think it bounced off something before it hit me. I can still feel it in there. I can walk, but it hurts."

"Let me help you," Tye said. "Let me come get you."

"No cops," Peter said. "And no hospital, because they'll call the cops."

"That works, for now," Tye said. "But eventually, you may have to call the cops. And you may have to see the doctor. If that wound gets infected, it won't do you any good if your leg rots off."

"I don't know. I might prefer that to going back inside." Peter gave a shaky little laugh, but Tye knew he wasn't kidding.

"Where are you?"

"You know where the old McCaslan house is?"

As soon as Peter said it, Tye almost hung up. He felt a wave of nausea pass through his guts. "What the hell are you doing there?"

"I don't know," Peter said. "When we were teenagers, we used to come out here and screw around. The place is supposed to be haunted. For most of my friends, it was just fun. But I always had bad dreams for days after I would come here, about a dark man."

Tye sucked in a breath. "Yeah. I know what you mean."

"So in some ways, I didn't want to come back, but I also found myself being drawn here, you know? Like I couldn't get it out of my head."

"Yeah. I know. Look, let's talk more once I get there. Will you let me help you?"

"It almost feels like I have to," Peter said. "I came here thinking I'd break in and have a place to sleep for the night, but there's this guy here who knows you. That can't be a coincidence."

"If it is, I've been experiencing a whole bunch of coincidences lately," Tye said. "I can be there in half an hour. Don't go anywhere."

"The longer I sit still, the more this leg hurts. I ain't going anywhere."

Tye grabbed his truck keys and headed out the door. He stopped by May and Gary's trailer in the hope that May would be home, but they were both out. He was halfway down the driveway when it occurred to him to let Kaity know.

His fingers hovered indecisively over the keyboard while he tried to decide if this qualified as "doing something stupid," without her. Even though, as far as he knew, Peter wasn't formally a suspect, he wondered if he was somehow obstructing justice by promising to help Peter without calling the cops.

He decided to play it cagey. *Found what we were looking for. Give me a call as soon as you can,* he texted.

Tye kept checking the phone as he drove until he was finally out of signal, but no reply came.

"Well, I tried," he said and turned on the radio to distract himself from what was happening. Like Peter, he often found himself drawn to the old McCaslan property and had even found himself driving past it from time to time and slowing down by the gate, but the place made his skin crawl. He sometimes felt if he spent more time there, he would learn more about why he had visions of dead people, but he wasn't sure he wanted to live with what he would find out.

He parked his truck beside the locked gate, right in front of the "no trespassing" sign. The forested road was lonely, with no other houses in sight. No one had made an issue of him parking here in the past, but he figured it would be par for the course for the sheriff to arrive just as he walked out of the woods with a wounded person of interest.

There was a comprehensive medical kit in the back of the truck. Tye took a few minutes to stuff that in his backpack before he started walking down the rutted old road to the house. It was later in the day than he'd realized, and even if he just grabbed Peter and started hauling him down the road without taking any time to talk, they'd be walking back in the dark.

"Great," he said under his breath as he walked through the old orchard full of strangely twisted apple trees. He wondered if he should have just used the bolt cutters in the back of his truck to cut the lock on the gate and drive in, but that would be much harder to explain to anyone passing by.

He set off at a fast walk, a pace he could keep up for a couple of hours if he had to. There was something about the stretch of forest between the road and McCaslan's house that made him uneasy every time he walked through it. To keep his mind off it, he reviewed what he'd need to assess the severity of Peter's wound. Tye was trained as a Wilderness First Responder, and keeping his mind busy by reviewing his training was a great way to distract himself.

Before he knew it, he broke out of the trees, and he could see the house. Jean sat on the front steps, next to a long gangly figure that Tye recognized as Peter Etchells.

Tye found himself strangely reluctant to approach. All his life, Tye had been curious to meet someone who saw the same kind of visions as him, but now that he had a chance, he found himself shying away from actually doing it.

Still, he kept his feet moving, until he was standing in front of the steps. Peter was dirty, and his bare forearms showed scratches from branches and brambles. A bandage improvised from torn cloth was wrapped around his right upper thigh.

"You looked taller on TV," Peter said.

"I get that a lot," Tye said and stuck out a hand. Peter's massive hand dwarfed Tye's, but he didn't squeeze too hard.

"I also thought you looked taller on TV," Jean said.

"How did you get a cell phone call out to me?" Tye asked. "There's usually no service out here."

Fiddler shrugged. "Sometimes when I need these things to work, they work."

That wasn't much of an answer, but Tye decided to let it go. He turned to Peter. "First things first, let's look at your leg," Tye said as he put his backpack on the ground and pulled out his medical kit. First, he donned a pair of gloves, then unwrapped the bandage, ready to cover the wound again hastily if it started bleeding heavily, but it only oozed. While Jean held a flashlight, Tye used a set of shears to cut a slit up the side of Peter's pants and inspected the wound.

There was an ugly puckered hole in the meaty part of Peter's thigh, and a visible bulge an inch or two away.

"I think the shot bounced off a fence post and then smacked into my leg," Peter said.

"Yep," Tye agreed. As far as gunshot wounds went, this was minor. Even a low-powered rifle round like .300 Blackout could have easily broken Peter's femur and left a palm-sized exit wound on the way out. It looked like most of the bullet's energy had been spent deflecting off the fence post, and it had traveled only a few inches just under the skin.

"I think your biggest risk is going to be infection," Tye said. "That bullet needs to come out, and the wound needs to be cleaned. The bullet pulled pieces of your pants into the wound channel."

"No hospitals," Peter said.

"I know somebody that can help you," Tye said. "But first we have to get you to my truck."

"I can help you," Jean said. He pointed at Peter's backpack. "I can carry that."

"I just walked a couple of miles wearing a pack," Peter said. "I can make it to the end of the road without it."

Tye cleaned the wound the best he could with what he had available, then wrapped an Israeli-military combat dressing around the wound. Because he was a hunter and constantly around firearms, Tye always carried first-aid supplies sufficient for a gunshot wound.

He fastened the leg of Peter's pants back together with some safety pins. In wilderness medicine, it was important to cut clothes in a way that could still be used to insulate the victim if possible. The night was getting chilly.

Peter stood and took a few shuffling, tentative steps. "I can do this," he said. "You're both going to have to be patient with me."

"This will help," Jean said as he handed Peter a fallen branch big enough to use as a walking stick. He was wearing Peter's pack.

They made slow progress, with Peter pausing to rest every fifty feet and often hissing in pain when his foot hit the ground.

"I ran almost two miles on this leg, and it didn't hurt this bad," Peter said.

"Your adrenaline was up," Tye said. "It usually starts hurting when you stop."

Tye had a bunch of questions he wanted to ask Peter, but the younger man was staring at the ground a few feet ahead of him, gritting his teeth and gutting his way through each step.

"I think it'll be better if I can get the slug out. I can feel it moving around in there with each step." Peter grunted, almost falling when a rock turned underfoot, but he caught himself and managed to keep going.

Tye studied Peter out of the corner of his eye. In his mind's eye, his image of Peter had been fixed as a high school student, but in reality, he was only a few years younger than Tye. Despite being almost thirty, Peter looked younger, like the years being locked up had somehow arrested his development. At the same time, there was a careworn edge to him.

"You've been doing a hell of a job living out in the woods for a guy that's been locked up for so long," Tye said.

Peter shrugged. "All I did before I got put inside was mess around in the woods. I lived in a bush shelter most of the summer. I'd stay in my mom's trailer in the winter. When I was locked up, I'd just daydream for hours about being out in the woods. They locked my body up, but in my mind I was free."

They shuffled along, with Tye and Jean taking short steps not to outpace the wounded Peter. Nobody talked as they moved through the dark forest. Tye gave Peter his headlamp so he could see the ground in front of him, while Tye made do with a handheld flashlight. Jean seemed content to manage by the glow of the other two lights.

It took both of them to help Peter into the passenger seat of Tye's truck. Once again, Tye was struck by how big he was. He had a sinewy strength that Tye wouldn't want to go up against. He tried not to think about the fact that he was going to be riding around with a recently released institutionalized man who was a foot taller than him.

"Thanks for your help," Tye said to Jean as he unlocked the tailgate of the truck so Jean could put Peter's backpack inside. "What were you doing here, anyway?"

Jean slammed the tailgate shut. "This is where my ancestor died. I was alive when he died, but I never met him. I only know him through stories. In this place, I can get to know him a little more before I have to go back up north."

He turned to look at Tye. "I think you are dealing with some dark men, Tye Caine. Men in your world have no one to guide them, and they often fall to the Wendigo spirit. Fall is probably not the right word. Many of them seem to run toward it, to embrace it."

"What should I do?" Tye asked.

"You should do whatever you can live with. You will live with your decisions for the rest of your life, however long that is." He turned back toward the gate.

"Where are you going? Can I give you a ride?"

Jean shook his head. "I have more to do here. Thank you, but I must get back to it. Good luck, Tye Caine." He ducked under the gate and walked back down the rutted two-track toward the McCaslan house.

When Tye slid behind the wheel of the truck, Peter was leaning against the passenger-side window, snoring lightly. Tye decided to let the man sleep, at least until they got back to the house.

He wanted answers, but he was afraid of what they might be.

28

———

Tye drove over a rise and his phone started ringing immediately as it came back into service. It was Kaity.

"I have Peter in the truck with me," he said without preamble.

"What? I thought we agreed that you weren't going to do anything without me."

"I sent you a text message that said I found what we were looking for."

"I thought you meant the sound bar thing we were talking about for the house."

"I was trying to be vague since it was a text message."

"Yep. That was vague. So, you're driving around with the escaped mental patient in the truck with you?"

"Hey," Peter said from the passenger seat. "I didn't escape. They let me go."

"You're on speakerphone," Tye said.

"Umm... Hi, Peter," Kaity said. "Sorry about that."

Peter shrugged. "It's okay."

"We're headed home," Tye said. "Peter hurt his leg. I'm hoping May can help him."

"Well, she's home. I just talked to her and sent her over to the yurt to see if your truck was there. I have some stuff I want to tell you, but not over the phone."

"Right," Tye said. "Sometimes there are things that we don't want to say over the phone, so we send vague text messages."

"Whatever. I'm on the way. I'll see you in about half an hour." She ended the call.

Peter looked at him. "That's the woman with the short dark hair? She's your girlfriend?"

"Yep. And business partner."

"I'm kind of looking forward to people not just thinking of me as a mental patient."

Tye didn't know what to say to that, so he concentrated on driving. He parked in front of May and Gary's trailer. May walked out with a cup of tea in her hand as Tye was helping Peter out of his seat.

"When you told Kaity he'd 'hurt his leg,' I wasn't expecting to find someone with a gunshot wound," May said as she helped Tye steady Peter.

"I was trying to be vague."

"It worked. Help me get him in the living room."

"I don't want to bleed on your carpet."

"Honey, we bought this trailer used, and that's probably not the weirdest thing that's ever hit this carpet. As soon as we get the new house built, we're going to strike a match to this place."

She did put an old blanket down before helping Tye ease Peter to the floor. She donned a headlamp and undid the bandages. "You did a pretty good job of this, Tye."

"Thanks."

May probed gently around the wound with a gloved hand. Peter hissed.

"I'm sorry, but I'm trying to figure out if this is something I can help with or if you need to go to the hospital."

"No hospitals."

"I can feel it. It's right under the surface in between the skin and the muscle, I think. I don't think there's any vascular damage or bone fractures. That's like winning the lottery when it comes to gunshot wounds. I can get it out, but it's going to suck."

"It sucks right now."

"That's the spirit. This would be better on the kitchen table, but I'm not sure it will hold your weight, so the floor it is. Sit tight while I get my bag. Tye, I'm going to need lots of light."

Tye busied himself rounding up all the lamps from the trailer and plugging them into various outlets in the living room, hoping he wouldn't blow a fuse.

"I'm going to inject some lidocaine around the wound," May said as she organized her gear. "That will help a little bit with the pain."

Tye held a light for May as she numbed the area around the wound, then gently probed for the bullet. Peter stared at the ceiling. Tye could tell he was trying to keep his breathing slow and even, but occasionally, he would gasp when May dug in a little deeper.

"I feel like we're in an old western or something," Peter said. "All I need is a bullet to bite on." He looked pale and fine beads of sweat covered his forehead.

"There's a bottle of bourbon over the stove," Tye said.

"Probably shouldn't. I haven't had any alcohol in ten years, so I'm not likely to handle it well."

Tye squatted there holding the light and thought about what it must have been like to be out of circulation for so long. Peter hadn't been able to walk in the woods, choose what he wanted to eat, or know the touch of another human being.

He heard the sound of Kaity's Jeep pull up, then the crunch of her feet on gravel. The front door opened, and before Tye could warn her, she looked over his shoulder.

"I found some stuff out," she said, then realized what she was looking at. "Urk. I'm going to go wait in the kitchen."

"It won't be much longer," May said.

"When you said he hurt his leg, I thought you meant a sprain or something," Kaity said.

"I was trying to be vague over the phone."

"Got it," May said, and Tye heard a ping as she dropped the bullet in the teacup she's placed on the floor.

"Oh, it already feels better not to have it in there," Peter said.

"I'm going to irrigate it to clean it out, then sew it up. The stitches won't be pretty, and there's going to be a gnarly scar. I'm a midwife, so usually when I put in stitches, it isn't in a visible area."

"Thank you," Peter said.

Before long, May had run a line of stitches on the wound. She taped a transparent dressing over the sutures.

"I have some antibiotics you can take. We need to be careful of infection. I have no idea where we're going to find you new pants."

Tye heard another engine pull up, and Gary walked in carrying a couple of bags of groceries. He walked over to look over May's shoulder and whistled.

"When you said he'd hurt his leg, I thought you meant he twisted it or something," Gary said.

"Tye was being vague. I'm almost done sewing him up."

Peter gave a wave. "I'm Peter. I appreciate the help you're all giving me."

"Anytime," Gary said with a nod. "We'll shake hands when I don't have an armful of groceries and you're not getting sewn up. I'll put some coffee on."

Peter nodded, and Gary walked into the kitchen. Tye heard him greet Kaity, then the sound of him putting groceries away. Soon the smell of coffee brewing came from the kitchen.

"That's the last stitch," May said. "You can get up now."

Tye helped Peter to his feet and guided him to a chair in the kitchen. Kaity was sitting there with her laptop in front of her, drinking a cup of tea.

"Hi, I'm Kaity," she said and stuck out a hand. "I'm sorry for what I said earlier."

Peter shook with her and looked down at the table shyly. "No worries. I guess you all have been trying to help me." His stomach rumbled, and he looked at Tye. "Would you mind fetching my pack from your truck? I have some cans of soup in there."

"We can do a lot better than that," May said from the living room where she was cleaning up her equipment. "There's some leftover chicken casserole, or you can cook him a burger, Tye."

Tye walked over to the refrigerator. "Which do you want?"

Peter blinked, and Tye realized he was fighting back tears. "What's wrong?"

"I'm just getting used to having a choice in what I eat. I was enjoying getting to pick whether to open a can of beef stew or chicken noodle soup, but this is something else."

"You can have both if you want," May said from the living room.

Peter wiped his eyes. "Chicken is fine."

Tye busied himself microwaving food. There were a million questions he wanted to ask Peter, but he decided to let the man eat first.

Kaity had other ideas. "So, I guess we're all kind of wondering why you tried to break into Deborah and Vivian's house."

"Those are their names? I feel really bad about that. I was looking for Eddie's phone."

"Eddie's phone?"

Tye set the microwaved plate of food down in front of Peter. He started eating like it was his job, talking between bites.

"Before she disappeared, Hannah told me she stole Eddie's phone. There was bad stuff on it, but she didn't know who she could trust in the cops, so she was hanging on to it. She was thinking about either talking to a lawyer or a reporter. She wasn't sure which."

"Bad stuff? What kind?" Kaity asked. Tye poured himself a shot of Gary's bourbon and sat down at the table.

"Videos. Of girls." Peter set his fork down and stared at the table.

"Oh no," Kaity said. "It goes that far back."

"What do you mean?" Tye asked.

"The videos. They're trophies, aren't they?" Kaity was looking at Peter.

He nodded. "If you wanted to be in the Wolves, you had to make a video. That's what Hannah said, anyway."

"The Wolves existed back then?" Kaity asked.

Peter nodded. "Yeah. It was before they got big. I guess Jared met the founder in an online chat."

Tye looked back and forth from Kaity to Peter. "You two are losing me here. What am I missing?"

Kaity looked at him. Her mouth was set in a thin line. "You've heard of Six Net?"

"I think. It's some kind of internet thing?"

She sighed. "Sometimes you're like an eighty-year-old man trapped in a thirty-year-old body. Six Net is a message board where pretty much anything goes. Racist stuff. Porn. Videos of animals being abused. The Wolves of the North have their own message board."

She looked at Gary. "I need to connect to it. It's nasty. I can use TOR so the internet traffic can't be traced to your IP address."

"Let's pretend I understood what that means," Gary said. "Go ahead and do what you need to do."

Kaity opened her laptop and started clicking through menus. Tye saw a menu that included titles like "How to Pick up Women," "Incels United," and "RAHOWA Now!" Kaity navigated to one called "Wolves of the North" and clicked on it. There was a long list of posts that started with the word "Score" and then a date and a city.

She looked at everybody in the room. "This is some pretty terrible stuff, so if you don't want to see it, you should probably leave."

Nobody moved, so she opened one of the posts.

The video was poorly lit and shaky. It took Tye a few seconds to figure out what he was seeing.

"Oh," he said. "Is she even awake?"

"Nope." Kaity stopped the video, went back to the message board, and opened another post. The video was pretty much the same.

"I think they're drugged," May said. "Rohypnol. Something like that."

Kaity let the video play for only a few seconds, then went back and started another one.

"I think we get the picture," Tye said. Kaity backed out of the video and went back to the message board.

The room was silent for a moment. Tye's mouth was dry. He felt like he had stepped up to the edge of a black abyss and taken a look down to see there was no bottom.

"How many are there?" Tye asked.

"Dozens. The board is moderated by somebody with the user-name of PNWAlphaWolf. When somebody joins, they are a probationary member. They are given a numeric code, and to become a full member, they have to post a video like the ones you just saw and show the code in the video."

"That way you can't become a member by stealing a video off the internet," Gary said from where he was leaning against the sink. "Smart, in a real sicko kind of way."

Peter had been staring at the table the whole time. "I think they were doing this when they killed Hannah. I don't think this website existed back then, but she said something about them trading pictures and videos on the internet. I don't have any way of proving it, though."

"I think I do," Kaity said. "I think I know who PNWAlphaWolf is, and I think I know where Hannah is buried."

"You know where she's buried?" Peter looked up from the table for the first time in minutes. "Where? How?"

Kaity started opening screenshots she'd saved. "PNWAlphaWolf is pretty free about sharing his exploits on the Six Net boards. It's all performative stuff, trying to impress people. Check out this photo from September of two years ago."

She opened a screenshot of a photo that showed rugged snow-capped mountains, captioned "looking forward to chasing elk here." A complicated compound bow and arrows sat in the grass in the foreground.

"This photo appeared on Jared Bauman's Facebook page. Also in September two years ago." It was the same photo, only this time the caption read "getting ready to whack 'em and stack 'em."

"Busted," Gary said.

"There's more," Kaity said. "Also some pictures from a bear-hunting trip in Alaska. Some pictures from outside a strip club, stuff like that. They are the same photos posted around the same date."

"But how does that help you find Hannah?" Peter asked.

Kaity scrolled through folders until she found a photo of a place Tye recognized. It was the circle behind Eddie's trailer with the four poles and the wolf skull.

"The caption says, 'You never know what's buried under a place like this. Some people don't know when to mind their own business.'"

"The date is the fifth anniversary of the party where Hannah disappeared," Peter said.

Kaity nodded. "Yes, it is."

"Did Eddie live there in high school? When Hannah was killed?" Tye asked.

"I did a property search. He did. It was owned by his mother. She's since passed away."

The room was silent for a while, save for the evening chorus of the birds as they settled in for the night.

"What do we do now?" Gary asked.

"I guess we give it all to Evans, see what she does," Tye said.

"It's going to be complicated," Kaity said. "The servers for Six Net are spread all over the world. It's going to have to go the FBI, I guess."

"What about the victims?" Gary asked. "It's all on video. Didn't any of them call the cops?"

"Maybe," Kaity said. "Most of them were drugged. I bet most of them didn't, out of shame. One of the things you'll notice about the videos is they rarely show faces. So to prove that's you in the video, you'd have to show something distinctive, like a tattoo or a birthmark or something. If there is, you'd get to undress in front of some police detectives who want to write the whole thing off as 'he said, she said,' since there are no signs of a physical assault."

"But Hannah had evidence," Peter said. "On the phone."

"From ten years ago?" Kaity asked. "Is it even still there?"

Peter crossed his arms over his chest. "It's in there. I know it. Just get me in the house and I can find it."

Kaity looked at Tye. "I guess I can call Deborah and Vivian," he said. "Maybe they'll be okay letting you into the house after Deborah shot at you and all. Stranger things have happened."

29

Deborah's surgical boot thumped on the stairs as she laboriously made her way up to the attic. The rest of them followed, trying not to rush her. Tye was right behind her, ready to catch her if she slipped.

Finally, she made it to the top step. "I can't wait to get this damn thing off," she said and leaned on her cane.

Tye and Kaity followed her into the cramped attic. Peter struggled to walk up the stairs. He said it was easier to move now that the bullet was out of his leg, but it was still painful for him.

"The last time I was here I focused on moving stuff away from the walls," Peter said after he finally made it up. "Then I heard a car outside and got spooked. Turns out it was just the neighbor down the road, but I didn't want to push my luck."

"Well, you're a very polite burglar," Deborah said. "You did a neat job of stacking all the boxes in the center."

Peter looked at the floor and stuck his hands in his pocket. "I'm sorry I scared you that night. I didn't think anybody was home or I never would have tried to come in."

"Well, at least I didn't shoot you."

Peter looked around the room. "It's so strange to be up here after so long. But I remember it like it was yesterday. Time is so weird when you're locked up. Her bed was over there." He pointed to the south wall, the one overlooking the window. "She had a couple of dressers along the walls. She didn't have a closet, you know."

Tye imagined he felt the feathery touch of something cold on the back of his neck. Peter's description matched perfectly with what he'd seen in his visions.

"You two were pretty close?" Deborah asked.

Peter blushed and looked at the floor. "Yeah. We were pretty close. I loved her."

Deborah reached out and put a hand on his shoulder. "I'm sorry you lost her."

While they talked, Tye had been walking along the walls, hunched over because there wasn't room enough to stand due to the slope of the ceiling. Previously, he hadn't taken seriously Peter's assertion that Hannah had hidden something in the room. He realized he'd been dismissing Peter as crazy, but now that he knew him in person, that was harder to do. Peter was a shy young man who was a little odd, but he was lucid, probably more lucid than Tye would have been had he been locked up and heavily medicated for ten years.

He also realized yet again that Peter wasn't that young. In certain light, he looked his age, almost thirty, but his affect was that of a teenager.

Since none of the furniture or boxes were left over from when Hannah lived in the house, what remained were the walls and floorboards. The floor didn't have any loose boards that Tye could see. They were worn and in need of refinishing, but he didn't see any high spots. They had been finely fit together. Tye was hard-pressed to find any spots where he could fit a fingernail between the boards.

That left the baseboards. They were simple dimensional lumber, stained a light brown to match the floorboards. They too had been well made, with boards that looked like they had been carefully chosen for their straightness. All the miter cuts were well done.

He ran his finger along the top edge of the baseboards and stopped when he felt some rough gouges. There was also a faint mark on the wall. Most of the boards were long pieces, six or eight feet long, but this one was short, pieced in to fill a gap near a corner. He popped open his Buck knife and slid it behind the board, then pried gently. It popped off the wall easily, having been held in place by only a few slender finishing nails.

Behind the board, there was a cavity hollowed out in the drywall between two wall studs. First, he pulled out a plastic bag holding a pipe and what he suspected was marijuana, then a small diary bound with a clasp, and finally a cell phone.

He put everything on top of a cardboard box. The diary smelled like honeysuckle, just like he'd smelled in his dreams. The phone was old, with an actual keyboard instead of a touch screen. Kaity picked it up and held down the power button.

"Nothing. It's dead."

"I guess it would be, after being stuck inside a wall for ten years," Tye said.

Kaity turned it on end so she could look at the charging port. "I have no idea what kind of cable it takes. It's not a USB. I bet we can find one online, though."

"They've got a pile of old cords at the Goodwill in town too," Tye said. It was his favorite place to shop.

Peter traced the flowers embroidered on the diary with his fingers. "I feel like it's kind of wrong to read this, but I guess we should."

"It might have something important in it," Tye said.

Peter picked it up and held it out. "Will one of you do it? I knew her. I loved her. But there were always things she kept to herself. If she had wanted to tell me some of the things in here, she would have said them when she was alive."

Kaity reached out and took the diary. "I'll do it. I can pick the lock without breaking it."

Peter swayed a little bit and put a hand on the ceiling where it sloped down to steady himself.

"Are you okay?" Deborah asked. She reached out and put a hand on his shoulder. She seemed kindly disposed toward Peter, especially considering he'd broken into her house.

"I'm tired," he said. "It's been a long day. I guess I lost some blood too."

"Let's head back to our place," Tye said. "We can find you a place to bed down for the night and figure this all out in the morning."

Deborah clomped her way down the stairs, followed by an unsteady Peter. Deborah headed off in the freshly repaired Subaru. Now that she'd laid eyes on Peter, she and Vivian would be moving back into their house the next day. Peter climbed laboriously into the passenger seat of Tye's truck, while Kaity sat in the backseat of the crew cab.

"You think your friends would mind if I took my sleeping bag and slept under that gazebo by the goat pen?" Peter asked.

"I imagine they'd let you stay in the guest bedroom," Tye said.

"That's nice, but I enjoy sleeping outside. I spent ten years locked in the same building, and I want all the fresh air I can get."

When they pulled into Gary and May's place, Kaity excused herself right away and headed for the yurt. She was uncharacteristically withdrawn and quiet. Tye had learned that at times like this, she wanted to be left alone for a little while, and once she had some time to order her thoughts, she'd share them with Tye.

Tye and Gary helped a weary Peter get settled under the gazebo. Gary made a token offer to let Peter sleep inside, but he seemed to understand why Peter preferred to be outside.

"I got a bottle of bourbon that needs help fulfilling its purpose in life," Gary said as they walked back toward the trailer.

"I could join you for a snort," Tye said. "Kaity seemed like she might want a little time by herself, but I don't want to wait too long to head over."

"I think you're growing more perceptive in the ways of women," Gary said. "I'll go grab the bottle."

Tye took a seat in a lawn chair under the front porch awning and listened to the night sounds. The river was audible, as it always was, and the goats rustled around in their pen, settling in for the night.

Gary reappeared with a bottle of Woodinville bourbon and two jelly jars. He poured out a dollop for each of them. They both sipped contentedly for a few moments.

"I'm not ready to give up making my hooch just yet," Gary said as he held his glass up to the porch light. "But now and then, some store-bought liquor is a treat."

"I reckon," Tye said.

"This is a hell of a thing you're wrapped up in this time," Gary said. "That's some dark business, those videos."

"It is," Tye said.

"I can't imagine doing that, drugging a woman then making a video of it to share with all your buddies. Who does that?"

"Evil men," Tye said. It came out of his mouth before he had a chance to censor himself.

"Evil men," Gary agreed. They both were silent for a moment, watching an owl flit from tree branch to tree branch, pausing between flights to scan the ground for wayward mice and voles.

"I think there are more men that would do something like that if they could get away with it than I'd care to know," Tye said. "You ever wonder what makes us different?"

Gary swirled his bourbon around in his glass for a while before answering. "I don't guess my dad ever told me that doing such a thing was wrong, but he didn't have to. I expect it was the same way with your father, God bless him."

"I agree," Tye said. His parents had both died in a boating accident when he was young. "But we both got up to all sorts of things our fathers told us not to do."

"Remember that time we stole that case of beer from old man Caudill's store?"

"I do," Tye said. "I remember feeling guilty about it and going back a few days later to pay for it without telling you."

"And I remember doing the same thing without telling you. I guess old man Caudill sort of made out on that deal."

"I guess. That's about the worst we did, though," Tye said.

"It is."

"I think deep down, you and I aren't hurtful men," Tye said. "I've knocked a fellow out a time or two. And there was that guy you killed that was trying to rape your sister. But he needed killing."

"He did. I've never felt particularly bad about it. I've thought about that a bunch, though. What made me different from him? What made him desire that? And what makes me sick at the thought of it? Was I raised that way or was I born that way or both? I guess a bunch of ink has been spilled on that particular question."

"It has," Tye said and took the last swallow of bourbon.

"I'm just grateful to be a better man than that," Gary said. "I think deep down those men are always going to be wanting something that they'll never get. We focus on the hurt they cause, which is appropriate, but deep down, they're some miserable sons of bitches."

The owl flew off. Tye knew there was another open clearing about fifty yards to the east where it would probably go next to look for mice. It pleased him to know the land he lived on so well.

"I guess we're better than that," Tye said. "I was raised never to consider myself better than anybody, so it feels wrong to say that, but I guess when it comes down to it, we are."

"You know what I'm afraid of, though?" Gary asked.

"What?"

"With these fellows you're tangled up with, it's not going to be enough to be a better man. You're going to have to be a better shot."

30

Detective Evans met Tye and Kaity in the Goodwill parking lot just as they walked out of the store carrying Hannah's phone and a handful of different curly-corded charging adapters.

"I can't believe they had it," Kaity said. "I thought we'd have to order it off the internet."

"I think there's a certain amount of karma involved with Goodwill," Tye said. "I donate stuff to them all the time, so when I need a particular thing, it seems like I usually find it. For example, they just happened to have two pairs of pants big enough to hold Peter."

She gave him a sidelong glance from behind her sunglasses. "I've never really heard metaphysics applied to Goodwill before."

"I'm sort of a working-class philosopher sometimes."

She gave him a wan smile, but he could tell it was forced. She hadn't slept well, waking Tye with her tossing and turning all night long. This case seemed to be getting to her more than the other ones they'd worked on.

Evans parked between Tye's truck and Kaity's Jeep. She was wearing her sheriff's department polo shirt, cargo pants, and heavy boots.

"We got a warrant to use ground-penetrating radar at Eddie's house," she said. "I only have a few minutes before I have to head up there to meet the technicians. Did you get the parts?"

Kaity held up a pair of cords like they were trophies. "Both of them. The one that plugs into a car cigarette lighter and the one that plugs into the outlet at home."

Evans held out her hand. Kaity drew hers back. "We were just about to see if it works in Tye's truck."

That put a sour look on Evans's face, but she nodded. Tye and Kaity climbed in front, and Evans got in the back seat and peered over. Tye started the engine. Kaity plugged in the phone and pressed the power button. Tye was surprised to see the display light up.

"Still works after all this time," Kaity said.

"Surely he set a password," Evans said.

"Nope." The phone started up and displayed its main menu. Kaity navigated the clunky arrow keys with surprising dexterity. "I had this same phone when I was in high school. Here's the photos folder."

She gave a sharp intake of breath. "Oh God, another one."

"There's no video?" Evans asked.

"This phone doesn't have video," Kaity said. She scrolled through the photos. They were grainy and poorly lit, but there was no mistaking what they were seeing.

"There are two of them," Tye said. "Two men."

"Yeah," Kaity said. "There are some pictures that show her face."

"Wait. Go back," Evans said from the back seat. Kaity scrolled backward in the line of photos.

Evans sat back in the seat, took off her sunglasses, and rubbed her eyes.

"What?" Tye asked.

"That's my brother. That's Neal." She looked away from them, out the window. In the rearview mirror, Tye could see that her hands were shaking.

After a minute she took a long, deep breath and let it out. "Okay," she said. "I have to get that bagged up. I'll give you a property receipt for it, then I need to go out to Eddie's place. I had to fight like hell to get that warrant for the ground-penetrating radar. Derrick Crown all but laughed at me when I asked for it. So if Hannah is out there, I want to get her out of the ground before I enter this phone into evidence."

"Why?" Tye asked.

"Because this phone has pictures of my brother committing a felony sex crime. As soon as I disclose that, Crown is going to take me off the case. The statute of limitations is a little complicated in cases like this, but clearly, it's a conflict of interest. There's also no statute of limitations for murder."

Kaity didn't move. She sat there with the phone in her hands.

"How do I know you won't make this phone disappear if I give it to you?" Kaity asked. "How do I know you won't delete the pictures?"

"Because I want my brother to stay in prison," Evans said. "He's my brother. I love who he used to be. But I don't love who he is now. Something in him went bad, and it's my job to make sure people like him stay locked up where they can't hurt people."

She filled out a form, then tore out the bottom carbon copy and put it on the center console. It was a property receipt for an item seized as evidence. Then she pulled an evidence bag from the cargo pocket of her pants and held it open.

"I think it's okay," Tye said. "You should give it to her."

Kaity unplugged the phone and dropped it in the bag.

"Thank you." Evans said the words like they cost her money.

"I'm sorry about your brother," Kaity said.

"I am too." Evans got out of the truck without another word. They watched her stalk over to her unmarked SUV and pull out.

"I feel really bad for her," Kaity said.

"Me too. You didn't give her the diary. You didn't even mention it. You were up late last night reading it."

Kaity picked at a loose thread on the seam of her khaki pants. "I'm not done reading it. I think I would be okay with Evans having it, but I don't know about the other detectives. I just don't like the idea of some crew-cut dude with a Punisher tattoo and a mouthful of chewing tobacco reading about her first sexual experiences and her life plans. I guess I feel kind of protective of her."

"That makes sense, but at what point are we withholding evidence? I guess we can claim we found it on a subsequent search of the house."

"I need to leave soon so I can get to work," Kaity said, but she just sat there, not moving.

"Maybe today would be a good day to call in sick?" Tye asked. "You've got the time saved up."

She shook her head. "No. I'd rather work. It'll take my mind off things. Otherwise, I just see those videos and pictures in my head when I close my eyes."

"Me too," he said.

"I never thought I'd hear myself say these words, but I think I want to buy a gun," she said.

"I've got extras."

She shook her head. "Yours are old-fashioned. I've been doing research."

"Nothing wrong with a good revolver. They're classics."

"I think I want it to be mine, not something you gave me."

"I guess that makes sense."

"I always thought guns were for uneducated people who didn't know how to solve problems any other way."

"Hey..."

She reached over to pat his hands. "Knowing you has changed my mind about lots of things. The other night when May and I were alone at the trailer and Peter spooked us, I was just standing there while she was loading shotguns and stuff. I felt like I had nothing to contribute."

"You contribute a lot to what we do," he said.

"I do. Thank you for saying that, but I still think I want a gun."

"Makes sense. I'd feel better if you had one, honestly. I know you're smart, and you're capable, but these recent events have made me want to follow you around surreptitiously with a shotgun slung around my neck."

She laughed. "It's hard to be surreptitious with a shotgun." She leaned over and kissed him on the cheek. "Thank you for being you. Time for me to go to work."

"I love you, Kaity."

"I love you too."

Tye watched her walk over and get in her Jeep. When she pulled out, he had to fight the urge to follow so he could sit outside the library all day keeping watch. Instead, he put the truck in gear and headed for home.

Peter was hobbling around and splitting wood when Tye pulled up at May and Gary's trailer. He'd split a round, bend carefully to pick up the pieces, then hobble over to the woodshed beside the trailer to stack them.

"Generally, when a fellow gets a bullet dug out of his leg, he's excused from manual labor for at least a couple of days," Tye said as he walked up with the pants slung over his arm.

"It just feels so good to be outside, getting some exercise," Peter said.

"Here," Tye said, holding out the pants. "New britches."

Peter's face lit up like Tye had presented him with gold bullion or something. "Thank you!"

"Why don't you change into those, then we'll sit a spell," Tye said.

Tye made coffee in Gary and May's kitchen while Peter changed clothes. May was out working, and Gary was running errands. They had an informal arrangement where either was welcome in the other's house. In practice that meant Tye spent quite a bit more time in their trailer than they did in his yurt since the trailer had a full kitchen and amenities like a shower. He kept his coffee and groceries over here, although all that was about to change now that the tiny house was about to be delivered.

Increasingly, Tye had started to feel like an interloper in Gary's life with May, so he supposed it would all be changed for the best. It wasn't that Tye felt unwelcome, May had accepted their unconventional arrangement with good grace, but he knew it was time for things to change. Neither of them had said anything, but Tye knew that his friends would probably be having children soon. Through the kitchen window, Tye saw the stakes marking the outline of where their own house would go.

Tye put a cup of coffee down in front of Peter, who inhaled the aroma wafting from the cup with a smile on his face. Tye explained what they'd seen on the phone.

"Neal?" Peter said. "I wish I could say I'm surprised. Eddie and he were pretty tight right before Hannah disappeared. I wonder who the girl is."

"I guess we should have had you look at the pictures," Tye said. "If she was a classmate, you probably would have recognized her."

"I guess," Peter said. "Although I've seen all of that sort of thing I care to see." For a second Peter looked like he was going to cry, but then he blinked away the tears.

At that moment, Tye felt a kinship with Peter. He realized over the last day, he'd started to divide other men into two camps: those like him and Gary, and those like Eddie and Jared. In his gut, he knew Peter was like him and Gary.

"I guess I've been curious how Cody Weber wound up over in the woods near where you were camping," Tye asked.

"He wrote to me while I was inside," Peter said. "He was involved in the group that helped get me released."

"What did he say when he wrote?" Tye asked.

"He said he was sorry for what had happened to me. He talked a bunch about repentance and redemption." Peter stared at his back-pack that was sitting in the corner of the kitchen. "I don't think I kept his letters. There was only so much stuff I could carry when they let me out and dropped me off at the bus station."

"You mentioned a group that helped you get out," Tye said. "Who was that?"

Peter limped over to his backpack and started pulling out paper-work. It was a hodgepodge of crumpled, stained official documents and sheets of legal paper covered with his illegible scrawl. It was organized by some system that made sense to him because he quickly found what he was looking for.

"The Coalition for Mental Health Justice," Peter said. "It's affiliated with some church, what's the name again?" He ruffled through the paperwork.

"The Church of the Open Heart," Tye said.

Peter found the paper he was looking for and looked up at Tye. "Yes. That's it. I guess Cody was staying there? He invited me to stay there too and said he could get me a room. But I just wanted to be out in the woods, so he bought me the backpack and stuff. He gave me a pre-paid cellphone, and I'd text him. He'd meet me places with canned food and stuff."

"Did he talk about what happened to Hannah?"

"Not directly. It was like there were things he didn't want to come out and say.."

"Do you think he was involved in Hannah's disappearance?"

Peter shook his head. "Not directly, but I think he knew things he never told anyone. Cody and Eddie were friends from elementary school. They were tight until Eddie hooked up with Jared Bauman."

Tye opened his mouth to ask another question, but his phone started buzzing. It was Evans.

"There's a body, right where Kaity thought it would be," Evans said. "It's skeletal, and we're exhuming it now."

Tye breathed out. "Sometimes it sucks to be right," he said.

"Is Peter Etchells there with you?" Peter could hear her well enough from across the table. He nodded his head.

"He is."

"We found a necklace on the remains. I'll text you a picture. Can you ask Peter if he recognizes it?"

"Will do." She hung up, and Tye placed his phone on the table between them. They sat there staring in silence, waiting for the message to come in.

Finally, it buzzed. Tye opened a photo that showed a necklace, with a butterfly-shaped pendant, held in a blue-gloved hand.

"That's hers," Peter said. "That's Hannah's necklace. I gave it to her."

He burst into tears.

31

"I haven't done anything like this in ten years," Peter said. "I'm not sure I remember how to function in a social setting."

Kaity was sitting in the passenger seat of Tye's truck as he drove them through the parking lot of Doyle's living facility. She turned around and reached into the back seat to pat Peter on the hand.

"Don't worry about it," she said. "They're nice people."

As Tye backed the truck into a parking spot, he looked at Peter in the rearview mirror. With a fresh haircut and a shave, he looked even younger. They'd scrounged a clean button-down shirt out of Gary's closet that fit him well enough. The sleeves were a couple of inches too short.

Tye parked the truck, and they all headed over to Doyle's, carrying a six-pack of beer and a plastic container full of Tye's venison carne asada. Kaity was wearing a skirt, and out of the corner of his eye, Tye could see Peter repeatedly glancing down at her legs, catching himself and looking away. For a young guy who had been locked up solely with other men for almost ten years, Peter was doing a good job of not being obnoxious, but he seemed a little gobsmacked by both Kaity and May at times. Tye wondered if the poor guy would need therapy due to being locked up in a mental facility for so long.

Doyle was having one of his good days. When he answered the door, he was wearing an apron that said: "Kiss the cook." His cheeks were ruddy, and his eyes were bright. As he shook Peter's hand and welcomed him, Peter visibly relaxed.

Evans on the other hand looked like she hadn't slept. She greeted everyone curtly, and Peter seemed to deflate. They all busied themselves making tacos and setting the table. Peter gave a long look at the wine but finally declined.

Tye cooked the carne asada on Doyle's cast-iron skillet. He would have preferred an open flame, but the results were still pretty tasty. This was an early dinner for everybody because Kaity had to work an evening event at the library. Evans had asked that they all gather together.

Tye dished out the food, and everybody but Peter and Kaity opened a beer.

"You never know what a tipsy librarian might do," Kaity said as she sipped her water. "Just checking out books willy-nilly."

Everybody laughed but Evans. She looked like she'd been gut-punched.

"I'm off the case," Evans said. "And even if I wasn't, Crown seems to have decided that there is no case. Eddie killed Hannah all those years ago. Then he killed Cody Weber, then shot himself. All the loose ends are tied up, and we needn't bother ourselves with it anymore."

"What about the phone?" Kaity asked.

"I logged it into evidence," Evans said with a sharp look at Kaity. "Our forensics guys downloaded all of it, all proper. Crown says without the identification of the victim in the photos, there's no case. The statute of limitations is kind of tricky too."

"What about text messages and call logs on the phone?" Kaity asked.

"There's plenty of text messages back and forth from Eddie to Jared Bauman, talking about motorcycle parts and deer hunting and all sorts of stuff like that, but nothing damning. Crown made it clear we're done, and if I push him, he'll have me investigating overdue library books."

"Well, we could use some help with that," Kaity said. "But I'm not giving this up. What if we find the girl in the photos?"

"It depends on what you mean by 'we,'" Evans said. "If I do anything officially, Crown will come down on me like a sack of bricks. He just assigned half a dozen cold burglary cases to me. They're cases that are going nowhere, but he wants follow-up reports on them within three days. If I spend so much as a moment chasing leads on this, he'll say I'm being insubordinate."

"What's Crown's problem, anyway?" Peter asked. "Why is he so reluctant to dig into this."

"He's friends with the Baumans," Evans said.

"So you're off the case due to a conflict of interest, but Crown is buddies with the Baumans and gets to supervise the whole thing?" Kaity asked.

"Seems a little odd, doesn't it?" Evans said. "The sheriff's office has changed in the years since I've worked there, but there's still a good-old-boy network at play. Crown is the head of investigations. He has a lot of latitude."

"So, are you asking us to do it?" Tye asked.

Evans looked out the window and swirled her beer around in her glass. "I can't ask you to do it officially. But if you give Crown evidence he can't ignore, it will force his hand."

Tye and Kaity looked at each other. There wasn't any doubt in his mind what she'd say.

"We'll do it," she said. "Carefully. I guess the first step is to figure out who the girl in the video on Hannah's phone is."

Evans handed Peter a folder. "Those are prints from the phone. Just her face. Nothing else."

Peter looked at the photos and shook his head. "I don't recognize her. It was a big high school, though." He started to hand the folder back, but Evans shook her head and pointed toward Tye and Kaity.

"You two take them. See what you can do." Kaity took the folder.

"That gives us a place to start," Tye said.

"Well, there's one more thing," Evans said.

"There usually is," Tye said."

"Your friend Jacqueline Elliot? The minister at Church of the Open Heart? She's Derrick Crown's ex-wife."

"I didn't see that coming," Tye said.

"Me neither. When I briefed him on the investigation, he sort of failed to mention that little fact to me. I only discovered it because I run everybody involved in an investigation, witness, victim, or suspect through the computer. She made a domestic violence complaint against him about ten years ago. They were married at the time."

"Let me guess," Kaity asked. "The complaint went nowhere."

"That's what it looks like. It's a paper report, which I have to request from our archives, and that would attract attention. I wouldn't be too surprised to find out that it's 'lost' anyway."

"So, Crown is friends with the Baumans, and Jacqueline Elliot used to be married to Crown. Good grief. I moved away from West Virginia to get away from all this kind of stuff," Tye said.

"It's a weird county," Evans said. "Lots of people have moved here over the last couple of decades, fleeing the high housing prices in Portland. But an old group of families has been here for a long time. They're all pretty interconnected."

"I'll go talk to Jacqueline Elliot after I drop you off at the library," Tye said. "Peter can come too. It'll give us something to do while we're waiting on you."

Kaity nodded. She was tapping her finger on the folder full of pictures. For a moment, Tye thought she was going to say something, but she didn't. Instead, she looked at her phone. "We should probably leave soon. I have to set up tables and stuff. I have four local authors giving a reading."

They helped Doyle clear the dishes. Tye left a healthy portion of carne asada and all the trimmings in his refrigerator. He realized it had been a couple of weeks since he'd gotten Doyle out of the house. On occasion, Tye would pick up the old detective, strap his oxygen tank to the truck's back seat, and take him on a drive. They'd go look at elk on the Chelatchie prairie or drive up to one of the overlooks with a view of Mt. St. Helens.

Before they left, Evans gave both Tye and Kaity a scrap of paper. "That's a burner cell phone number," she said. "Call me or text me with anything you find out."

"So, are you two like junior cops now?" Peter asked.

"Not really," Tye said. "I think it's more like we're standing in a field of land mines. I'm not even sure how to go about identifying this other victim. Since you didn't recognize her, she probably wasn't one of your classmates."

Peter said, "I'll look again. Maybe if we can find a yearbook, I can look at that too. It might jog my memory."

"I guess high school yearbooks are worth something after all," Tye said.

Kaity was silent as they got in the truck. When Tye started to turn the key in the ignition, she reached over and put her hand on his. "I know who she is," she said. "The other victim."

"How?" Tye asked. "Who is she?"

"She told Hannah what happened. It was in Hannah's diary."

"You mean the one we didn't tell the cops we had? I guess we better tell them now."

"But what if she doesn't want that?" Kaity asked. "What if she doesn't want the cops barging into her life and bringing all this up again? She didn't go to the police when it first happened, so why would she want to do it now?"

"So Jared just gets to go on doing this over and over?"

"Will it do any good?" Peter asked from the back seat. "It doesn't sound like Crown is interested in prosecuting any of this, so will it change a thing if this other woman comes forward?"

"Dammit," Tye said. "I hate this. I don't expect much out of the cops, but I'd like to think at least that we could count on them to put evil bastards like this in prison." He started the engine. "If we don't get going, you'll be late for your event."

"Yeah, we wouldn't want that." Kaity's voice was distant. As he drove, Tye kept glancing over at her. She seemed smaller somehow, like she'd shrunk into herself. She was pale, and there were dark circles under her eyes. She hadn't slept well in days. Tye had woken up a couple of times through the night to find her sitting up in bed, reading Hannah's diary with the help of a headlamp.

She reached over and squeezed his hand. "I'm fine," she said. "Since I knew you were going to ask. We'll get this figured out. We always do."

"Yeah. We always do." But what was foremost in his mind was that over the last several months, they'd been shot at, kidnapped, almost frozen to death in the mountains, and Tye had been stabbed. He wondered how much of this sort of thing they could keep doing before they stopped getting lucky and something really bad happened to them.

32

———

The parking lot for the Church of the Open Heart was empty except for the same battered Honda that had been there the last time. Jacqueline Elliot was pulling futilely on the starter rope of an old lawn mower. It made desultory putting sounds but refused to start.

"Howdy," Tye said as he and Peter walked up.

She looked from Tye to Peter, then blinked when she realized who Peter was.

"Peter," she said as she reached out and grabbed his hand. "It's good to see you."

A flush crept up from Peter's collar. "I appreciate you helping me get out," he mumbled as he looked at the ground.

"I don't suppose either of you knows anything about small-engine repair?" Jacqueline said. She nudged a canvas bag of tools with her foot.

Peter squatted in front of the mower and started pulling tools out of the bag. "I do. I can look at this while you two go in and talk."

Jacqueline looked at Tye. "Would you like a cup of tea?"

"Sure."

Tye glanced over his shoulder before they walked through the door. Peter already had the spark plug removed from the mower, and it looked like he was in the process of taking off the carburetor.

"How's he doing?" Jacqueline said as she plugged in the electric kettle in her office.

"As well as can be expected," Tye said. "He's almost thirty, but sometimes it's like he's still in his late teens. I guess that makes sense considering he's lived the same day over and over for the last ten years. He sure doesn't seem crazy enough that he should have been locked up for the last decade."

"How about that?" she said. She sat behind her desk and wrung her hands in front of her, then touched the scar over her eye. She caught herself doing it and then jerked her hand away.

"How about you used to be married to Derrick Crown and forgot to mention that little fact to us the last time we were here? Along with how you forgot to mention you were part of the organization that helped get Peter out of the mental hospital."

She gave a small laugh. "It's not much of an organization. It's just me. I guess I was surprised when you and your partner showed up here. I thought I knew all the elements in play."

"You got Peter out of the institution, then put him and Cody Weber in touch. Why?"

She rubbed the scar again, this time not even bothering to hide it. "Derrick gave me this. I was twenty-one. I didn't know it at the time, but I was pregnant. I lost the baby after he beat the hell out of me."

"I'm sorry." It didn't seem like the right thing to say, but it was all he could think of.

"Our families went to the same church and pretty much decided we would get married, even though he was fifteen years older than me. You'd think the era of arranged marriages is over, but it's not."

"The Church of the Sword and Spirit?"

She shook her head. "That came later. The Baumans started it when they decided our church wasn't conservative enough." She gave a bitter laugh. "You know, letting women wear pants is the first step down the road to eternal damnation."

"We had some of that where I grew up," Tye said. He was trying to find some kind of common ground with her. He felt like if he could just get her to talk, it would give him the keys to figure all this out.

"So you can imagine how that marriage went," she said. "He hit me for the first time on our honeymoon."

The water in the kettle started to boil, so Jacqueline got up and poured two cups.

"I joined the Army. I didn't tell him ahead of time. I just went down to the recruiters, signed up, and a week later I was on my way to basic training. I had him served with divorce papers long distance. Since I didn't ask for anything, he just signed them. The Army made me a chaplain's assistant. You wouldn't have thought I would learn about progressive theology in the military, but here we are."

"I don't understand what that has to do with Peter and Hannah," Tye said.

"Derrick didn't tell me much about his work," she said. "I was supposed to cook, clean, and pop out babies. But one night I over-heard him talking on the phone about Hannah. I'm pretty sure he was talking to Samuel Bauman."

"Jared's dad," Tye said.

"Yes. Jared's dad. I'm not that much older than Jared. I only over-heard snatches of the conversation, but I heard Derrick say some-thing about 'burying the problem' and making sure Peter Etchells 'looked good for it.' I heard him say he knew somebody at the state hospital that owed him a favor."

"Wow," Tye said.

"Yep. Good old Derrick. At the time there wasn't much I could do about it. But as I got involved in prison justice and reform, I kept thinking about Peter and that whole mess. Nobody was going to take my word for it, ten years after the fact. Then one day Cody Weber walked into one of our services."

"That's a hell of a coincidence," Tye said.

"Is it?" She looked at him over the rim of her mug. "The stock line for me to say would be 'everything happens for a reason.' I'm not sure if I believe in that, but I think some things happen for a reason."

"Maybe," Tye said. At one point in his life, he would have

dismissed that. But after the events of the last few months, he wasn't so sure.

"Getting Peter's case reviewed wasn't as hard as I expected. I wonder if whoever owed Derrick a favor had quit or retired from the hospital system."

"There's one thing I don't understand," Tye said. "Somebody knew where Cody was going the night they killed him. There's no way it was a coincidence they randomly encountered him out in the forest."

"A couple of days before he was killed, Cody sat in that exact chair and told me he felt like he needed to give Jared Bauman and Eddie Guff a chance to atone for what they'd done."

"He knew," Tye said.

"He knew. But I don't think he participated."

"If he had, would you have still helped him?"

She shrugged. "Probably. But I wouldn't have let him stay here."

"So Cody reached out to Jared and Eddie. Then they killed him."

"I think that's a fair guess."

"Did you tell Evans that Cody contacted them?"

"I told Evans as little as possible. She works for Derrick."

"There's very little love lost between them."

"I think you can imagine why I would have trust issues with the sheriff's department," she said and rubbed the scar on her brow.

"Why are you telling me all this?"

"Intuition. My gut tells me you're a good man, that you're the key to finally getting some justice. You and your partner, Kaity."

Tye's response was cut off by the sound of a lawn mower starting outside. At first, it ran rough and backfired, but then it settled into a steady hum.

"It sounds like Peter had some success," she said. "Let's go see how he's doing." She put her cup on the desk and walked out the door, not waiting to see if Tye would follow.

Outside, Peter was mowing the narrow strip between the parking lot and the church building. Jacqueline squatted to pick up a pair of safety glasses and a pair of hearing protectors, then motioned for Peter to cut the engine.

"My liability insurance isn't very good," she said after the engine stopped and handed him the glasses and earmuffs. "You got it running."

"Yeah. I think it was just old gas," Peter said. He looked around the grounds of the church. "It looks like you need some work done here. I need a job. I used to make money cutting lawns and painting houses. I could work cheap and take cash."

The corners of Jacqueline's mouth quirked up. "How about you finish mowing and I'll give you twenty bucks and a hot meal. If you need a place to crash tonight, we've got spare rooms in the multi-purpose building."

Peter looked at Tye. "Is that okay with you?"

Tye blinked. It was almost like Peter was asking permission from a parent. "Of course. I need to go get Kaity."

"My stuff is in the back of your truck." Peter had insisted on packing up his backpack and bringing it with them each time they left the house. Tye didn't think he was worried something would be stolen from it so much as it was all that he owned in the world and he wanted it on hand.

They retrieved Peter's bag, and Jacqueline led them to a room across the hall from where Cody Weber had stayed.

"It isn't much, but it's dry and warm," Jacqueline said.

"I think it's awesome." Peter blushed and looked at the floor. "It might sound a little weird, but I might sleep outside sometimes. It's just nice to feel fresh air after being inside for so long."

"Doesn't sound weird to me at all," Jacqueline said and dropped a key into his palm. "Why don't you unpack your stuff, and Tye and I will wait for you outside."

The neighborhood around the church was starting to get a little busy as people came home from work, got out of their cars, and went inside. Tye realized that was the most outside time many of these people would get for the day. Then they would wake up the next morning and walk out to the car so they could drive to their work where they would spend the next day inside. Tye figured since Peter wanted to sleep outside, he was the sanest person around.

"He's going to need a bunch of help reintegrating," Jacqueline said.

"Yeah, it sounds like they just kicked him out the door of the hospital and gave him a bus ticket," Tye said. "We want to help him, but we're not sure how."

"That's kind of my wheelhouse," Jacqueline said. "I help people transition from an institutionalized life to being on their own. I have a degree and everything."

"I think this is a good place for him," Tye said. "He needs something to do. We'll have some work for him later in the year I think, and I can put the word out to some people we know that might need a hired hand from time to time."

"Then he already has a huge advantage compared to most of the people who get out of an institution," she said. "Most of them have nobody."

"Nobody but you, it sounds like." Tye found himself liking Jacqueline, even though she hadn't been fully honest with him about everything that had happened. Over the years, he'd developed what he thought was an intuitive sense for decent people who wanted to give a little more to the world than they took, and he could tell Jacqueline was one of those people.

Tye looked at his watch. "I have to go get Kaity. Thanks for your help."

"I feel like I should be thanking you." She put his hand on his arm. "Be careful. The Baumans aren't good people."

33

The next day, Kaity was quiet as they drove south down the interstate. Tye drove with one hand and drank coffee with the other, content to sit in the right-hand lane and let all the impatient drivers pass him. Tye spent most of his time either walking or driving on lonely country roads, so the interstate traffic seemed like a madhouse of speed and aggression to him.

"You keep looking over at me like you think something is wrong with me," Kaity said.

Tye put his coffee in the cupholder and watched a BMW pass him going eighty. "I guess that's because I'm worried about you. You didn't sleep much last night, and today you're pretty quiet."

"Says the king of the monosyllabic reply."

"Well, yeah. But that's kind of my baseline. You're usually a little more voluble."

She laughed. "I think one of the things I love about you is you drive a pickup, half your wardrobe is camouflage, and yet you still use words like 'voluble.'"

"I feel like you're trying to change the subject."

"That's because I'm trying to change the subject."

"Well, alright then." He reached down and fiddled with the radio.

Kaity sighed. "I guess this whole thing is just getting to me. It's like these guys are just operating with impunity."

Tye nodded. "I think what bothers me the most is the idea of them all working together. You figure there's always some creepy dude lurking in the bushes, but these guys seem organized."

"And nobody is doing anything about it," Kaity said.

He reached over and took her hand. "We are."

"Yeah, but it shouldn't be up to a librarian and an animal tracker."

"Maybe this woman you found will help shake something loose," Tye said.

"Maybe. I've been stewing about this all night. Can we talk about something else?"

"There's always the house."

"That's a good topic. I guess we're going to have to decorate once it's delivered."

"That reminds me, I've been meaning to pick up a velvet Elvis and a print of that picture of the dogs playing poker."

She did a double take. "You're kidding, right? Please tell me you're kidding."

"We can compromise. I'll give up the dogs playing poker as long as I get my velvet Elvis."

She laughed, and it made him feel good. They spent the next hour talking about their plans for their house, which still seemed unreal to Tye. Once they set the joking aside, they settled on a minimalist approach to things, which suited Tye just fine.

They hadn't talked much about their future beyond that. The idea of marriage had seemed like a foreign concept to Tye most of his life, but now he found himself thinking about it quite a bit.

"So, I think we can get most of what we need with just a couple of stops in town," Kaity said as she punched the list into her phone. She was interrupted by the computer voice on her phone giving them directions to their destination. "Oh wow, we're almost to our exit."

"Time flies when you're planning interior decor," Tye said.

"I'd tell you to get in the right lane, but you're already there. Have been for miles. You drive like a little old lady."

"I figure the speed limit is plenty fast compared to walking."

First, they passed through farm fields where soybeans and industrial hemp grew right up to the edge of the road, then they wound their way up into the hills. The farther they went, the rougher the road, and the houses were more dilapidated.

Tye watched Kaity out of the corner of his eye as they passed a mobile home with a bunch of junk and broken-down cars in the front yard. He'd spent most of his teenage years in a trailer very much like that one, and Tye wondered how that squared with Kaity's upper-class upbringing. At times she'd expressed some dismay and frustration at the choices she saw made by poor people, but he got the sense it was more due to a lack of understanding than a place of judgment.

"Not much farther," Kaity said. It wasn't necessary. He could see the phone display as well as she could, but she tended to state the obvious when she was nervous.

He turned onto a narrow two-track, drove through an open gate, and passed a field with a single, mournful-looking cow standing there chewing its cud. At the end of the road was an older manufactured home that could have used a coat of paint but was otherwise in good repair. An old truck with mismatched fenders sat next to a little Honda. There was a sticker Tye recognized on the window of the Honda: a circle with a triangle inside of it, the symbol of Alcoholics Anonymous.

Tye turned the truck around so he was facing the exit, but he could still see the house in his mirrors. As he did so, a woman stepped out on the porch. She was painfully thin, with close-cropped blonde hair, and wore baggy sweatpants and a shapeless sweater.

Kaity took a deep breath. "That's her. I'll text you if she says it's okay for you to come inside."

"Text me now and again either way?" Tye asked. "That way I know you're okay."

"How about every fifteen minutes?" Kaity asked.

A lot of bad things could happen in fifteen minutes, but Tye nodded anyway.

She leaned over and kissed him on the cheek, then was out of the truck and walking toward the house. Tye watched her walk up in the mirror. The other woman stood with her shoulders slumped forward and her arms crossed over her chest. After talking for a moment or two, they both went inside.

It wasn't until the woman turned and Tye saw her face in profile that he was sure it was the woman from the video. The last ten years had not been kind. He would have easily believed she was a generation older.

He didn't listen to the radio, for fear it would keep him from hearing some noise from inside the house. Tye sat there with the windows rolled halfway down, watching the cow wander in the enclosure, his eyes glued to the screen of his phone, as the minutes ticked by.

At the fourteen-minute mark, the phone buzzed, and he jumped in his seat.

All okay. Talking.

He realized they should have arranged for some kind of codeword for her to use to indicate it was okay, and she wasn't under some kind of duress. He spent the next few minutes deciding if he should creep up to the house and peer in the window to figure out if the message was legit.

Tye sat there and stewed for almost fifteen more minutes, at times putting his hand on the door handle to get out and creep around the house, before thinking better of it. He knew Kaity would be royally pissed if she looked over and found him peeping through the window.

Finally, the door to the house popped open and Kaity walked out, eyes downcast. The other woman looked at Kaity's back for a moment before finally shutting the door. Kaity climbed in and buckled her seat belt without a word.

"Well?" Tye asked.

"Just drive," she said, staring straight ahead with her arms folding across her chest.

Tye started the truck and dropped it into gear. At the end of the driveway, he had to swing wide to go around another pickup truck that was sitting there. A man in his fifties sat in the cab, his long gray hair pulled back in a ponytail. He gave them a flat stare as they drove past, then dropped in right behind Tye's bumper.

"Check out this knucklehead," Tye said. "I hope I don't have to stop suddenly, because we'll wind up getting rear-ended."

"Unless I'm mistaken, that's Derrick Crown's brother."

Tye glanced in the rear-view mirror. "Now that you mention it, I think I see the resemblance."

"The woman back there is Derrick Crown's niece."

"Oh. Does that make the man behind us her father?"

"Yes. He lives here." Kaity pointed at a house on the right side of the road. "Right where he can see who comes and goes up his daughter's driveway."

Instead of pulling off into his house, the man behind them continued, locked onto Tye's bumper as he drove toward the interstate.

"I'm getting tired of this guy being stuck to me like a leech," Tye said.

"Please don't do anything. It's important that none of this blows back on her. If anybody asks, she didn't tell me anything."

Tye glanced over at her. "She isn't going to testify?"

Kaity shook her head. "No."

"She was the last chance. Without her, Evans has nothing. They can just keep doing it."

Kaity shook her head again. "I think we'd all love to see the strong victim taking a stand, helping convict those guys. But does she owe anybody that? It's not her job to put people in jail. That's the cops."

"Derrick Crown is the cops."

She gave a bitter laugh. "That's the real problem, isn't it? She knows she's going to be on trial as much as them. They're going to ask her why she waited ten years to say anything."

Tye looked in his rearview mirror. Ponytail Guy was still back there, three feet from his bumper.

"Looks like dear old dad is more worried about running us off than taking care of his daughter."

"She's afraid they'll kill her," Kaity said.

"Why did she agree to talk to you in the first place?"

"I think she just wanted to tell the story to somebody. Somebody who won't think she's crazy. But she isn't going to talk to the police. I'm not sure I did the right thing contacting her. It didn't do us any good and just dredged up memories for her."

As Tye signaled to get on the interstate, the man behind them finally dropped back. Instead of taking the onramp, the man continued past. Tye was reminded of a dog that had escorted another animal off its property.

"Well, at least he's gone now," Tye said.

Tye settled into the right lane, letting faster traffic pass him, and looked over at Kaity.

"You did everything you could."

"It happened her senior year. She had a full-ride scholarship to a state school. Now she cleans houses, goes to AA meetings, and pays rent to her dad so she can stay in that house."

As was often the case, Tye didn't know what to say, so he remained silent and concentrated on driving.

Kaity slammed her hand on the dash of the truck. Tye jumped and nearly swerved into the other lane. She hit the dash again, and he put the turn signal on for the next exit.

"Dammit!" she said. "Why did I do that? I just got a cast off that hand." She clutched it to her chest and started crying.

Tye pulled into the parking lot of a fast-food restaurant, put the truck in park, and undid his seat belt. He reached over and put an arm around Kaity. She buried her face in his chest and sobbed for what Tye guessed was a solid five minutes. He'd never seen her cry before. The words "it's okay" almost made it out of his lips, but he realized things weren't okay, so he didn't say it.

Finally, she pulled back. "I'm sorry," she said.

"Why?"

"For breaking down. Crying all over you."

He shrugged and pulled a bandanna out of his back pocket. "Reckon it goes with the territory. It's pretty awful."

She took the bandanna and blew her nose. "It could have been me. In high school or college. There were always guys like Jared and Eddie, swimming around like sharks. Sometimes I wonder how I made it without something like this happening."

He squeezed her hand. "I'm glad it didn't."

She looked at herself in the rearview mirror. "Good grief. I was never one of those women who could cry demurely."

"I was never into demure women anyway," Tye said. He dropped the truck into gear and pulled out into traffic.

"I'm trying to figure out what we should do now," Kaity said. "If she won't talk to the police, and the police are going to just sweep the whole thing under the rug, where does that leave us?"

"Sometimes you just need to wait," Tye said. "And see what develops."

34

"So that's it?" Peter asked. "They get to just get away with it?"

They were digging a trench for the electrical lines for Tye and Kaity's new house. The morning sun shone in the valley, but there was still a chill in the air. Peter was wearing one of Gary's old Carhart coats and holding a shovel.

Tye leaned against his shovel, feeling worn out after a night of poor sleep. "I don't know. I hope not, but I don't see any way forward right now."

Peter blinked back tears. "I hate myself for saying it, but I'm glad Eddie is dead. It wasn't just him, though. I can't prove it, but Jared Bauman was involved in Hannah's death. I know it."

"Yeah. I know. "

Peter thrust the shovel into the ground. "The only person that paid a price for what they did besides Hannah is me."

Tye couldn't deny it. One of the reasons he'd tossed and turned all night was the unbearable sense of wrongness in the idea that Jared Bauman was just going to walk away from all this. Tye was under no illusions that life was fair. Growing up poor in a West Virginia county where a few rich families got to do whatever they wanted had given him an understanding of how the real world worked.

"Let's try to be patient and see what develops," Tye said. It sounded lame even to his ears.

Tye worked in silence for the rest of the morning, finishing the trench just before lunchtime. It was the last piece of work that needed doing before the tiny home was delivered. He'd stubbornly insisted on doing as much of the site prep work himself as he could, to save a few dollars.

As they sat at the picnic table in front of Tye's yurt, eating a lunch of leftover beans and rice, Peter just picked at his food.

"I haven't even heard back from any of those jobs I applied to."

"Something will come along," Tye said.

"Will it? It's kind of hard to explain that ten-year gap in my resume."

"Well, Jacqueline has some work for you. Deborah and Vivian too. And we can always use a spare hand around here, as can George out at his ranch. You might have to piece together a living from three or four different gigs for a while."

"I appreciate all you're doing for me, but I'm not sure this really qualifies as a living. I feel like a little kid, dependent on all of you to shuttle me around. You're paying me way too much to come out here and dig ditches."

"It's nice to have somebody I can trust here on the property," Tye said.

"All that kept me going for those ten years was the idea that I would get out, find the evidence that Hannah stashed, and help put Jared and Eddie in prison. It's stupid, I guess, the kind of fantasy of a boy that read too many comic books growing up."

The waves of anger washing off Peter were palpable. Tye was uncomfortably reminded of how big he was. Often his mannerism was boyish and goofy, and it was easy to forget that Peter was easily a head taller than him and had arms almost as big around as Tye's thighs. Not for the first time, he wondered what would happen if Peter's temper let go for real. Tye had a suspicion that it would be like standing too close to a hand grenade when it went off.

Tye looked at his watch. "I reckon we ought to head downtown soon. Send me a text when you're done over at Jacqueline's, and I'll swing by and pick you up when I'm done running errands."

The truth was, Tye had only a few things he needed to pick up, which he could have gotten much closer to home. But Jacqueline had promised Peter several hours of paid work, so Tye was giving him a ride into town. It didn't make sense to drive all the way home, just to go back and pick Peter up again. Peter was going to start painting for Deborah and Vivian first thing in the morning, so he'd need to sleep at Tye's tonight. Tye was looking forward to spending a few hours in a park downtown reading a book, away from the long list of things that needed to be done on the property.

As they drove toward town, Tye reflected that what Peter really needed was his own car. But for starters, he didn't even have a driver's license, and even a beater vehicle was well beyond his means. In many ways, Peter reminded Tye of himself when he'd been a teenager, full of desire to make his way through life but lacking the means to do it. Except Peter was almost thirty years old, almost as old as Tye.

"I called three different military recruiters and explained my history," Peter said as they passed the city limits sign. "The Navy guy just hung up on me. The Marine laughed at me, then hung up on me. The Army guy talked to me for a few minutes. He sounded sympathetic but said there was nothing he could do. I'm not even going to bother with the Air Force or Coast Guard. No use embarrassing myself further."

Tye's knee-jerk reaction was to utter some kind of platitude like, "It'll all work out in the end." But he didn't. He knew what Peter was feeling all too well, the sense that there was no place for him in the world, no way to move forward, that he would be stuck living hand to mouth in a dead-end existence forever. Tye had been on the edge of that most of his life, and it was only the blind luck of landing a role on a reality TV show that had changed things for him. The money from the show had been enough to buy his property, but sometimes, he still worried he would lose it all.

Tye pulled into the parking lot of the Church of the Open Heart. Peter mumbled, "Thanks for the ride," and got out.

"Hey, man," Tye said. "I'm sorry this is rough right now. Just give me a call when you're done, and I'll come get you. We'll figure something out."

Peter gave him a half smile and a wave then walked toward the doorway where Jacqueline was standing. Tye sighed and pulled back out onto the street. He resolved to put the whole thing out of his mind for a while and relax. After a quick trip to a big box store for a few things they needed for the new house, Tye found a coffee shop, ordered an overpriced drink and muffin, and lost himself in a book of Gary Snyder essays for a while. He'd been fretting over the situation with Peter, meeting Jean Fiddler, and buying a house with Kaity for weeks now. It was nice to just sit somewhere and read a book. He would have preferred to be outside, but a cool drizzle had settled in.

Before he knew it, the coffee cup was empty, and his phone buzzed. It was a text from Peter.

We're all done.

Tye looked at the time on his phone, surprised to find that four hours had passed since he'd dropped Peter off. It was the longest period Tye had relaxed for weeks. *Be there in ten minutes,* he texted back.

"I need to do this more often," he muttered as he threw his coffee cup away. It earned him an odd look from the barista with the facial piercings, but Tye had reached a point in his life where odd looks from people didn't bother him anymore.

It was raining harder when Tye pulled into the parking lot of the church. He didn't see Peter, and there was only a single light burning inside. He figured Peter must have decided to wait inside because of the rain.

I'm out in the parking lot, he texted. He waited several minutes. Then with a sigh, he grabbed his rain hat from the back seat and ran over to the door outside Jacqueline's office. It was locked.

He had to knock several times before he heard the shuffle of feet from the other side of the door.

"Can I help you?"

"It's Tye. I'm here for Peter."

She opened the door, wearing a bathrobe, with her hair still wet from the shower. "He isn't out here?" She scanned the parking lot. "It was just drizzling when he left. He said he was going to wait here under the awning. It's raining hard now."

Tye pulled out his phone and sent another text. *Where are you?*

They both stared at the screen of Tye's phone. Nothing came. "Maybe his battery is dead," Tye said.

Jacqueline shook her head. "He plugged it into the charger in my office when he got here. It had to be full up when he left."

Tye turned and scanned the parking lot, as if he expected Peter to appear out of the driving rain somehow.

"This is weird," Tye said. "Where the hell is he?"

"We worked for a few hours painting the downstairs meeting room. He was pretty quiet but mentioned a couple of times how grateful he was for the help you were giving him, and how he was looking forward to working around your property to repay you. When we were done, I gave him his cash, he grabbed his phone, and he said he'd wait out here."

Tye knew it was pointless, but he walked around the grounds of the church anyway. There was no way Peter could have missed him pulling into the parking lot, but maybe he was having some kind of medical episode or something and couldn't respond.

He was walking over to his truck to grab his rain jacket when he saw the track. The grass between the building and the parking lot was patchy and uneven. In one of the bare spots, Tye saw two tracks. One was undeniably Peter's. The track of his left boot was long and wide, just a little smeared, as if he'd been dragging his feet. Next to it was the right print of what looked like a light hiking boot or trail runner. It was average-sized, and the tread was crisp.

He heard a door bang shut behind him and turned to see Jacqueline; she'd thrown on pants, an overcoat, and shoes and was carrying a flashlight.

"Somebody else was here," Tye said. He pointed at the track. "Did you hear another car?"

"I was in the shower, downstairs. Between that and the rain, there's no way I would have heard anything."

"These tracks are from two different people. The big one is Peter. The other one is someone else."

"Maybe the other track is old?"

"No. See how the edge just overlaps? That track was made over the top of Peter's. And with this rain, they're already losing their definition. In twenty more minutes, they'll just be a vague outline."

Tye squatted behind the track and looked toward the parking lot. There was a set of impressions in the grass. Four different prints, two sets of feet. The grass was already springing back upright. After that was the sidewalk, where he found a small square chunk of mud that had no doubt fallen out of the tread of the other person's shoe.

"I'm going to drive around and look for him," Tye said. "If he comes back, tell him to call me."

"I will," Jacqueline said. "Do you think he just left? Do you think something happened to him?"

"Dunno."

Tye circled the block, seeing no sign of him. In his head, he was doing the math for how far Peter could have walked in the time since he'd sent Tye the text message. He expanded the square out another block and dialed Evans's phone number as he drove.

"Peter's gone," he said when she picked up. He explained what happened.

"That's weird," Evans said. Tye heard soft music playing in the background. "But I can't call out the cavalry. He's an adult, and there's no sign that anything criminal happened to him."

"Did he get arrested?" Tye asked. In his mind's eye, the tracks lined up perfectly: Peter was in handcuffs, stumbling slightly, with a police officer holding onto his right arm and walking just slightly behind him.

"I don't think so. Hang on." He heard the sound of typing. "No officers have been checked out at the church recently. And there's no warrant out for Peter."

"Something's not right," Tye said. "Why would he text me to pick him up and just take off."

"Well, he's not the most stable of people." Tye could tell from her tone that she wasn't on board with the idea of doing more to find Peter. She'd already written this off as the crazy guy doing something unpredictable.

"I'm going to keep looking," Tye said.

"Well, if you find anything interesting, let me know. I'll be in the office until late tonight. Crown has me buried in cold cases that are going nowhere."

Tye kept driving in an ever-expanding square. He cruised through the parking lots of a couple of convenience stores, thinking maybe with some money in his pocket Peter had wanted to buy himself something. There was no sign of Peter in any of them, or at any of the nearby fast-food restaurants. He texted Peter a couple more times, with no response.

He did a slow pass outside of a liquor store, which earned him a hard look from the guy behind the counter, when his phone buzzed with an incoming call from Kaity.

He pulled over down the street from the liquor store.

"Peter's gone," he said. He briefly explained what had happened.

"That's weird," Kaity said when he finished. "Do you want me to drive downtown and help you look?"

"Where are you?"

"I'm already back at the yurt."

He sat there for a minute, watching the rain fall. "I don't think there's any point in that. I've done everything reasonable we can do. I guess I should just come home and see if he contacts us. I feel like I'm abandoning him, though."

"I think you've done more for him than anybody should expect," Kaity said. "Just come home. We'll sort it out in the morning."

Tye sighed. "I'm on my way." Still feeling like he was doing something wrong, he ended the call with Kaity and pulled away from the curb. The whole drive home he kept one eye on the road and one eye on the screen of his phone, waiting for a call that never came.

On his way up the driveway, he had to slow to avoid a young button buck deer who eyed him insouciantly as he drove past. Just as he was backing his truck into place beside Kaity's Jeep, the rain stopped. He stepped out and smelled the woodsmoke from the fire Kaity had started in the wood stove.

She was sitting cross-legged on the bed, reading a book when he stepped in. Despite all his other worries, he stopped for a moment just inside the doorway, struck by how good it felt to walk inside and see her sitting there.

"What?" she asked.

He laughed. "Just had one of those gooey moments again."

She smiled at him. "Come to bed. It's late."

"Let me put my stuff away." He walked over to the sheet metal gun cabinet, unlocked it with the key on his ring, and pulled his little revolver out of his pocket. He placed it on the shelf at the top of the cabinet and was swinging the door closed when his brain registered that something was missing.

"Son of a bitch," he said, pulling the door back open.

"What?" Kaity asked.

"The knife. It's gone."

"The big one? The Fiddler knife?"

"Yep. I keep it here on the shelf next to my pistols. It's not there." He opened the drawer underneath his workbench. There, among the clutter of tools and arrowheads, sat the spare key to the gun locker.

"I guess I need to find a better place to hide the spare key," he said.

"The guns are all there?" Kaity asked.

Tye double-checked to be sure. "They're all there. He just took the knife."

"Who? Peter or Jean?"

Tye stood there in front of the open cabinet, his hand on the open door. "Great question. Jean said he didn't want the knife. If he wanted it, all he had to do was ask."

"Peter then. What is he doing? And if he's up to something bad, why not steal a gun?"

"Another great question." Tye started to close the locker door.

"Maybe leave one of those out here where you can get to it?" Kaity said. She looked at the flimsy door of the yurt.

Tye didn't like leaving guns unsecured, but he didn't argue. Instead, he pulled out his big Ruger revolver, checked the load, and set it on the nightstand next to his flashlight.

"Just for tonight," Kaity said. "Maybe tomorrow we can stay at my place."

"Just for tonight," Tye agreed.

35

***

T he next morning, Tye was sitting outside the yurt, drinking coffee, watching the birds, and brooding when his phone rang. It was Evans.

"Any news on Peter?" he asked.

"Hello to you too," Evans said. "No news on Peter. But I think my boss has had a personality transplant. He wants to put together a proposal to management to put you on contract as a tracking consultant."

"I didn't see that coming. I got the picture he doesn't like me very much."

"I don't think Derrick Crown likes anybody very much. But he does find certain people useful, and apparently, he thinks you might be one of them."

"I guess that's reassuring. How does this work?"

"Apparently there's a sense of urgency. He wants to know if you, Kaity, and I can meet him at Eddie's place this morning. He wants you to walk him through things again."

Tye looked at the empty parking spot in front of the yurt. Gary's Scout wasn't running. Again. He'd borrowed Tye's truck to make a supply run into town. "Kaity's at work. There's nothing on my calendar, but I'm without transportation at the moment."

Evans sighed. "Sit tight. I can be there in half an hour to pick you up, and we'll drive together up to Eddie's."

"I'll be here." Tye ended the call and stared across the valley, watching the mist rise from the river as the sun warmed the air in the canyon. He felt a familiar throb behind his eyes. Something about this was making him uneasy, but he wasn't sure what. He tried to fathom Crown's sudden change of heart about the value of tracking evidence.

Tye swallowed the last of his coffee, then walked into the yurt to grab some gear. Before Gary left, Tye had grabbed his little sixteen-liter daypack from inside the truck. It was always packed with the bare necessities to spend time out in the woods. There was already a rolled-up lightweight jacket lashed to the bottom.

He stood there with his keys in his hand, looking at the gun cabinet. He didn't have a concealed handgun license, and even if he had, Crown probably wouldn't be too enthusiastic about him toting a gun while working as a consultant for them. He put the keys away, asking himself why he'd even thought about going armed in the first place. He didn't want to turn into one of those men who felt like they had to carry a gun around all the time.

He pecked out a text to Kaity, explaining what was going on. After a few minutes with no reply, he stuck the phone in his pocket, figuring she was busy with work and would reply later.

Shouldering his pack, he left the yurt and walked down the driveway so he could meet Evans, trying to enjoy the morning as he walked. Through the long winter months, it was like the property was in suspended animation. Nothing changed from day to day. Now, with the onset of spring, he could take a walk in the morning and another in the afternoon and notice plants that had budded out or flowers that had opened in a matter of hours. This was one of his favorite times of the year, and he told himself that he should make more of an effort to enjoy it.

As he walked down the driveway, he noted fresh deer tracks that had been made since the rain stopped at midnight. Soon the does would start having their fawns, and bucks would start growing a fresh set of antlers, only to shed them again in the late winter. All around him, birds flitted from branch to branch.

Evans's black SUV made the birds scatter when she gunned the engine to make it up the steep slope of the driveway. She rolled down the window, her eyes unreadable behind sunglasses.

"Since we're going to put you to work, I won't make you ride in back," she said. "Hop in."

"Thanks." The passenger seat was crowded by the laptop computer mounted to the dash, but he managed to squeeze in.

There was something about being in a police car that made Tye uncomfortable, even though he was riding in the front. As the resident long-hair in the county where he grew up, he'd been stopped by the locals for no good reason more times than he could count. He'd never venerated the police the way some people he knew.

"Just when I think I have Derrick Crown figured out, he throws me a curveball," Evans said. "I've been chasing leads on cold cases for days, then out of the blue, he calls me up with this proposal to bring you on board as a consultant."

"I wonder what made him change his mind."

Evans shrugged. "We've had a bunch of cases lately where having a trained tracker would be helpful. We also have a bunch of Department of Homeland Security grant money we haven't spent that is supposed to go to outside security contracts."

The mention of DHS didn't make Tye feel any better. Interacting with giant arms of the government, especially ones that carried guns, was something he avoided as much as possible.

He changed the subject. "I think what's bothering me about Peter is he left his stuff back at the house. He insisted on toting that backpack everywhere, but then he took off without it?" He thought about mentioning the knife to Evans but decided not to.

She glanced over at him. "Peter was in a mental institution for ten years. I'm not super surprised by anything."

Tye felt his jaw tighten at her disdain. "You know, he doesn't seem all that crazy to me. I think he got a raw deal."

"He told the detectives who investigated Hannah's disappearance that he knew she was dead because he had visions of her where she tried to talk to him."

"Yeah, I guess that must seem pretty crazy," Tye said.

Evans braked to avoid a wayward chicken in the road. "You don't seem all that enthused to be a contractor for the sheriff's department. Sometimes we hire people for technical support, and we have to rein them in because they've watched too many cop shows and they think they're now a junior detective or something. With you, I sense a bit of reluctance."

"You know I grew up in West Virginia?"

She nodded.

"The cops in my county were pretty corrupt. There were always rumors they had a hand in the local dope trade. I know we had all sorts of crime they never seemed too interested in doing anything about. I think my real issue with them is they failed to protect Gary's sister."

"From the guy he killed," she said.

"Yeah. She'd gone out with this guy a few times, and she broke it off. He got super weird and made all sorts of threats. We suspect he killed her cat. We tried to get the sheriff to help, but the guy's dad was a big deal in the county, and they blew us off."

"This is your friend Gary we're talking about."

"Yep. His sister was working by herself one night in a church office when the guy showed up. He beat the hell out of her. I think he would have killed her if Gary hadn't shown up."

"Then Gary killed him," she said. "Blunt force trauma to the head."

"He's a good man, but he doesn't tolerate people threatening his family."

"Makes sense to me. I think you'll find law enforcement out here is different."

Tye thought about what they'd learned so far about Hannah's disappearance and wasn't so sure, but he kept his mouth shut.

They turned onto Haley Road and passed the old mill. Tye saw a fresh arc of disturbed gravel where someone had pulled the gate open and closed, and the tire tracks of two vehicles in the mud.

They drove past the farm fields. Cows watched them blankly as they drove by. The drizzle quit just as Eddie's trailer came into view. The morning mist still hung in the valley.

An unmarked police SUV identical to the one Evans drove sat in the driveway of Eddie's trailer. Evans pulled in beside it, and Tye got out and stretched. His back felt tight and sore. He'd been sitting in car seats far too much lately.

He stopped when he saw a dry patch of gravel next to the other SUV. Until recently, another long vehicle with a wide wheelbase had been parked there. There was a mess of tracks in the muddy spots where there wasn't any gravel. Tye's brain automatically tried to make sense of them.

A Stellar's jay gave an alarm call from a nearby alder tree, and Derrick Crown stepped from around the back corner of the trailer. He gave Tye a fixed stare as he walked toward them with his hands in the pockets of his tan windbreaker.

"Good morning," he said, his voice flat.

"Morning," Evans said.

Crown stepped from the wet, muddy yard into the gravel of the driveway. His hiking shoes left little squares of mud behind him, just like the ones back at the church parking lot.

"Who else is here?" The words came out of Tye's mouth before he had a chance to think about the consequences. His brain was putting pieces together, but he didn't know what they all meant yet.

Crown's right hand jerked in the pocket of his jacket, like he'd thought about pulling it out but thought better of it. "Nobody but me," he said. For a moment, his eyes jerked to his left, toward the trailer, then they centered back on Tye.

"Run," Tye said to Evans, then he did just that, breaking right across the front of the trailer, almost sliding in the wet grass but recovering at the last second.

He heard the flat crack of a pistol shot behind him and felt the wind brush past his head. In slow motion, the front door to the trailer swung open, and Jared Bauman stepped out, his stubby little rifle held in both hands.

Tye was past him in a flash, feeling the skin between his shoulder blades tighten as he rounded the corner of the trailer. The odd, industrial sound of a suppressed rifle followed him, and he heard something smack into the siding of the trailer but didn't feel the burn of a bullet in his back.

Then a fusillade of shots opened up behind him. He slowed for a moment, realizing he was leaving Evans behind, then kept going. He was the only one without a gun, and there wasn't much he could contribute to this.

Tye continued at a dead run into the woods behind Eddie's trailer, then broke right to run sidehill instead of slowing himself down by trying to charge up the slope. There was another burst of gunfire, but it stopped.

He wove between downed trees and thick clumps of low-growing vegetation, almost slipping on the wet ground several times. Finally, he dove behind a fallen log and pulled his phone out of his pocket.

No signal.

"Next time I'm bringing a gun," he panted as he tried to figure out what to do.

He heard a yell. It was a man's voice, indistinct. Tye couldn't tell what was being said.

Tye didn't know what to do. He had an image of Derrick Crown on the radio, calling in reinforcements and identifying Tye as a suspect in some kind of crime. Tye needed help, but he wasn't sure how to get it. The last thing he wanted to do was pull Kaity into this nightmare. He wished Gary were here.

Forcing himself to breathe slowly, Tye crouched behind the tree and considered his options. Jared had shown some skill in tracking, but Tye knew he was better. When he'd shown Crown the tracks behind Eddie's house, it had been clear the detective had no idea what he was doing. In the short term, Tye's best bet was to stay in the woods. It was his element.

In the long term, though, he needed a way to communicate. The houses on this road were scattered and far apart. Tye didn't relish the idea of coming out of the woods to knock on a door so he could explain that he really wasn't a criminal and the police detective that was hunting him was actually the bad guy.

He heard a stick snap in the woods between him and Eddie's trailer and saw indistinct movement between two trees. Staying low, he moved deeper into the woods, moving from tree to tree and being careful to pick his steps so his passage was as quiet as possible.

He had an idea.

<h1 style="text-align:center">36</h1>

Tye squatted in some bushes across the road from the old mill on Haley Road. He checked his phone. Still no signal. Even though it wasn't raining right now, his jacket and pants were soaked through from the water dripping off the trees and from brushing against the wet vegetation.

He allowed himself a few seconds to long for the gear in his backpack that was sitting on the floor of Evans's truck, then dismissed it. He had what he had, and that was it.

He also wondered about Evans, if she was alive or dead. He shoved that away too, making himself focus on the moment.

There was no movement inside the old mill, and Tye didn't hear any sound either. He studied the pole right outside the gate carefully. Since he and Kaity had been planning the installation of their tiny home, he'd become familiar with utility cables. The wrist-thick wire running from the pole, over the fence, and into the facility was most certainly for electrical power. It was the smaller skinnier wire that Tye was interested in. It was almost certainly a landline telephone wire.

The fence was eight feet high, with two strands of rusty barbed wire on top. Tye took off his jacket. Under that, he wore a thin fleece sweater. He took that off as well and tied both around his waist. After several seconds of looking and listening, he took off at a dead run across the road.

The holes in the chain link fence were a little small for the toes of his hiking shoes, but he made it to the top. There he held on precariously with one hand and managed to untie the jacket from around his waist and wrap it around the top strand of barbed wire. He almost dropped the sweater, which would have forced a choice to either crawl down after it or leave it there for anyone driving by to see, but he managed to snatch it at the last moment and wrapped it around the wire as well.

His pants caught on the lower strand as he hoisted himself up and over, and he felt a hot stab of pain in his calf. He ignored it and managed to get over the top of the fence, lingering for an excruciating second with his groin over the barbed wire as his foot found purchase on the other side of the fence.

Then he was over, again holding on with one hand. He unwound the sweater and jacket and let them drop inside the fence. The sweater looked okay, but the jacket had long tears in the fabric.

His feet slipped a few feet from the bottom, and he hit the ground hard. Tye dusted himself off and gathered up his clothes before dashing behind an old logging truck that would shield him from the road.

As he donned the sweater and tattered jacket, Tye looked around the compound and listened. Several metal garages and shop buildings were scattered around the property among old trucks, log trailers, and giant pieces of machinery that Tye vaguely recognized as having something to do with making paper pulp.

In the center of it all sat a two-story concrete building. It had only person-sized doors instead of giant rollup garage doors, so Tye guessed it was the office. The skinny wire terminated in a box under the eaves. If there was a phone on the property, it would be in there.

He moved quickly from piles of scrap metal to giant vehicles, trying to minimize the amount of time he was out in the open and plan each move to limit his exposure. After a couple of bounds, he was directly across from the front door, hiding behind an old skid steer. All the windows were dark. A breeze blew through the scrapyard, causing the metal to rattle, but there was no other sound.

To get there he would have to cross fifty yards of open ground before he made it to the door with the "authorized personnel only" sign on the front. After one last listen and look around, he took a deep breath and went for it.

There were three concrete steps leading up to the door, and Tye stopped short when he saw the fat drops of dried blood on them. There were also little square cubes of dried mud.

"Peter," he said under his breath and pulled on the door, expecting it to be locked. Instead, he almost fell backward when it opened. He slipped inside and saw a long dark hallway with doors off either side. A stairwell ascended to his left. The place smelled old and musty.

The blood droplets led from the door up the stairs. From the second floor, Tye heard a sound like a chair leg scraping on the floor, then a muffled grunt. Tye pulled his flashlight from his pocket and went up the stairs, walking near the edge of the tread where it met the wall to minimize the squeaks and groans of the old wooden stairs settling under his weight.

There was another long hallway at the top. Tye followed the blood trail past old offices piled high with dusty metal furniture, boxes of adding machines, and old cathode-ray tube computer displays. It was like a trip back in time to the 1980s.

Tye followed the blood trail to a doorway and peeked inside. Peter was zip-tied to a metal chair. His left eye was nearly swollen shut and dried blood was caked under both nostrils. Duct tape covered his mouth. His one good eye widened when he saw Tye.

"This is going to suck," Tye said as he grabbed the end of the duct tape and yanked.

"Ahhhh..." Peter said once his mouth was uncovered. There was a wide band of red skin around the bottom of his face. "I thought Crown was arresting me, but he brought me here instead."

"I know," Tye said. He pulled his Buck knife out of its belt pouch and started cutting zip-ties.

"How?" Peter asked.

"Crown's shoes leave distinctive little cubes of mud behind them. They were on the sidewalk at the church, and out here too." Tye carefully slid the knife blade between Peter's wrist and the arm of the chair. He kept the knife sharp enough to shave with, so he didn't have to apply much pressure.

"If I wasn't worried about the lack of feeling in my feet, I'd sit here and think about how cool it is that you noticed that," Peter said.

"Hang tight. I'll have you loose in a minute." Tye squatted to cut Peter's legs free. "Derrick Crown and Jared Bauman ambushed me and Evans over at Eddie's trailer. I think Evans might have gotten shot."

"Oh, man," Peter said. "This is so messed up. What are we going to do? Crown is a cop. Nobody will believe us."

"I don't know," Tye said. "I'm making this up as I go." The last zip-tie fell to the floor. "Try standing up."

Peter pushed himself up out of the chair a little ways, then sat back down. "Oh, this hurts. Do you know when your leg falls asleep? It's like that only ten times worse." He started moving his legs in circles and rubbing his wrists.

Tye folded the Buck knife and put it back in the pouch. "We need to get out of here as soon as you can walk. Why did you take my other knife?"

Peter looked away, down at the floor. "I was afraid Jared would come after me. I saw where you kept the key to your gun cabinet, so I snuck in and grabbed the knife."

"Why not a gun?"

"Guns scare me, man. When Crown searched me, he took the knife. I'm sorry. I should have run when I saw him outside the church."

"Well, there's nothing we can do about it now."

Peter tried again to stand. This time he succeeded, although he was a little wobbly. "All right, I can walk. I think. Now what?"

"We need to find a phone. My cell doesn't have service, but this building should have a landline. Hopefully, it's still hooked up."

"Who are we going to call? Can you call the cops on somebody who is a cop?"

Tye was spared from having to answer that by the sound of an engine outside and the rattle of the front gate.

"Shit," he said. He ran over to the window, expecting to see Derrick Crown and Jared Bauman. Instead, it was Samuel Bauman. Tye watched as Jared's father drove his truck through the gate, then got out to shut it.

"If we go out the front door, he'll see us," Tye said.

"Maybe we can just hide up here?" Peter said. "I think the real office is downstairs, and they don't use the rooms up here."

"There's a big trail of blood droplets going up the stairs, courtesy of your nose. He can't miss them."

"Oh. Now what?"

Tye wished Peter would stop asking him that. He ran out into the hallway, hoping there was a back stairwell he'd somehow missed. Nope. There was just the stairwell at the front of the building. He vaguely wondered if that violated some kind of fire code.

Next, he ran to one of the offices on the side facing away from the front gate. There was an awning beneath the window, apparently to cover the back door, but the window was painted shut.

"Over here," Peter whispered from across the hall. Tye heard a truck pull up outside the office building, then the engine cut out. Tye ran over to Peter, his soft-soled shoes almost soundless on the old hardwood floor.

Peter had a window open a few inches. An old air conditioner unit sat on the floor, and the office had a bigger desk. Tye guessed at one time it had been a manager's workspace.

"It's stuck. I'm afraid if I push hard, it will make noise."

"Just do it." Tye heard the sound of boots on gravel from out front.

Because of his shy demeanor, it was easy to forget that Peter was a large, powerfully built man. He strained for a few seconds, the veins on his forearms popped out, and the window slid up with a low groan. The footsteps on the gravel stopped.

Peter started to climb through the window, but Tye put a hand on his arm. "Wait," he whispered and strained his ears to listen.

After a few seconds, the footsteps started again, and he heard the front door swing open.

"Now," Tye said and pointed out the window.

Peter tried to be careful, but the flimsy aluminum awning still rattled when he slid out onto it. He rolled over to his stomach, trying to spread his weight out, but Tye still heard the supports attaching it to the wall groan in protest. Then Peter slid down, tried to hang from his fingers on the edge, and dropped to the ground with a thud.

As Tye had hoped, the elder Brunner started clomping up the stairs, toward the source of the noise, rather than simply walking back outside and around the building, as he might have if they'd bailed out the window while he was still outside. Tye took a deep breath and followed Peter out the window. He was close to a hundred pounds lighter, but the awning still shimmied and shook under him. He slid down on his belly and dropped, landing next to Peter who was standing and dusting himself off.

Apparently, this was the smokers' station, as there was an old ashtray full of moldy cigarette butts. Tye pointed to a rusty old crane, and they both ran for it. Fortunately, the ground here was covered with ragged grass and not gravel, so they made little noise.

They both dropped on the far side of the crane. Tye peered through the glass of the cab at the office building and saw Samuel Bauman at the upstairs window, eyeing the big disturbance in the dirt and leaves on the top of the awning.

Bauman shut the window, and Tye pointed to a pile of scrap metal, deeper in the yard. They both ran. Tye wasn't happy to be moving farther from the gate, but right now, he just wanted to create distance between him and Bauman.

They dropped behind the pile of old, twisted metal, and just a second or two later, Tye heard the back door of the office squeak open. Samuel Bauman stood there, a long-barreled pistol in his hand,

and scanned the junkyard. Fifty yards away, Tye knew he was all but invisible behind the pile of junk, but the animal part of his brain screamed that he was exposed and needed to get up and run.

Bauman took a step out of the doorway, and Tye felt his gut clench, horrified that he was going to face a choice of getting shot by Bauman, or ambushing the man while trespassing on his property. He figured jail was better than the morgue.

Tye heard the crunch of tires on gravel out by the front gate, and a car door slammed. The front gate rattled, and Bauman turned away to walk around to the front of the building.

"Now what?" Peter asked.

"I don't know," Tye said. "I'm making this up as I go. I want to get out of here, but I don't want to leave Evans behind if she's still alive."

Peter nodded. "Okay. I don't have much I care to live for anyway."

That wasn't exactly encouraging to Tye, considering how he had plenty to live for. He thought about Kaity and their new house and wondered if he'd live to see it. He looked around the junkyard, planning a route that would let them circle the office building but stay out of sight.

"Follow me," Tye said. "Let's try to get to a place where we can see and come up with a plan."

"What if they start shooting at us?"

"Try not to get shot again."

37

They moved from piles of junk to pieces of broken-down machinery at a dead run, pausing in between to check to make sure the coast was clear. Tye heard angry voices from the front of the building but couldn't tell what was being said.

They paused behind an old pickup truck partially buried by pieces of scrap metal, and Peter did a double take. "That's Hannah's grandpa's truck."

Tye looked at the forty-year-old pickup with mismatched paint. "You're sure?"

Peter pointed. "See that scratch on the bumper? Hannah did that backing out of the gate when she was learning to drive. She never got her license, just her permit."

There were quite a few scratches on the truck. Tye wasn't sure if Peter was deluding himself or what, but he couldn't afford to think about it right now.

"We need to put that on the list of things to think about later," Tye said.

They made one more rush to hide behind an old log trailer, and they could see the front of the building. Both Derrick Crown's and Evans's police SUVs were parked behind Samuel Bauman's pickup truck. Jared, Samuel, and Crown all stood milling around talking and gesticulating. The back door of Crown's SUV was open, and Tye saw Evans sitting in the back seat, slumped over with her hands cuffed behind her back. Tye couldn't tell if she was wounded, but she didn't look good.

The wind shifted, and Tye caught a snatch of conversation.

"How are we supposed to make this look right now? It was supposed to look like Peter killed her and Caine," Jared said.

Peter sucked in his breath and half rose from the crouch he was in. Tye put a hand on his shoulder.

"Stay cool," Tye said.

"Get her out and bring her inside," Crown said. "Maybe this will be easier if they all just disappear." He sounded like a man who was trying to convince himself. As a detective, Crown would know exactly how hard it would be to fake a murder.

They pulled Evans out of the back of the SUV and half dragged, half carried her to the door of the office building. Tye saw blood on her shirt, and she stumbled like something was wrong with her leg. Jared Bauman and his father disappeared inside the building with Evans, but Crown stayed behind. He stood at the top of the steps, hands on his hips, and turned, looking around the junkyard.

"I know you're out there, Caine," he yelled. "Just come in and I won't kill her. We can figure something out."

Again, Peter started to rise from his crouch, and again, Tye put a hand on his shoulder.

"He has to kill her," Tye said. "And us too. It's the only way he comes out of this. If we give up, it'll just make it easier for him."

Peter settled back onto his haunches, and they both sat silently, staring at Crown, who just stood there as if he expected them to appear.

After a few minutes, Crown broke the silence. "Fine. We'll do it that way." He turned away and went inside.

"What do you think his plan is?" Peter whispered in Tye's ear.

"We need to move before he gets up on the roof," Tye said. From the roof, Crown wouldn't be able to see them behind the pile of junk, but they'd be trapped because he'd have a better view of their travel routes around the piles of scrap and machinery.

"Where to?"

Tye looked around. At the very back edge of the property stood a metal shop building. He pointed. "Let's head for that. If there's no phone inside, it's a good spot to slip over the back fence and into the woods."

"We're just going to leave her?"

"We're unarmed and outnumbered. If you've got a bright idea about how we can cross this open ground, storm that building, and rescue Evans with my Buck knife, I'm all ears."

Peter didn't like it, and Tye didn't blame him, but he followed as Tye darted from machinery to junk pile, expecting a bullet between the shoulder blades all the while.

A Stellar's jay bolted from her nest as they crept up to the shop. Next to the door was an old burn barrel. The contents caught Tye's eye. He reached in and pulled out a scrap of charred leather. The ashes inside were still warm.

"I bet that's Eddie's old vest," Tye said.

"The Wolves of The North," Peter said. "Somebody wanted to hide the fact that Eddie was a member."

"Yeah." Tye dropped the leather back into the burn barrel. "We don't have time to worry about this now. Let's go inside and see if there's anything we can use."

The door wasn't locked, saving Tye the trouble of breaking in and making noise. The inside was dimly lit by light coming through the dirty windows, and there were rodent feces all over the floor.

Tye pulled out his flashlight and shone it around, lighting up a drill press, bandsaw, and shelves full of old pipe and sheet metal. Peter walked over to a workbench, picked up a heavy engineer hammer, and smacked the head against his palm.

"It might be wishful thinking, but I feel better having this," he said.

"Yep," Tye replied, distracted as he searched the shop for a phone. Up a flight of stairs, there was an office in a loft where a supervisor could look out on the shop floor, but there was no phone, just an ancient Motorola walkie-talkie. Tye knew the battery would be dead, but he picked it up and tried it anyway. Nothing.

"We can go over the fence behind the building," Tye said. "That gets us in the woods. From there we can maybe flag somebody down or find a phone and figure out what to do next."

"How long do you figure that will take?" Peter asked.

"Dunno. Couple hours maybe."

Peter shook his head. "I'm not going. You can go if you want. But I'm not."

Tye looked at him and realized he wasn't going either. He'd been regretting his panicked run away from Eddie's trailer the whole time. It had been pure instinct, driven by a desire not to be in the middle of a gunfight when he didn't have a gun. But he'd been kicking himself for leaving Evans behind.

"Our only way out of this is for Evans to live," Peter said. "If she dies, Crown and the Baumans can cook up whatever story they want. They'll figure out a way to blame us for killing her. Crown can't wait too long. He has to kill her soon or somebody will be able to figure out that she was injured for hours before he tried to get help."

Tye didn't say anything. He knew Peter was right.

"You saw how she was bleeding," Peter said. "She may not have a couple of hours."

"I don't know what else to do," Tye said.

Peter looked around the shop. "Surely we can figure something out. We need a distraction."

Grateful for a new problem for his mind to work on, Tye stood at the handrail at the edge of the loft and looked around the shop. At one time it had been a fully equipped metal shop, full of welding equipment, sheet metal bending tools, and stocks of raw material that could be shaped into parts and structures. Tye had a vague idea of what most of it was for.

He heard the sound of a truck engine and looked out one of the grimy windows. Samuel Bauman was driving his pickup up and down the narrow lanes between piles of machinery and junk, while Jared rode in the truck bed, holding a rifle.

"They're looking for us," Peter said. "If they come in here, what do we do."

"Try to ambush them and hope for the best, I guess."

Peter hefted the heavy hammer, and it seemed like for a second, he was relishing the idea of going to work on the Baumans. In some ways, Tye didn't blame him.

The truck slowed in front of the shop. Tye looked around for a weapon, but there was nothing up here in the office. He pulled his Buck knife off his belt.

"I shut the door behind us when we came in," Tye said. He whispered, even though there was no way the Baumans could hear him.

Samuel drove by at a crawl, but he didn't stop. Jared moved from side to side in the bed of the truck, looking for something to shoot. Finally, they rounded a corner and were out of sight.

"That means Crown is alone with Evans," Peter said.

"Yeah, if she's not dead already."

"So there's just one of him and two of us."

"He's substantially better armed than us at the moment," Tye said over his shoulder as he walked down the stairs.

Tye did a circuit through the workbenches and shelves. He walked over to an oxy-acetylene torch, still hooked up to the pair of tall metal bottles. Tye picked up the nozzle of the torch and opened the valve. He was awarded by the hiss of escaping gas. Picking up the striker from the workbench, he ignited the gas into a thin, pale blue flame.

"That's cool," Peter said. "But those bottles must weigh a hundred pounds each."

"I have an idea," Tye said. "Let's see if we can find some trash bags."

38

Tye and Peter waited until the Baumans were on the other side of the compound, then they split up. Each of them was holding a trash bag full of oxy-acetylene welding gas like a kid holding a giant black balloon. They'd stuck the nozzle of the torch in the neck of each bag and filled it, sealing it closed with duct tape. The gas would probably leak out over time, but by then, this would all be over.

Over Tye's shoulder was a mechanic's tool bag containing a couple of road flares pilfered from the cab of a defunct pickup, a crowbar as long as his arm, some heavy leather gloves, and a mostly full can of wasp spray. It seemed like a poor set of tools to counter the arsenal that Crown and the Baumans were holding, but he tried not to think about that too much.

The jumble of junk in the old mill worked to Tye's advantage, and against the Baumans'. He could hear them coming from a long way away and would duck behind scrap metal, or once into the back of an old panel van, where he hid, holding his breath against the smell of mildewed carpet, until the Baumans passed by. He didn't hear any gunshots, so he guessed Peter was having similar luck.

He looked at his phone. He still didn't have a signal, but the clock said it was almost time. He'd felt like he was in a cheesy action movie when he gave Peter his watch and synchronized it to his phone. Using a hunk of twine, Tye tied the trash bag to a pile of junk. Acetylene gas had a chemical added to make it smell like garlic. He sniffed the air, it seemed clear, but he tied the twine around the taped-up mouth of the bag anyway. The bag floated in the gentle breeze.

This next part had seemed like a good idea back at the shop, but now, Tye pulled out the road flare and stood there with the striker cap in one hand, hesitating. Images of Evans bleeding out competed with images of himself covered with third-degree burns.

When his phone showed the agreed-upon time, Tye ignited the road flare. He stuck the non-burning end under the trash bag, then ran like hell.

The skin at the back of his neck crawled the whole time, as he expected to be burned to a crisp, but apparently, Tye's bet that the bag wouldn't ignite until the flame was directly underneath was correct, because he made it to the back of an old box van. He'd chosen this spot because he was close to the office building, with only a dozen yards of empty ground to cover. He was facing the side of the building that didn't have an entrance. Tye pulled on the heavy leather gloves and grasped the crowbar.

The engine of Samuel Bauman's truck had been a constant drone in the background. The big diesel was loud even at idle. Now Tye heard it over by the bag he'd left, and the sound of brakes as the truck stopped.

The wind carried a snatch of conversation to his ears. "...the hell is it?"

Then the bag full of welding gas exploded. Tye saw a giant fireball over the piles of junk. It was bigger than he had expected, easily taller than the two-story office building. Next came the sound of a man screaming. Apparently one of the Baumans had been investigating the bag when it went up. Tye couldn't tell if that was good luck or bad.

Seconds later, Peter's bag went up, just a little farther north than where Tye's had been.

Tye took a deep breath and ran for it. This whole plan depended on lots of things going right. First of all, Crown needed to be looking to the west, toward the explosions, and not the south or north as Tye and Peter ran toward the building.

No bullets came as he crossed the open ground. The crowbar was already in his hand when he approached the downstairs window, and he made short work of the glass. The heavy leather gloves protected his hands, but he felt the hot burn of a cut on the side of his leg as he hoisted himself inside.

Once inside the cluttered storeroom, he dropped the crowbar, pulled the glove off his right hand with his teeth, and pulled out the can of wasp spray. There was a racket from the opposite side of the building. Apparently, Peter had made it as well.

This was one of the many things Tye had been dreading. Weaving through the piles of musty old paper, he made his way to the doorway, then stuck his head out.

Crown was only a few feet away, his pistol was held out in front of him, but his head was turned toward the sound of Peter climbing through the window.

Tye blasted him in the face with the wasp spray, filling the hallway with the harsh chemical smell. Crown screamed and jerked off a shot involuntarily, causing dust to drop from the ceiling tiles.

Tye dropped the spray and went low, wrapping his arms around Crown's waist and driving with his legs. The other man fell backward, and his head hit the floor tiles with a thud. They fought over the gun. Tye was lighter than Crown by a good twenty pounds but had the advantage of being on top and not having a face full of wasp spray. He pinned Crown's hand to the floor but couldn't get the gun free.

Crown bucked, and Tye almost lost his grip. Even blinded by the wasp spray, it wouldn't take much for the detective to put a bullet in him in the narrow confines of the hallway.

Tye's finger ran across a familiar shape: the stag handle of Remy Fiddler's old Bowie knife. It was stuck in the back of Crown's belt. Tye's hand closed around the handle, and he jerked it out of the sheath. His first thought was to drive the blade deep into Crown's belly, but a voice in the back of his head screamed at him that Crown was a police detective, and rogue or not, Tye couldn't just gut him.

Instead, he brought the heavy pommel of the knife down between Crown's eyes. Crown gave a huff of surprise, and his resistance slackened. As Tye raised the knife again, Crown turned his head to the side, and this time the butt end of the knife smacked into his temple with a meaty thump.

Crown went limp, and for a second, Tye thought he'd killed the man despite his best efforts, then he gave a low groan.

Peter stepped into the hallway, brushing glass fragments off the front of his shirt. He stopped when he saw Crown, and stood there with the hammer in his hand, giving the detective an appraising look.

"If you smash his head in with that hammer, this whole thing is going to get even more complicated," Tye said. "Help me drag him upstairs so we can help Evans."

Peter stuck the hammer in the mechanic's bag he'd slung over one shoulder. "I've never wanted to hurt somebody this bad before. I don't like this feeling," he said as he stooped to grab one of Crown's arms.

"Yeah, I know what you mean." Tye stowed the knife, crowbar, and Crown's pistol in his bag. The pistol was one of the modern plastic-framed ones with no safety catch or hammer, and the damn thing made him nervous. He put it in the bag with the muzzle facing away from him and hoped for the best.

"Where are the Baumans?" Peter asked as he grabbed Crown's other arm.

"I heard one of them screaming right after my bag of welding gas went off. I think it was Jared." Tye grimaced, imagining what it would be like to have a big ball of fire go off in his face. "That should slow him down some. Let's go find Evans. We can grab her and get out of here. Hopefully, we can find the keys to either her SUV or Crown's."

Tye didn't particularly want to kill Crown, but he and Peter weren't gentle dragging him up the stairs either. His head wounds left quarter-sized drops of blood on the treads. He groaned as they made it to the top of the stairs.

Evans was in the same chair that had previously held Peter. The side of her shirt was soaked with blood, but her eyes were bright and alert.

"Get me out of this damn chair," she said.

Peter and Tye dropped Crown with a thud. Tye started to pull out his Buck knife, then remembered the big Bowie in his bag. It was razor sharp, and the big blade would make short work of the tape.

Evans's eyes widened at the sight of the big knife. "Whoa! Careful with that."

Tye squatted behind her and worked the knife between her leg and the leg of the chair. The duct tape popped apart. "How bad are you hit?"

"I'm not dead yet. It went into the lower left side of my chest. I think it might have traveled around the outside of my ribs, because I'm not coughing up any blood."

"Lucky," Tye said as he moved to her other leg.

"If you can call getting shot lucky." She looked at Peter. "Hey, see if there are any car keys in Derrick's pockets. And while you're at it, pull his handcuffs off his belt and lock him up."

"I've got him," Peter said and turned toward Crown. Tye had both of Evans's legs free and started working on her arms. He cut her right hand free, and still kneeling on the floor, moved over to her left.

In the confines of the room, the gunshot was so loud Tye felt his eardrums squeeze inwards. Peter crumpled to the floor, and in slow motion, Tye saw Crown on his side with a tiny little pistol in his hand. His pant leg was hiked up to expose an ankle holster.

Backup gun, Tye thought. *I should have thought of that.*

The muzzle of Crown's pistol swung toward them. Tye felt like he was moving underwater as he shoved the chair over with his shoulder. There was no time to go for the gun in the bag on the floor next to him. The second shot was as loud as the first. He didn't feel the burn of a bullet, and he hoped the grunt that came from Evans was due to hitting the ground and not getting shot again.

Crown was holding the gun in his right hand but was aiming with his left eye due to all the blood running down his face. For a half-second, Tye thought about how deliberate and calm the detective looked, then he realized he better do something or he was going to get shot.

He did the only thing he could think of: he threw the knife. If it had been an action movie, the big Bowie would have stuck point first in Crown's neck or chest. But it wasn't a movie, and the last time Tye had thrown a knife was horsing around when he'd been a teenager.

Tye had been hyperfocused on the muzzle of the gun when he threw, so that was where the knife hit. It hit with the blade edge instead of the point, and the heavy blade cleaved through Crown's hand, then spun so the butt end of the pommel struck him in the teeth. Crown dropped the pistol and slumped back to the floor.

"Wow," Evans said.

"Yeah."

"Oh shit. Is that a finger on the floor?"

Tye didn't want to look, but he did. "Yeah. I'll get the gun and help Peter."

"My left arm is still taped to the chair."

But Tye was already to Peter. He rolled the other man over and saw a hole in his chest, just above the top button of his shirt. Peter coughed, and blood ran out of his mouth. There was a panicked look in his eyes.

Out of the corner of his eye, Tye saw Crown reaching for the knife with his good hand. Tye swatted it away, then punched him. Crown ducked at the last second and Tye's hand glanced off the top of his head. He looked for the gun Crown had dropped.

"Cut me loose so I can help!" Evans said. She was scooting along the floor, dragging the chair still taped to her arm.

For a moment, Tye froze, torn between finding the gun Crown had dropped, helping Peter, and cutting Evans loose.

He spotted the gun on the floor and that broke the freeze. Just as he was reaching for it, he heard footsteps in the hallway, and a smell like barbequed meat filled his nostrils.

Jared Bauman stepped into the room. The hair on the left side of his head was burned down to stubble, and the left side of his face was a massive red blister. His clothes were charred, and his left hand was raw and red.

His right hand seemed to work fine because he held his stubby little rifle pointed at Tye.

39

"Can't run this time, Caine," Jared said. His speech was slurred because of the big blister forming at the left corner of his mouth. "I'm going to enjoy killing you."

There were more footsteps behind Jared.

"Let's just hold on a second," Samuel said. "This whole thing has gotten out of control."

The elder Bauman stepped around his son and surveyed the room. "Jesus H. Christ," he said. He wore a pistol at his belt and had the look of a man that was watching everything he'd worked for fall apart.

Peter made a choking noise from the floor. His breaths were long and ragged.

"Oh good, Peter's still breathing," Jared said. "I've been looking forward to shooting him too."

Samuel put a hand on his son's shoulder. "Hold on."

"He killed Eddie."

"No, he didn't," Tye said. "Your father did."

Jared blinked. Then he smirked. "Nice try." He flicked the safety off the rifle. Beside him, Samuel's eyes grew wide.

"Your dad did it," Tye said. "I recognize his footprints. Those are the boots he wore the night he shot Eddie."

"These aren't the boots I wore the night..." Samuel trailed off.

Jared turned to look at his father, who was standing there with the look of a man who had just realized his mouth was working faster than his brain.

"Eddie was a loose cannon," Samuel said. "You needed to put that business with those girls behind you. You were never going to do that with Eddie around."

"You killed him?"

"I did what I had to do to protect this family. I've worked too hard to let it all go to waste over Eddie and some white-trash girl." He surveyed the room. "I reckon if Caine and Peter were to kill Crown and Evans, and this building somehow burned down, we might just make it out of this intact. Between the dirt I've got on people and greasing some palms, I reckon we have a chance."

Jared stared at his father, mouth agape. From the floor, Crown made a sound halfway between a growl and a moan. For a long few seconds, the only sound was Peter's labored breathing.

"Hey, Tye," Evans's voice came from behind him. "Hold still."

Tye froze. The first bullet hit Samuel right between the eyes, and he dropped. The second hit Jared low in the neck, and he staggered but stayed upright. Tye saw Crown roll to his right and reach with his left hand for the little backup gun on the floor. Staying low, Tye lunged to intercept him, grabbing Crown's arm. Wounded as he was, the man was still strong. Tye turned his head just in time to avoid a thumb in the eye from Crown's injured hand and responded with a head butt to the man's nose.

As they fought, Tye heard a fusillade of shots, and Jared's body hit the floor next to them. He was vaguely aware of Evans yelling something, but his brain tuned it out.

Tye had never been particularly good at ground fighting, and that was almost his undoing now. Crown rolled to a position on top of Tye, and slowly, inexorably started pushing the muzzle of the pistol toward Tye's head.

"Crown! Stop!" Evans yelled.

Both of them turned to look at her. She was on her side, left arm still taped to the overturned chair, with the pistol held out in her right hand.

Crown smirked. "You can't shoot me, Darla. We're both cops."

"Fuck you, Derrick." She took careful aim and shot Derrick Crown in the head.

He slumped on top of Tye, and his grip instantly weakened. Tye scrambled out from under him, wiped the other man's blood off his face, and tried not to vomit.

"Cut me loose," Evans said.

Tye stood and looked around. There were guns, blood, and bodies everywhere. He spied the Bowie knife over in a corner and scooped it up, then crossed the floor to cut Evans loose. Her wound was bleeding again.

"Why didn't you say something about seeing Samuel's footprints at Eddie's murder scene before?" Evans said after he cut her loose.

"I didn't see his footprints," Tye said. "I made all that up. It was a guess."

Evans made a sound halfway between a grunt and a laugh as she stood. She staggered over to Peter.

"There's a medical kit in my vehicle. Help me get him downstairs."

Tye pulled the keys out of Crown's pocket, then he and Evans hauled Peter down the stairs and outside. Tye blinked when they stepped into the sunshine. The cloud cover had lifted, and it was a beautiful day.

Evans tried to simultaneously talk on the radio and put a chest seal on Peter's wound while Tye drove as fast as he dared, the siren wailing and the lights flashing. Just before the SUV slid to a stop in the gravel parking lot of the volunteer fire station, Peter gave a final long sigh.

Tye helped her pull him out of the back while a volunteer dropped the hose he'd been using to wash a firetruck and ran over. Peter's face was gray. His eyes were shut, and his shirt was soaked with blood.

As the EMT started cutting off Peter's shirt, Tye felt a breeze on the back of his neck that carried with it the faint scent of flowers, and Peter's face relaxed. His body went limp, and Tye knew he was gone.

They worked on him until the ambulance got there, applying more dressings and taking turns doing chest compressions and using a bag valve mask. As they worked, Tye was vaguely aware of sirens and more vehicles arriving full of uniformed sheriff's deputies and paramedics. Evans stood, relieved by a paramedic, and he heard her telling another deputy about the scene back at the scrapyard.

A contingent of deputies jumped back in their vehicles and tore off down the road toward the scrapyard. A volunteer paramedic who didn't look like she was old enough to buy beer tapped Tye on the shoulder.

"I've got it from here," she said and took the bag valve mask from him.

Tye stood and looked at the chaos around him, and that was when he noticed Kaity's Jeep parked across the road in the Forest Service visitor center parking lot. She stood there looking at him.

Nobody tried to stop him as he walked toward her. He stopped a few feet from her, trying to read the expression on her face.

"When I couldn't get you to respond to a text, I just started driving this way. Then all the ambulances and police cars started passing me with their sirens going. I thought you weren't going to do anything stupid."

"Well, when I started this morning, I didn't know I was doing anything stupid."

She looked him over from head to toe. "You're covered in blood."

"None of it is mine. At least I don't think so."

"Is Peter dead?"

"Yeah. I think he is. So are the Baumans. And Crown."

She looked over his shoulder, and Tye turned. He saw one of the deputies from across the road heading his way.

She reached over and touched his face. Then pulled his head toward her and kissed him.

"I think you need a lawyer," she said.

"That might be a good idea."
"Okay. I'll call one. I love you."
"I love you too."

40

L ater, Tye stood with Kaity in the kitchen of their new house. It smelled of cut lumber and fresh paint.

"Okay." The electrician's voice carried in through the open window. "You can turn it on now."

Kaity reached over and threw the main circuit breaker. The ceiling fan started with a whir and the lights came on.

"I can't believe we're finally done," Kaity said.

"Yeah, it seemed like it took forever."

The electrician gave a friendly wave and headed over to his truck. The grass outside was torn up and rutted from where the giant truck had backed in to deliver the tiny house. There had been one heart-stopping minute when Tye thought the truck wasn't going to make it up the steep driveway, but the driver finally made it up.

The sound of the electrician's truck faded into the distance, and then for a few moments, there was silence, before a robin gave a tentative chirp outside. Soon, several birds were chattering back and forth.

It had been a long, loud day, starting at dawn when the giant truck pulling the tiny home chugged up the driveway, and continuing through the early afternoon as things were adjusted, hooked up, and tested. Tye stood there, just enjoying the sounds of the birds and watching as Kaity walked around opening cabinets and testing the faucets.

"I feel like I've spent almost all my time trying to make this happen for months, and now that it's here, I'm not sure what to do with myself. I'd sit down, but the furniture doesn't get here until tomorrow."

Tye looked at his watch. "We need to leave for the funeral in a few minutes."

"I hadn't realized how late it was. No rest for the weary, I guess."

They walked from the house to the yurt to change clothes. Kaity pulled on a dark dress, a rarity for her.

"You look good," he said as he buttoned up the back for her.

"Don't get used to the dress thing," she said.

On the way to her Jeep, Tye stopped and stared at the house. Kaity walked up beside him and put an arm around his waist.

"I've never lived anywhere this nice before," he said.

"Just wait until we get some furniture."

"Oh, I don't know, I spent years living in the back of a pickup truck. I can just throw a sleeping bag down on the floor."

She laughed. "I'm not going to try to change you completely from your feral ways, but I still want some furniture."

"I reckon I can compromise."

They walked like that, arm in arm, over to the Jeep. As he slid into the passenger seat, Tye had a sudden flashback to driving down the road in Evans's SUV with Peter dying in the back seat. For a sudden, panicky moment, he wanted out of the car.

Instead, he took some deep breaths and focused on the view of their new house through the windshield. Kaity put her hand on his.

"Okay?" she asked.

"Yeah. It's getting better."

"It's just going to take some time. Maybe you'll sleep better in the new place."

He nodded, doubting that would be the case.

Kaity's phone pinged. She looked at the screen and frowned. "Check this out. George just sent me a link."

Tye looked at the screen. George and Kaity were members of several local social media groups. Someone had posted a picture of firetrucks staging at the entrance of the old McCaslan property. A black cloud of smoke rose from behind the trees.

"Huh," Tye said. "It looks like the McCaslan house is on fire, but they are having trouble getting to it because somebody cut down a bunch of trees and they fell across the road."

"You think Jean set it on fire?"

"It's hard to think of anything else. I'm glad he did it now when the forest is still wet and it won't spread, although I'm sure he thought of that."

"We probably shouldn't mention Jean to Evans," Kaity said as she started the Jeep.

"Probably shouldn't. Although that's assuming they ever let her off administrative leave."

"At least you're in the clear," Kaity said.

"Yeah. I think they just want to bury the whole thing. Which is easy when most of the people involved are dead."

Gary and May were already parked in the driveway at Deborah and Vivian's house. As Kaity parked, Gary got out of May's car, carefully carrying the two cremation urns. Jacqueline Elliot got out of the back seat.

Evans pulled in behind the Jeep. She moved a little gingerly as she got out, but otherwise seemed mostly recovered from the gunshot wound. Deborah had graduated from the surgical boot on her foot to a splint and a cane.

Nobody said much as they made their way down the steep steps to the river. Kaity and Evans had both tried to find Peter and Hannah's relatives, with little success. The closest they'd come was a great-aunt of Hannah's back east. She'd hung up as soon as Kaity explained why she was calling.

In the end, Tye, Kaity, and Evans paid to have Peter and Hannah cremated. The Clark County Medical Examiner, relieved to have two fewer unclaimed bodies, hadn't taken much convincing to allow them to be released.

Tye took Peter's urn from Gary, and Kaity took Hannah's. Tye stood there, not listening to Jacqueline's words. Instead, he was remembering a funeral from long ago, when Tye had buried his mother, father, and brother.

He snapped back to the present moment when Kaity stepped forward toward the river. He joined her at the water's edge, and they poured the ashes into the river, where they mingled together and floated downstream, toward the sea.

Tye felt a breeze on the back of his neck that carried the familiar scent of honeysuckle, then as the last of the ashes ran out of the urns, it was gone.

Deborah and Vivian had prepared some refreshments. Tye didn't want to stay, but he did anyway out of politeness. Evans joined him in a corner with a paper plate full of snacks.

"Any news?" Tye asked.

Evans shrugged. "Several people at the sheriff's office have politely suggested I quit. I made it clear I intend to come back to work, and if they mess with me, I'll sue the britches off of them. That lawyer of yours is a big help."

"Willie is quite the character," Tye said.

"Tomorrow, I have to drive out to Pullman and talk to the Whitman County prosecutor about my brother."

"What do you think will happen?"

She shrugged again. "I don't know. It'll be up to them. I feel like my brother is dead, and whatever sickness infected Jared and Eddie turned him into a completely different person. We'll see."

"Yeah, I guess we'll see."

Evans checked her watch. "I hate to run, but I'm supposed to take Doyle out to dinner tonight. He wanted to come, but there's no way we would have gotten him down the stairs."

"Tell him I said hi."

Evans's departure seemed to be the catalyst that broke up the party. Tye caught Kaity's eye from across the room, and she cocked her head toward the door. They made their goodbyes and went outside to get in her Jeep.

Instead of starting the engine, Kaity sat there for a minute.

"Did we do any good here? There was just so much death."

Tye watched as two bald eagles headed downstream, scanning the water for fish. "Crown isn't a cop anymore. The Baumans can't hurt anybody anymore."

"I feel like we just scratched the surface. There have to be more people that knew what was going on but didn't say anything. It's like nobody is accountable."

The eagles turned and roosted in a tree together.

"We can only do so much," Tye said. "Most people go out of their way not to even know about this sort of thing. We did more than our fair share."

Kaity reached over and took his hand. "I guess that's one way to look at it. More than our fair share. Let's go home."

"Let's go home," he said.

KEEP READING!

Keep reading for a sneak peek of *Taking Refuge: A Tye Caine Wilderness Mystery #5!*

DID YOU ENJOY WARRIOR SOUL?

Please leave a review!

Would you like a free Tye Caine Wilderness Mystery short story?

Visit www.dlbarbur.com to join the Tye Caine Tracker Pack!

We'll keep you updated with developments in the world of the Tye Caine Wilderness Mysteries, plus share occasional info on tracking, wildlife, wilderness skills and more.

TAKING REFUGE CHAPTER 1

"What do you mean she's gone?" Tye Caine asked. He looked off toward the mountain in the distance to avoid staring at the naked Swedish woman standing in front of him.

"I woke up, and Brianna was gone. I looked around for her and waited an hour or so before I hit the emergency call button." Sigrid was scratched, dirty, and barefoot. Her long blonde hair was matted and full of twigs and pine needles.

Tye took a long, slow look around the campsite. The sun was just barely over the horizon in the east, throwing rays of pink light on the slopes of Mt. Adams to their north. The makeshift debris hut was in a clearing among the tall Ponderosa pine trees. A fire pit still smoldered with coals, and Tye could hear the burble of a creek from fifty yards away. There were a couple of remote cameras set up on tripods.

He looked over his shoulder at Powell Fuller, the producer of the reality TV show *Stripped and Stranded*, standing next to Jennifer, the camera operator. Powell made a "keep rolling" gesture with his finger, then tapped his chest, reminding Tye to speak loud enough that the microphone clipped to his shirt collar would pick up his voice.

"Maybe she went to the bathroom?" Tye asked.

Sigrid had a way of looking at people when they said something she thought was stupid. Tye hadn't received that look nearly as many times as Powell, but apparently, now it was his turn.

"We haven't eaten in three days, so I doubt it would take an hour to go to the bathroom," Sigrid said, then pointed. "The pooping spot is over there if you want to go check."

"Yeah. Let's check the latrine."

"Latrine," Sigrid repeated to herself softly. Sigrid's English was nearly flawless, with only a slight accent. "There" came out "dere," and her vowels were a little funny, but otherwise, Tye didn't have a problem following her.

Tye figured the latrine was as good a place to start as any, so he walked through the trees, Sigrid walking beside him. She was tall, the same height as him, and wore only a small shoulder bag that concealed nothing but was big enough to hold an emergency tracker and a microphone. Even though it was mid-August, the nights here were cold, and he was grateful for his light jacket. Sigrid wrapped her arms around herself, as much for warmth as modesty, he guessed. Contestants on the show knew they'd spend three weeks in the woods naked, so it tended to attract people who were comfortable with no clothes on. Later in post-production, they'd blur over the contestants' intimate areas so the show could be aired on major streaming outlets, but they filmed in the buff unless they managed to craft makeshift clothes.

They were nearly three thousand feet above sea level in the dry Ponderosa pine forests of eastern Washington state. Previously, the show had filmed in exotic locations in Central America and Asia, but apparently, now Powell's budget only allowed for renting out a corner of ranchland in Eastern Washington. He heard Powell and Jennifer walking behind them, huffing under the weight of the camera and sound gear they carried.

"There," Sigrid said, pointing at a neatly dug latrine under a tree. "You can see she is not here. Perhaps it is time to check her satellite tracker."

"Yeah. About that." Tye checked the Garmin device clipped to the shoulder strap of his backpack, hoping to find a different result. When Jennifer had banged on the door of his cabin before dawn, yelling that Sigrid had activated her distress beacon, the first thing he'd done was check the screen. Sigrid's tracker was still working. The tracker for Brianna, the other contestant, hadn't pinged a satellite since three a.m.

"I'm going to the last position," Tye said, looking back at Powell, who nodded. Jennifer had the camera pointed right at him. This wasn't how the show was supposed to work. Tye was a safety and survival consultant. He wasn't supposed to appear on camera. He was supposed to work behind the scenes, monitoring the contestants' health and responding to potential emergencies. Part of him wondered if this was all a scam that Powell had cooked up to boost the show's flagging ratings.

He tracked Brinna from the latrine to a spot deeper in the forest, both by following her footprints and the GPS display. Sigrid fell in beside him, and she was clearly seeing the same tracks as him. Brianna was small and light, only a couple of inches over five feet. The forest floor here was mostly pine needle duff, and her tracks were faint.

"We're here," Tye said. There was a disturbance in the duff ahead of him, and he squatted a few feet away to study it rather than walking up and disturbing the marks on the ground. Sigrid did the same.

"What do you see?" Powell asked. Irritated, Tye held his hand up for silence.

After a minute, he stood, walked over to the bare patch in the duff, and picked up a sliver of plastic. It was hard to be certain, but it looked like the same stuff that his device's screen was made of. Then he picked up a fist-sized rock with a scuff of gray plastic on the side.

"She knelt here. I think she smashed her tracker with this rock."

Beside him, Sigrid let out a breath. "I think so, too."

"Why would she do that?" Powell sounded genuinely puzzled. Either he hadn't known about this, or he was a hell of an actor.

"Dunno," Tye said. "Let's follow the tracks." He didn't wait for

Powell to agree. This could be a massive con job on Powell's part, or Brinna could have smashed her tracker and run naked into the woods. Either way, Tye wanted to get to the bottom of it quickly.

The Dibley Ranch bordered the Gifford Pinchot National Forest to the north. The ranch was mostly flat toward the south, full of once-manicured horse pastures that had gone scraggly and weedy due to years of neglect. The north end of the ranch sloped upward into the mountains and was still in timber. This was where they'd decided to film *Stripped and Stranded.* The contestants had been confined to about twenty acres, but Tye knew the episode's voice-over would make it sound like they were in the middle of a vast wilderness.

The track was hard to follow in places. Tye picked up a stick off the ground, a little less than three feet long. He found a long line of clear prints and used the stick to measure Brianna's stride length, marking a notch with his pocket knife. When he had trouble finding the next track, he put one end of the stick on the last clear impression and moved it around in an arc. Unerringly, the next faint track would be near the notch. The track mainly moved north, with some meandering from side to side.

"She is using the north star to navigate," Sigrid said. "Remember, it was dark. Moving through the thick trees, she goes a bit off to the west or east. But she always turns to the north when we pass through a clearing. She can see the stars better in the clearing."

Tye blinked. Sigrid was right. "Nice catch," he said. She nodded.

The farther north they went, the steeper the slope became. Now they were slowed by Jennifer and Powell struggling under the weight of the camera and sound gear more than the need to find the next track. There were several spots where Brianna had slipped trying to climb the steep slope. The soles of Tye's hiking shoes were lugged, and he had trouble staying upright. Sigrid's bare feet lost traction several times, and she fell to her hands and knees. Tye offered her a hand up the first time, but she just looked away and got up under her own power.

"She's going to the road," Tye said. The border between the

national forest and the Dibley ranch was a forest road that ran east and west along the slope's contour.

Sigrid nodded. "Yes. She just has to go north, and she is bound to find the road. It is what you call a handrail?"

Tye nodded. Some English idioms were new to Sigrid. In navigation terms, a handrail was a long feature like a river or a road that ran perpendicular to your line of travel. It didn't matter at what exact point you encountered it. All you had to do was find it, and then you knew you could follow it to a destination. Roads surrounded the Dibley Ranch. When Tye had briefed the contestants before the start of the show about what to do if they became lost, Plan A had been for them to sit tight and wait to be found. Plan B had been for them to walk in a cardinal direction until they hit a road, then sit down by the side until either a member of the production crew or a resident drove by.

Tye scrambled up the slope to the road, leaving the rest behind. He'd spotted a tan-colored object and was pretty sure he knew what it was. He picked up a canvas bag identical to the one Sigrid wore and unzipped it.

Inside was the wireless microphone transmitter and a smashed GPS tracker unit. From his pocket, Tye pulled out the sliver of plastic he'd found earlier and saw with grim satisfaction that it was a perfect match for the piece missing from the screen.

"There's nothing else inside?" Powell asked, out of breath from the scramble up the slope.

"Nope."

"No note or anything?"

Sigrid looked at Powell. "We are naked. What should she leave a note with?"

Tye handed the bag to Powell, then walked up and down the road for fifty feet in either direction. He couldn't find any sign of Brianna. The road surface was hard-packed gravel that wouldn't hold a tire track, much less the footprint of a hundred twenty-pound woman. He saw no sign that she'd crossed the road and continued up the slope on the other side.

"Where did she go?" Powell asked. He looked dazed and confused like a man contemplating his business going down the tubes.

Tye didn't answer, and he just stood there thinking.

Sigrid squatted next to where he'd found the bag. "She stood here a while. Maybe stamping her feet and walking around in a small circle?"

It had been cold last night, and Tye imagined the naked woman standing there with her arms wrapped around herself and stomping her feet. Waiting for what? Someone to drive by?

Down the road to the east, the rising sun was framed by two tall Ponderosa pine trees. Tye was already growing warm in his light jacket. It would be well over a hundred degrees by noon. He looked at his watch. It had been nearly four hours since Brianna's satellite tracker had ceased transmitting. They'd been filming for eighteen days, during which Brianna had averaged only a few hundred calories a day of foraged food. He'd been worried she was losing too much weight, but he thought it would be okay with only three days of filming left.

"What do we do know?" Powell asked.

Tye had written the emergency plan himself. If a contestant went missing and failed to turn up after an initial hasty search by the production crew, the next step was obvious.

"Time to call the sheriff," Tye said.

ABOUT THE AUTHOR

David Barbur lives in the foothills of the Cascade Mountains. He can often be found wandering the forest with a longbow in his hand, tracking animals and trying to figure out what happens next in his latest story.

Follow David on social media: